The Werewolf Upstairs

Ashlyn Chase

sourcebooks
casablanca

Published by Sourcebooks Casablanca, an imprint of Sourcebooks, Inc.
P.O. Box 4410, Naperville, Illinois 60567-4410
(630) 961-3900
FAX: (630) 961-2168
www.sourcebooks.com

Printed and bound in the United States of America.
RRD 10 9 8 7 6 5 4 3

To my family of origin. You made me who I am today. Sort of. Don't worry; I'm not blaming you for the warped parts. You may not be able to see what I've done with my life—or maybe you can, I don't know—but I can't let a little thing like death stop me from appreciating you the best way I know how. Mom, Dad, Dex...this one's for you.

Chapter 1

"HERE ARE YOUR KEYS, DEAR. THANKS FOR COMING upstairs to get them. Now don't let your neighbor across the hall scare you."

Roz Wells took the key from Dottie, the apartment manager, and froze. "Scare me? Why would he or she scare me?"

"He's Nathan Nourie." She stepped closer to Roz and whispered, "I call him Nasty Nathan, and I assumed he might scare you because he scares *me*. I'm told he's harmless, but…oh, well, I don't want to influence your opinion by relating my own harrowing experiences."

"Harrowing?" *Oh my freakin' God*. "What's wrong with Nathan?"

"That's what I'd like to know. All I can tell you is he works in a morgue and has an odd sense of humor. Downright morbid, if you ask me."

Maybe she's just easily freaked out. "Okay, that doesn't sound so bad."

Dottie folded her arms and humphed. "You haven't met him yet. If I told you everything…but I won't. I wouldn't want to prejudice you."

"No, of course not." Roz rolled her eyes.

"In fact, most of the tenants here may take some getting used to. If I were you, I'd stay away from the women in 3B, too."

"Why? What wrong with them?"

"Well, they seem to have gotten better lately, but they used to scream and holler all the time. Oh, and don't get me started on my neighbor right across the hall here, Konrad Wolfensen, unless you like nudists. But you're on the first floor, so you shouldn't have to see what I've seen. I swear to God, my eyes can never un-see that."

Roz wondered if leaving her comfortable apartment in Allston and moving to Boston proper had been a good idea, but she wanted to keep an eye on her best friend Merry, having learned her new husband's secret.

She'd confided in her last winter. Merry said she was marrying a shapeshifter, and as crazy as it sounded, Merry was the most down-to-earth and stable person Roz had ever known. There had to be something to it, and Roz needed to know that her best friend in the world hadn't made a horrible mistake.

"Well, thanks for the warning." *I think.* "Oh! I almost forgot to tell you…you know that I'm Merry's friend, right?"

"Which is why you were standing next to her at her wedding and why you knew her apartment was available before I advertised it. Yes, I remember."

"Please don't tell her I moved in. I want it to be a surprise."

Dottie shrugged. "Suit yourself. She'll be in Florida with my nephew while he's in spring training. You know her husband, star pitcher for the Boston Bullets, is my nephew, right?"

Roz gave her a sardonic smile. "I may have heard about that." *Like each time I've heard you talking.*

The door across the hall clicked open and a familiar-looking, gorgeous blond hunk stepped out of his apartment. A short-sleeved black T-shirt exposed lus-cious biceps and stretched across massive, taut pectoral muscles. When he turned around to lock his door, Roz noticed his tight butt and hair so long it almost reached his waist.

Don't drool, don't stare, don't drool…

"Oh, hello, Konrad," Dottie said with syrupy sweet-ness. "I was just welcoming our new resident."

Some welcome.

"This is Rosalyn Wells. Rosalyn, this is Konrad."

I wish I could shed thirty pounds twenty seconds ago. A hottie like him would never be interested in a lump like me.

"Oh, you're Merry's friend." He nodded at the key in her hand. "Are you moving into 1B, her old apartment?"

"Yes, I am." *Why, oh why did I wear my oldest, rat-tiest sweatpants today?*

"I remember meeting you at the burger restaurant a few months ago, and then I saw you again when you were Merry's maid of honor. You looked ravishing in that blue dress, by the way."

Roz was taken aback. *Oh, no, he isn't gay, is he? Good-looking, sensitive, notices and remembers details; sheesh. It's always the good looking ones. But I'll take a compliment wherever I can get it.*

Merry was usually the one who attracted male atten-tion. Roz had never considered herself memorable in the least. Her figure was less than svelte, and her dark brown hair was too straight to hold a style. She usually just swept it back into a bun for work. At least she liked her eyes. They were big and blue, but her eyeglasses hid them. Wearing glasses gave her an authoritative appearance, good for the courtroom, but lousy for dating. "You remember me?"

"Of course I remember you. Welcome to our humble abode, Rosalyn."

He extended his hand, and she grasped it. His big warm paw held hers in a surprisingly gentle clasp. Some kind of energy passed between them, something she'd never felt when shaking the hand of a colleague.

"Call me Roz."

"I'd hardly call this building humble," Dottie said. "That chandelier in the foyer must have cost my nephew a fortune."

"That chandelier has been there since my hair was short. Your nephew just bought the building when? Last summer?"

Suddenly the crystals in the chandelier downstairs tinkled and clanged together.

Dottie jammed her hands on her hips. "For God's sake, Chad, haven't you gone into the light yet?"

Konrad elbowed Roz's arm. "Chad is our resident ghost."

Dottie rolled her eyes. "Yes, God forbid I leave him out when telling you about the other residents."

"There's a g-ghost haunting the building?" *What kind of fresh hell did I just get myself into?*

"Yes, but he won't bother you if he likes you," Konrad said. "I didn't even know he was here until the séance." Konrad looked at the chandelier. "You leave the new woman alone, all right, Chad? She's a friend of Merry's."

*Nice of him to intervene for me, but…*The back of Roz's neck prickled. "You held a séance?"

"Sure, didn't Merry tell you?"

"No. I think I would have remembered that."

Dottie shook her head. "She was the only resident who couldn't make it, besides my husband. She said she had to work. My husband said he had to keep an eye on the building. I don't know where he thought it was going. Well, I have work to do now, but before I leave you, Roz, you should know that I'm not happy with loud parties or tenants who cause trouble. And I live right above you."

Konrad leaned toward Dottie. "Is that some kind of threat? I don't recall her saying she's a party animal."

Wow, is Konrad this protective of all the tenants, or is it just me? Nah, he and Dottie probably have some kind of history. "Oh, you don't have to worry about me," Roz said quickly. "I live a quiet life." *Not by choice…*

"Good. We'll get along swell, then."

Dottie gave Konrad a dirty look, stepped into her apartment, and closed the door

"Can I help you move in? I'm pretty strong." He flexed his sizeable muscles.

Holy Christmas! I haven't seen muscles like that in… ever! Whoa, didn't Dottie say he was a nudist? What I wouldn't give to see…but no. Even if he showed me his, I'd never show him mine.

"Weren't you headed somewhere else?" Roz asked.

"No. Would you rather I was?"

She chuckled. "Of course not. I just thought…oh, never mind. It'd be nice to have company while I wait for the movers."

—⁓—

"Hi, new kid." Chad followed Roz down the stairs. Most of the residents seemed like kids to him. After all, he'd been haunting the place since the 1960s. Okay, so Konrad was older, but he was a werewolf. Other than Konrad, not even the super, Ralph, or his wife Dottie, or the vampire Sly could claim Chad's age or experience.

"That's right, kid, we have a vampire. The only reason the landlady didn't mention him was because she doesn't know he's living in the basement. Heh, heh.

"I'll bet you thought I was swinging from the chandelier, didn't you, kid? As much fun as that would be, I'm afraid my astral body doesn't work that way. It's not like I have an invisible body. I'm a spirit. That means I have no astral ass to sit on.

"But just like a corporeal person who loses one sense and strengthens the others, I may have lost my body, but I've strengthened my mind to razor sharpness. Yeah, I'm smart as shit.

"Ha, ha. I wish. Actually I've learned to use my mind to affect objects, so even though I wasn't literally swinging from the chandelier, I concentrated really hard on the chandelier swinging until it did. It's called telekinesis. If I were able to ride it, I'd do it every day until the damn thing came crashing down. You have no idea how badly I need entertainment."

Chad followed Roz into her empty apartment, continuing to chat at her, as though she could hear every word. After all, he never knew when he might run into a sensitive soul who could sense, hear, or see his presence.

Roz glanced up at Konrad. "I just want to take a quick look around to figure out where I'm going to put things when the movers come."

"Would you like me to step outside?"

"Only if you want to."

Chad continued, still hopeful. *"The others in the building don't know much about me, except Morgaine and Gwyneth. They're the witches in apartment 3B, and they're noisy because they're phone-sex actresses. Some of their clients like screamers."*

Still no reaction from the new tenant. Damn. I like making Dottie and Ralph's ceiling fan spin around. Dottie thinks I'm riding it, and Ralph, who doesn't believe in ghosts, scratches his head and tries to find a logical explanation. A short in the wiring? Oh, come on. It wouldn't work at all, if that happened.

Roz pulled on her hoodie sweatshirt and fumbled for the zipper. "It's cold out. Don't you want to get a jacket?"

Konrad shook his head. "Nah, I'm good." He opened the apartment door as wide as it would go and said, "Hang onto this a minute." He carried over the marble pedestal table from the foyer and propped the door open, presumably to carry furniture through it.

Roz shivered. "It's freezing in here, too, but I'd better wait to turn the heat on. Otherwise it'll all just rush outside."

Oh, maybe she sensed me! Chad floated in front of her and made a scary face. *"Muu haua huaha. Damn, I hope you're sensitive and just ignoring me because we're not alone. I'm sick of talking to myself all the time."*

Konrad opened the front door for Roz and held it as she stepped right through Chad to the outside. Disappointed, he floated back upstairs, hoping to find one of the witches to talk to.

Roz and Konrad settled on the front stoop. Konrad sat so close that Roz could feel his body heat radiating into her skin. It felt oddly comforting.

Konrad spoke first. "I heard Dottie giving you her take on the neighbors, and thought I'd try to put your mind at ease."

"You heard her? Right through your apartment? I didn't realize we were speaking loudly, or are the walls that thin?"

"No, I—uh, seem to have extra acute hearing."

And kind of cute ears, slightly pointed at the ends. "So, about the neighbors…they're not as bad as she thinks they are?"

"They're not bad at all. Dottie's the crazy one, if you ask me."

"How so?"

"Always sticking her nose into other people's business. She acts like she has to protect her nephew's investment or something. Like one of us is about to burn the place to the ground at any moment."

Roz reeled back. "Why would anyone do that? You live here too."

"Exactly."

She shook her head. "Well, you don't have to worry about her influencing my judgment. I'm an attorney. I form my own opinions based on evidence, not hearsay."

"Sheesh, you even sound like a lawyer."

She chuckled. "Comes with the territory, I guess. But I wish I could find some other lucrative line of work."

"Really? Why? Isn't law fulfilling?"

Wow, he seems genuinely interested. How rare is that in a man? Plus kind and good looking. Maybe living here won't be so bad, even if he turns out to be gay. Maybe we could go shopping together. "Well, to tell you the truth, the job is changing me in ways I don't like."

"Ah. You're becoming jaded."

"You said it. That, and it's no fun. I wish I could find a job that I could be passionate about *and* have fun while I'm doing it."

"I get that. I'd like the same thing. So what type of law do you practice?"

"I'm a public defender, low on the totem pole, so I get all the weird cases. Tomorrow night's the full moon. I can hardly wait to see what the next day will bring."

Konrad laughed. "Imagine that, Roz Wells gets the weird cases. You must have some stories to tell."

"Yeah, too bad about that attorney-client privilege thing."

"Oh, come on. You can talk in generalities. Some of those stories probably wind up in the news anyway."

"True."

"Give me some examples of full-moon cases."

She sighed. "Well, there are the usual extraterrestrial sightings, but with what I call the loonies, there's always an unusual twist."

"Like zealots with shotguns wearing tin foil hats for protection?"

She chuckled. "Yeah, or like one time when a guy claimed to see a spaceship melting. Funny how it happened on a hot day on a tar road."

"Ah, so he was seeing a mirage?"

"Probably. I didn't hear about any melted spaceships."

"Why did he need a lawyer? It's not against the law to report an extraterrestrial sighting."

"But shooting out the windows of a 'melting' minivan is kind of frowned upon."

Konrad's laugh was deep, sort of like Santa Claus without the "Ho, ho, ho."

"The moon isn't full every night. What do you do the other twenty-seven days?"

"If it's not the nuts, then it's the dregs of society. Drug dealers who hang around playgrounds getting into turf wars with the pedophiles, each one claiming the same street corner. Once I had a not-so-bright client who called the cops on the druggies, only to be picked up himself for violating his parole. And of course there are the vandals who like to show off their colorful vocabulary by hating a particular subgroup in graffiti."

"Yeah, that doesn't sound like a barrel of laughs, but you knew it wouldn't be, right?"

"Sure, I knew I'd meet my share of dirt bags. But I also pictured the occasional innocent person I could really help. Most of the time the son of a bitch is probably guilty and lying his head off, but everyone deserves a fair trial, presumed innocent until *proven* guilty, right?"

"Right."

She shook her head. "That assumption is rapidly evaporating. Now I look at a defendant and the first thing that pops into my mind is, 'What the hell did this one do, and what line of bull is he going to feed me?'"

"You could go into a different type of law practice."

"I already have. I used to do civil law. Lots of nasty divorce cases."

Konrad groaned. "Don't tell me. Now you think all men are scum."

"Not anymore. It took a while to find the old die-hard romantic in me, but I eventually did. Now I think all men are criminals."

Konrad laughed, but there was a nervous edge to it. He scratched the back of his neck, uncrossed his long legs, and crossed them the other way.

Roz stretched to get comfortable too. "So what do you do?"

"For a living?"

No, for kicks, nervous boy. "Yeah. What kind of work do you do?"

"I work nights. In security."

"You're a security guard? Well, you have the size for it, but that wouldn't have been my first guess. You sound so well educated. I mean, who uses the word *ravishing* these days? Oh! Not that you couldn't be extremely intelligent and still be a security guard. I didn't mean to—"

"Put your foot in your mouth?"

"Yeah, sorry. That happens when I meet a cute guy."

He laughed. "Don't worry about it. Actually, I used to be an educator."

"A teacher? Where?"

"A private school for boys."

Before she had a chance to ask him more about it, he was already rerouting the conversation to the present.

"And now I'm more of a security specialist. I analyze a company's weak spots in its off hours and recommend the best protection to suit each company's individual needs. My brother and I own the business together."

Maybe the past isn't something he wants to talk about. "He works nights too?"

"Sometimes, but not for the company. He's a cop, but he installs our alarm systems during the day. It's far more lucrative than teaching."

"I can imagine. Teachers don't get paid enough for all they do."

"What brought you to our building? Did you move here to be near your friend?"

Roz wondered why he suddenly shifted the conversation back to her. It seemed kind of abrupt. "Yes, actually."

"But you wanted to keep your being here a surprise until she gets home? Why is that?"

Roz bit her lower lip and then came out with the truth. "I figured after I was all settled in, she wouldn't try to talk me out of it."

Konrad leaned away from her and appeared puzzled. "Why would she want to do that?"

"Oh, uh…no reason. I was just kidding."

"No, you weren't."

Roz's shoulders slumped. "You have one of those built-in lie detectors, don't you?"

"Comes with the teaching gig."

"Yeah, I'll bet you heard your share of dog-eating-the-homework stories."

"Oh, yeah. Dogs, wolves, something was always eating homework."

"Wolves?" Roz shivered. "Where did you teach? Montana?"

He laughed. "No, Newton, Massachusetts, but you should have heard the more creative excuses. Almost made me want to give extra credit for imagination."

"Such as?"

"You're distracting me from my original question, aren't you?"

"Damn, you're good."

"What's the answer?"

"What was the question again?"

He gave her the hairy eyeball.

"Okay, okay. Do you remember that day Merry and I were having lunch in the burger place?"

"When I was sitting right behind you and overheard her telling you that Jason's a shapeshifter?"

Roz gasped. "You heard that? You know?"

"Yes. I was quite impressed with how well you handled the news. I liked how you were there for your friend, no matter what she said or how crazy it sounded. You must be a very open-minded woman."

She hung her head. "I may not be quite as open-minded as I seemed. I actually want to keep an eye on Merry. I can't do that from Allston. But if she knew my intent, she'd kill me. Her family has been overly protective her whole life. I don't want her to think I am too."

"But you're worried about her."

"Naturally. She's my best friend. I don't want to doubt her sanity, but shapeshifters? Really?"

"You're not willing to entertain the possibility of aliens *or* shapeshifters?"

"I never said that." Roz sighed. "Look, I'm used to logic and objectivity. If I can't see it with my own eyes, there has to be some kind of explanation. I can't just flex the laws of physics on someone's say-so. You have to admit the whole idea is kind of weird, and she means the world to me. I don't want to see anything bad happen to her."

"Bad? Like what? Are you afraid it's going to rub off on her?"

"No…yes…hell, I don't know. I can't imagine why Jason would make that up. I mean, how did you take it? Weren't you a little weirded out?"

"I was surprised, but not weirded out. Is *weirded* a word?"

"It is now."

He smiled and bumped her arm playfully. Then he cleared his throat. "You may have moved to the wrong place if you're easily, um, weirded."

"Yeah, now that I know there's a ghost here as well as an alleged shapeshifter. Holy crap."

Konrad glanced the other way and mumbled something under his breath.

"What was that?"

"Oh look, there's the moving van."

"Yup. It looks like their GPS is working."

Konrad kissed her on the forehead, rose, and jogged down the stairs to meet them, as if he were the one moving in.

Surprised, Roz touched the spot, and it tingled. *He's like a big, friendly Great Dane. Jeez, I hope he's not gay.*

———

Konrad slid into a booth across from his identical twin brother. "Nicholas, we've got to be even more careful now. A lawyer has moved into my building. She's a public defender, but they know people."

"Crap. First a private dick, and now a lawyer. Like attracting like again?"

"Maybe. This one's cute though. Kind of has that sexy secretary thing going on. Looks innocent as vanilla, but underneath there's something very spicy. She even smells like cinnamon."

"Steer clear, bro. She could be trouble."

Konrad leaned against the padded vinyl back. "What if I don't want to?"

Nicholas leaned back too and folded his arms. "Are you out of your mind? Should I remind you what you do for a living? A thief and a lawyer aren't a match made in heaven—unless God has a really twisted sense of humor."

"The attempted-robbery gig is temporary. It's always been temporary. Besides, her job sounds temporary too. She's trying to find a whole new line of work. Being an attorney doesn't agree with her."

Nicholas grinned and leaned forward. "Maybe she could become a librarian."

Konrad almost sighed aloud as he fantasized. "Wouldn't that be nice? I can picture her in glasses, riding the rolling ladder in my living-room library."

"The ladder you'll *never* need unless you're chopped off at the knees?"

Konrad chuckled. "Hey, it goes with the old-world look of the place."

A waitress strolled over to take their lunch orders. They both ordered rare steaks, bloody, with cold centers and no side dishes. She wrinkled her nose, but jotted it down and left them to continue their conversation.

"How tall is she?"

"About five six or seven."

"You're about a head taller. She'd need the ladder

just to look you in the eye." Nick grinned, wickedly. "Or you could find more interesting uses for it. It's probably been gathering dust, just like you have."

"Is that a crack about my social life?"

"No, it's a comment on your lack of one. But you should wait to ask her out until one of you finds another line of work."

"Yeah, yeah. So what job do you have for me this time? A boutique? A jewelry store? What?"

"Nope, this heist is unusual. It's a restaurant downtown. They have a free-standing freezer plus one of those dessert display cases."

"Crap, those weigh a ton."

"I'm sure you can lift them. No mere mortal could, that's for sure."

Konrad sighed. "Fine. You're sure they have no cameras? No alarms? Remember last time? That was close. If I hadn't shifted and growled, scaring the damn dogs out of their minds…"

"No dogs, either. No security whatsoever. Not even a dead bolt. I'll bet you could get in with a credit card."

"Well, since I don't have any, I'll have to borrow one of yours."

"Yeah, right. Like I'm going to hand over my credit card to my deadbeat brother."

Thanks a lot, rude-o. "Be nice. And exactly what am I supposed to do with these things once I get them outside?"

"Leave 'em on the sidewalk. Make it look like you were scared off. Oh, but bring me home some steaks and a Boston cream pie. You know how much I love those."

Konrad shook his head. "Man, I'm glad I don't have to carry the equipment far."

"Yeah, we just want the owners inconvenienced enough to want an alarm system, and then I'll conveniently drop in."

"Sounds good. When do I do it?"

"Tonight."

"Tonight? Are you sure? It's almost that time of the month. What if I get caught and locked up?"

"You won't."

Easy for you to say.

Nick tucked his napkin into his collar to protect his uniform. "You're always careful."

"Yeah. I wouldn't want to miss a run through the Arboretum. We're on for tomorrow at midnight, as usual?"

"Absolutely. Are you planning to go to Newton after that?"

"You know I have to keep an eye on the pack."

"No, you really don't. They kicked you out and replaced you with another alpha. How can you possibly feel any responsibility toward them?"

"I just do. You've got tomorrow evening off, don't you?"

"Of course. It's the full moon."

"It's a good thing there are so many werewolves on the Boston police force, especially the ones who arrange your schedule."

"If you do the job tonight, you'll be nearly at full strength."

"True."

"Pretend your sexy librarian is watching. Muscles get the ladies hot."

"Yeah. That'll work." Konrad rested his chin on his fist and drifted off into a fantasy of Roz Wells without baggy sweats.

Chapter 2

"ARGH, THIS SUCKER WEIGHS A TON." KONRAD'S MUSCLES ached as he struggled under the weight of the freezer. "Shouldn't have had that chocolate cake."

He had propped open the back door of the restaurant using the tall, cylindrical dessert case. All that remained of the third shelf were crumbs, and his stomach hurt.

As he managed the few steps that led to the alley, he muttered, "Damn Nicholas. Why can't he take a turn once in a while? Just because he's a cop—"

"Hey, you! What are you doing?"

He froze. "Fuck." Konrad tipped the freezer back enough to see who had called out. He lost his precarious balance, and the huge chest slid out of his grasp. Falling backward, he hit the curb with his hip. *Ow, damn it!* A second later, the freezer hit the street with such force, it may have cracked the pavement.

Konrad rolled to the side as quickly as he could, but the heavy ice chest pinned his leg to the ground. It held him just long enough for the witness, who looked like a homeless guy, to yell for the cops.

"Shit. I should have checked the boxes and crates in this damn alley first."

If only the guy would move out of view, Konrad could shift and reappear as a big dog limping away, but the shift would take a couple of minutes, and who knew how fast the cops would get there? An unreliable witness might be dismissed or might not. To expose his shapeshifter capabilities might be worse than getting caught. His muscles vibrated as he tried to lift the dead weight off his leg.

Unfortunately he had to remain in human form or risk exposure, the very worst thing that could happen to a werewolf. To expose the existence of one would lead to witch hunts for others. Maybe even government experiments. *Ugh. Being dissected would really suck.*

By the time he pushed the freezer aside enough to free himself, a uniformed cop on horseback came charging down the alley.

Konrad shook his head and mumbled, "Too late. Caught by the damn Mounties."

―――∾∾――――

While Konrad waited in his cell, he reflected on his life with a good dose of self-pity. In 1922, he and his brother had been running away from home, and while making their way through the woods at night, they happened upon a werewolf council meeting. They were turned and taken into the pack to prevent exposure—even back then it was a werewolf's greatest fear. As long as humans didn't believe werewolves existed, they were safe.

He had worked his way up to the alpha leader of the Newton pack. Yes, Newton, Massachusetts. He was proud of how completely he and his brother had been able to blend in, even in a pricey neighborhood. He helped found a private school for troubled boys and subsequently became the dean of students.

Life was good, until he took in a lone wolf named Petroski, who had used Konrad's tendency toward kindness to oust him. The newcomer managed to poison the pack's opinion of him. Petroski challenged him for alpha status, and by cheating, won.

Now Konrad sat in a jail cell for the first time in his life, without the support of his pack and without the help of his brother. With a breakfast that no matter how hungry he was, he couldn't wolf down. He wanted to howl at the sun.

"Wolfensen, you've got a visitor."

The guard startled him out of his pity party. Konrad stood and groaned, still sore from the night's activities. He stretched as he waited for his cell door to open. He could easily overpower the guard and escape, but curiosity got the better of him. No one knew where he was, so who'd come to see him? Did Nick hear about it?

He followed the guard past the long row of occupied jail cells. It had obviously been a busy night for the Boston PD. He and the guard stopped at the end of the corridor in front of a door with a small window. The guard opened the door and told him to go ahead inside and sit on the far side of the wooden table. A woman wearing a gray suit with her brown hair twisted into a bun sat in the seat closer to the door.

"Ah, you must be the lawyer they promised me."

She turned her head enough to see his face. And he recognized *her*.

"Roz?" *Holy crap! Way to make a good impression…*

"Good morning, Konrad." She opened the folder on the table and said, "I'd hoped there were two people with the same name. I never expected to see you here." She waved him over to the seat on the opposite side.

Konrad gulped. He slowly made his way to the other side of the table and sat down gingerly.

"Would you prefer another attorney? Not that there are a lot of us, but if you're uncomfortable…"

"No, I want you…um, to represent me, I mean." *Oh, God. Of all the public defenders! But maybe…*"I really need your help, Roz. And I trust you to do your best, since I'm that rare innocent victim of the system you spoke of."

Roz nodded to the guard, and he left them alone.

—∿∿—

It figures I'd be attracted to another loser. Damn. Just my freakin' luck. Why can't I find a great guy like Merry did? Roz cursed her terrible taste in men. Just one more thing to blame on her stepfather.

"You're being charged with breaking and entering and attempted grand theft. Are you aware of the process?"

"Process?"

"The legal proceedings?"

"No. This is the first time I've been arrested." He hung his head.

She saw tears welling up in his eyes, and her heart automatically constricted. What should she do? Show sympathy? Try to face it like an impartial attorney? She sighed. Until she knew the whole story, she'd have to put on her best poker face.

"Well, that should help. Give me a minute to look over the police report." She tried to maintain a professional distance and demeanor, but the details of what she was reading sounded so ridiculous, she wanted to laugh. Either that or reach out and squeeze his hand, telling him everything would be all right. The charge was preposterous. He couldn't have done what the witness said he did. And what a witness! A street person? He was probably drunk or hallucinating or both. She doubted the police would even be able to find him if the case went to trial, which it wouldn't. She'd get it dismissed if it was the last thing she did.

"What were you doing in that alley late at night?"

Konrad's expression didn't waver. "Just taking a walk. Some people like long walks on the beach, I like long walks around the city."

"I like long walks too, but not at three in the morning, and certainly not in back alleys."

"There's less traffic. I can think better when it's quiet. And who would mug me?"

Did she imagine it, or did he just flex his pecs? Either way, she had to look down and not at the hot guy in front of her. *Christ, I'd better take some deep breaths and clear my head*. "Okay, so let's say you were just out for a walk, and then what happened?"

He shrugged.

"Come on. Are you telling me a five-hundred pound freezer fell out of the sky and hit you? Because the police report said there was no heavy equipment nearby. No way to lift it, yet the witness said he saw you carrying it out of a restaurant on your back."

Konrad laughed. "I was passing by and wondered what it was doing there. I *tried* to lift it, to at least get it out of the street, but it toppled over. Fortunately it was only my pants leg that got pinned."

Roz took a deep breath. "Well, first is the arraignment. That will happen today. If the judge feels there's a case, he'll set bail."

"Bail? How much do think that'll be?"

"Well, nothing, if I can get the charges dropped, and that's what I intend to do."

"Really? Do you think you can?"

Roz leaned back in her chair. "You never know what will happen, but the witness claims he saw you carrying the freezer, fully loaded with frozen meats, on your back. Hang on a minute."

Roz opened her laptop and typed in *commercial freezers*. She found one about the same size as the one Konrad had allegedly picked up and carried. "Okay, this size and type of restaurant freezer weighs about five hundred pounds empty and holds fifty-seven cubic feet of frozen food. And the police report states it was filled with frozen beef, fish, and chicken."

"How much weight do you think that would add?"

"I can guess, since I do my own shopping and cooking. Let's see, by my estimate, a cubic foot of equal amounts of those items weighs about twenty-five pounds. That's fourteen hundred twenty-five pounds. Combined with the weight of the freezer itself, you would have had to pick up and carry about one ton. Is that even humanly possible?"

Konrad laughed. "It sure isn't. No *human* could possibly accomplish that. I think the world record for weightlifting is about half that."

Roz nodded. "Let me double check that." She typed in *weightlifting world records*. What she read confirmed it. "Perfect, so between that and a less-than-credible witness, I think there's a good chance of getting you off." *Getting him off? What is wrong with me?* She felt her cheeks heat.

Konrad simply smiled.

Damn, my Freudian slip is showing, and he noticed.
Roz ruffled the papers in front of her and jotted down
some notes. It had obviously been too long since she'd
had sex. She noticed her panties dampening.

When she glanced up, he was still smiling at her.
*Maybe planting the seed of that idea isn't the worst
thing I've ever done.*

After the arraignment, Konrad asked Roz to join him
for lunch. Fortunately she had no more cases, so they
decided to grab takeout and enjoy a long walk home.
The sunny sky held the promise of a warm, spring day.

"You were brilliant." Konrad hoped he hadn't blown
his chances with his sexy attorney and neighbor.

"Aw, shucks. I'll bet you say that to all the public
defenders."

His smiled faded and his gaze dropped to the sidewalk. "It really was my first and only arrest, but I know
how you feel about the guys you defend. I guess you
aren't interested in me now. I was hoping to ask you out."

She touched his arm, and the spot tingled. "This is
different. You were innocent."

If only... Konrad hated to deceive her, but there was
no way he could explain his abilities without exposing
what he was, and therefore, the existence of his kind.
Not to mention that he needed time to discover if she
could be his mate. He had the sneaking suspicion that
the beautiful lawyer might just be the one, and he had
to check out that theory. If he didn't, he could spend his
whole life wondering.

She smiled up at him. "So, where do you want to eat lunch? Indoors or out?"

He contemplated her soft expression and glanced up just in time to witness a child drop his mother's hand and dart out into traffic. The mother screamed, and Konrad dropped their bag of takeout, rushing after the child without a thought. He scooped up the little boy seconds before a car's brakes squealed.

The car hit Konrad, but even as he staggered, he held the boy steady. The tot was untouched.

The mother cried out, "Oh, thank God!"

Even though Konrad limped to the sidewalk, it was mostly an act. The car bumper was dented, so he had to make it look good.

As he passed the boy to his relieved mother, he winced.

She hugged her son close and stared at Konrad. "Oh my goodness. Are you hurt?"

"I'll be fine. Probably just a bruise. Nothing broken."

The driver of the car rolled down his window and yelled, "Hey, lady. Keep your friggin' kid out of the street."

Konrad turned to him and said, "We're fine. Thanks for asking."

The driver flipped him the bird and sped off.

"If you hadn't been there…" Tears welled up in the mother's eyes, and she bit her lower lip.

"I'm just glad I was able to help, ma'am." He glanced at Roz for the first time since he'd bolted into the street. Her mouth hung open and her eyes were wide with awe.

"Are you sure you're okay?" Roz asked. "I mean, you took a pretty hard hit."

"Nah, I'm made of strong stuff. I drink lots of milk—rich in calcium."

The woman grappled for her purse. "Sir, let me give you a reward."

"Aw, heck no. I'm just glad I saw what was happening in time to stop it."

"I insist."

"Tell you what. Take the money and buy one of those child harnesses." He ruffled the boy's hair. "Some precocious children need to be protected from themselves."

She smiled and nodded. "Thank you. I will. I'm truly grateful." She squinted at the kid and said, "You're in the doghouse, young man. And just for that, I'm getting you a leash!"

"I can't believe you saved that child without getting killed."

"Yeah, I don't know what I was thinking. I guess I wasn't thinking at all, just reacting to the situation."

"You were so brave and so selfless." *And so amazing and so... hot!*

He smiled and placed a finger under her chin. Tipping her face up, he bent low, hovering just over her lips. "Can I have a kiss as my reward?"

"I'm sure the boy's mother would have kissed you if you'd asked." She was teasing, but also trying to keep her distance. After all, he had just been in trouble with the law.

"I didn't want to kiss *her*. I'm asking *you*."

Aw, I'm melting. Roz slipped her arms around his neck and closed her eyes. He held her in a surprisingly gentle embrace and closed the short gap between their lips.

The pressure was just right. Firm, but not bruising. He

opened his mouth slightly and slanted his head, allowing her to deepen the kiss if she wanted to. She answered by slipping her tongue past his teeth, but something sharp pricked her.

She almost pulled away, but his big paw of a hand cradled her head and kept her mouth fused to his. He slipped his tongue past her lips and lapped at the sore spot. Suddenly the pain faded and disappeared.

Roz let her body mold to his and felt petite in his arms. *Now, that's a first.*

The hot, drugging kiss continued, right there on the sidewalk, heedless of passersby and traffic. The world fell away, and soon the only thing she could name that existed outside herself was his arousal nudging her stomach.

She even wanted to incorporate the hard length inside her body and join with him completely. *Whoa, where did that thought come from?*

"It came from us, darling."

Roz snapped out of her trance. Pulling away, she mumbled, "Wha…what just happened?"

Konrad kissed her forehead and smiled. "I think it's called telepathy."

"You heard me?"

"Yes, as if you were speaking inside my head."

Shocked, Roz lost the power to communicate—or breathe.

Konrad stroked her cheek with his thumb. "It's never happened to me before, but I've heard of it. Certain members of my family can do it with their m…uh, people they're very close to."

She inhaled deeply and tried to steady herself. "Well, I've never heard of it happening to anyone at all." She remembered what he'd heard, and heat rose to her cheeks. "To tell you the truth, I'm a little embarrassed you overheard what I was thinking. I'm not sure I want anyone listening to my warped mind."

Konrad wrapped an arm around her and gave a side squeeze. "Don't worry; I won't tell a soul how warped you are."

"Hey!"

He laughed. "I was just messing with you. I think you're beautiful. Inside and out."

She gazed at him as if mesmerized. No man had ever said she was beautiful, at least not convincingly, but his eyes were telling the truth. *He really thinks I'm beautiful!*

"*Inside and out.*"

"Now cut that out. I just said I don't want you listening to me while I'm thinking."

"Then don't think so loud."

"Don't think so…what?"

"I doubt I hear all of your thoughts, just the ones that come across clearly."

Roz crossed her arms and pouted. "Oh, that's just great. Now I'll have to keep my mind a jumble, in order to have any privacy?"

Konrad shrugged. "This is new to me too. I guess we'll have to figure it out together. Let's go home." He kept his arm around her and guided her to walk beside him. She wanted to slip her arm around his waist too, but regardless of what just happened, it seemed too soon.

"Maybe I can talk to my brother about it. He might know if there's a shut-off button."

"Has he experienced telepathy?"

"No, but he…well, he's closer to the rest of the family than I am. He can probably ask them for me."

"Oh, you've had a falling out with your family?"

"You could say that."

"I don't know what I'd do without my mother and brother." *My stepfather can go to hell, though.*

"What did your stepfather do?"

"Oh, damn. Did I think that out loud?"

He smiled. "Don't worry, I won't tell. But I'd like to know, so I don't do the same thing."

She snorted. "If you did, the circumstances would be totally different." *Like mutually consensual.*

"Oh, no! You mean he—"

"Get the fuck out of my head, will you?"

Konrad stopped walking and leaned over to give her a warm, tender hug. He whispered in her ear, "I'm sorry that happened to you."

She gently pushed him away. "It wasn't when I was a kid or anything. I was in high school, and it only happened once. He came home from a party drunk. My mother went right to bed. He…he came into my room uninvited and tried to kiss me a little too amorously. He put his hand on my breast, and I shoved him off."

"Crap. That must have been frightening."

"Yeah, not to mention disgusting."

"Did your mother ever find out?"

"Yeah, I told her, even though he told me not to. He said it was my word against his, and he'd deny it, but I figured she deserved to know."

"That was brave of you. A lot of girls would have kept it bottled up inside and acted out in some other way. Did she protect you?"

"She booted his ass soon after I told her. Then we both went to counseling."

He squeezed her shoulder and continued walking. "Thank God for that. Some mothers don't believe their own daughters. I saw some of that as a teacher. That's when the kids act out to get the attention of someone—anyone—who might help."

"Yeah, in that way I was fortunate."

"How old were you?"

"Seventeen. Too old to call anything that might have happened statutory rape, but too young to be a legal adult."

"Damn. If he'd pushed it, I hope you'd sue his ass off."

"That would have been difficult. My stepfather was a lawyer. He said he'd make me look like I was totally crazy if I tried to ruin his reputation." She looked up at Konrad with a sad smile. "And what teenager hasn't acted totally crazy from time to time?"

He shook his head. "Well, at least you got counseling to help you put it in perspective. Is your mother okay?"

"My mom is strong. She put us kids first. After she threw him out, she threatened to take him for everything he owned if he contested the divorce."

"Did anything happen to your brother?"

"No, except he wanted to kill my stepfather when he found out. He was always my protector."

"Well, now you have me."

Surprised, Roz stiffened momentarily, then offered him a weak smile. "Thanks, that's sweet of you, but we just met."

"So?"

Roz chuckled. "Seems like I've picked up another protector, whether I like it or not."

"Oh, you'll like it, all right."

She halted, and her eyes widened.

"Oh, no. I didn't mean that the way it sounded. Please don't worry. I'll never pressure you." A second later, the thought, *"I hope"* popped into his mind.

Roz took a couple of steps away from him. "You hope? What the hell does that mean?"

"I…I would never… It's just that I'm so attracted to you, it's like…I can't explain it. Just know that I'll never hurt you or let anyone else hurt you, either." He shook his head vigorously. "Never, ever." He enveloped her in a tender hug. "I promise."

———⟶———

His mate. He'd found her! At last. Telepathic communication didn't happen by accident. He had heard of it only in mated couples. Even then, not every couple was lucky enough to experience it.

His canine tooth accidentally scraped her tongue. Her blood must have triggered the telepathy. Now he was burning to find out if they were compatible in bed, but if he rushed her, he could scare her off. *Especially with her history.*

She interrupted his thoughts. "What's so special about my history?"

"Huh?"

"You were saying…or rather thinking, something about my history. Something special?"

"Oh. It was nothing." *Damn, this telepathy is going to be a pain in the ass.*

"Tell me about it."

"Shit. You heard that too?"

Roz giggled. "This is really weird. Kind of fun, but totally bizarro."

Konrad took a deep breath. "Let's go home and try not to think until we get there. Are you up for a jog?"

"Sure. If I get tired, I'll walk and meet you there."

"Or I can carry you."

Roz burst out laughing. "Yeah, right. I may not weigh as much as a ton of frozen food, but I'm no lightweight."

"Sure you are." He turned his back to her and squatted slightly. "Hop on."

"What? Are you nuts? You want to give me a piggyback?"

"Why not? We're going to the same place, and we want to get there quickly."

"I'll slow you to a crawl."

"Try me."

Roz folded her arms. "I'm not getting on your back."

"Why not?"

"Because I weigh too much. And I don't want you to know how much too much."

"Suit yourself." Konrad turned back toward her and scooped her up in his arms.

She shrieked.

As he strode off in the direction of their building, only a few more blocks away, she wriggled in his grasp. "Put me down!"

"If you don't stay still, I might drop you."

"Fuckin' caveman."

"Did you know that contrary to popular opinion, the cavemen were neither slovenly nor dimwitted? Regardless of having no manuals, no education, no knowledge of science or mathematics at all, they managed to live beyond puberty to raise the next generation. That points to intelligence."

"What are you, Mr. Wikipedia? Did you just Google *cavemen*?"

"No, I'm trying to impress you. It's also agreed that language has been around for a million years or more. They developed language in order to communicate with each other. To do that, they must have been extremely intelligent."

"Yeah, yeah. You're a freakin' rocket scientist. Now put me down! I'm too old to be carried like a baby."

"I've got a better idea." He set her on her feet.

"Whew, finally. I—"

Konrad dipped down and came up with Roz draped over his shoulder.

She gasped.

"If you're going to accuse me of being a caveman, I might as well act like one."

Roz thumped him on his back. "Put me down this minute!"

"Just relax and enjoy the ride."

"I don't usually hear that until I make it to the bedroom."

Konrad laughed but ignored her plea and strode off in the direction of their building as if she weighed no more than a sack of tennis balls. He added to her embarrassment by whistling.

"Oh, very nice. What if I have to fart while I'm up here?"

"Then fart. We're traveling downwind."

Roz giggled and bounced along with Konrad's long strides. "I give up."

"Good."

"It's your hernia."

"You're not as heavy as you think. So many women have negative self-images. You think you have to be bony to be beautiful, when it's the opposite for most guys."

"Oh, really?"

"Well, I guess I can't speak for the entire male population, but most guys I know like a little meat on their women." He patted her ass.

A passing couple laughed.

"Oh, for Christ's sake. Do you have to embarrass me completely and totally?"

"If that's what it takes to convince you that you're ravishing."

She sighed. *Ravage me when we get back to your place, and I might believe you.*"

Konrad slowed his march. "Did you mean for me to hear that?"

"Put me down, and I'll tell you."

He quickly set her on her feet and grasped her shoulders to steady her.

She looked up into his serious face and took a risk. "Yeah, I meant it."

He straightened, and his eyes widened. "I'll race you."

They grinned at each other and took off running the final block to their building.

Chapter 3

KONRAD HOPED SHE LIKED HIS APARTMENT. HE KEPT IT
neat enough, but he wasn't obsessed with cleanliness.
If she inspected anything up close, she'd see dust, for
sure. If he had only known she'd be willing to come to
his home this early in their relationship...

He had to extract his keys from the manila packet that
held his belongings at the jail, one more reminder that
he'd been arrested.

"Are you sure you don't mind being with an ex-con
accused of grand larceny?"

A door clicked upstairs.

"I thought you said this was the first time you'd
been arrested."

Someone appeared at the top of the stairs holding a
basket of laundry.

Roz clapped a hand over her mouth. "*Oh, I'm so
sorry. I didn't mean for anyone to hear that.*"

Konrad glanced up and saw who stood there. *Whew.
It's Morgaine, not Joe, the private dick.* "It's okay.
She's cool. Hey, Morgaine. Come down and meet our
new neighbor. She's a friend of Merry's."

Morgaine smiled, descended the staircase gracefully,
and set the basket on the floor. "Any friend of Merry's
is a friend of ours."

Roz extended her hand. "I remember you. You were
at the wedding."

"Yeah, I'm told I'm hard to forget." They shook hands.

Konrad was so used to seeing Morgaine in her goth makeup and long black dresses he didn't think anything of it. Fortunately, it seemed as if Roz didn't have a major problem with it, either, but wait until she found out Morgaine was a medium and a witch. That friendliness might change.

He suddenly realized Morgaine may have gotten the wrong impression from his quip, if she heard it. "Did you overhear me kidding Roz about being an ex-con, Morgaine? You know I'm not, right?"

"Oh, forget it. I'm not even concerned if you are. I've known you long enough to know you're trustworthy. In fact, I feel safer with you around."

"That was nice of you to say, especially in front of my new girlfriend." He placed a possessive arm around Roz.

She glanced up at him. Surprise registered on her face. He decided to deflect it by continuing to talk to Morgaine.

"So, what happened was, I got arrested last night, but Roz here is a lawyer and got me off. So I was just kidding her."

"Hey, no big deal. You must have been innocent, right? I mean, with your job as a security expert and all, you'd never do anything to jeopardize that."

"Exactly." *Hey, that was the truth. I'd never knowingly jeopardize my job, even though I hate it. At least it pays the rent.*

Roz looked up at him, and he wondered if she had heard his thought. He'd have to think about other things.

"Well, we'd best be going. I want to give her a tour of my apartment." *Especially the bedroom.*

Morgaine smiled and picked up her basket. "You kids have fun."

As she left, Konrad turned the key to the deadbolt. *Crap, I hope she can't hear us too.*

"You think she can?"

She can communicate with the ghost.

He opened the door wide, and Roz followed him in.

"She can talk to Chad?"

"She says she can. I guess there's no way to know for sure."

As soon as he shut the door, Roz wrapped her arms around his neck and kissed him hard. It took him by surprise, but he had no intention of wasting the moment and kissed her back just as passionately.

When they finally broke apart, panting, he asked, "What was that for?"

She looked down shyly. "For calling me your girlfriend."

He smiled. "You are. I mean…I hope you are. I'm about to ravage you—unless you've changed your mind."

"Oh, no." She shook her head. "No mind changing here."

She began to unbutton his shirt. He helped her shrug out of her suit jacket while walking backward toward the bedroom. Her hourglass figure came into view with her white blouse tucked into a gray pencil skirt. Wow. Talk about an hourglass figure.

Konrad tensed. He had to hold back his strength, despite the powerful lust he felt building inside him. If he gave into it, he'd have her naked and spread beneath him in seconds. Her clothes would be in shreds on the floor.

When they reached the bed, she gazed into his eyes, and her breath caught. She must have seen the hunger in them. Burning need consumed him. He forced his hands

behind his back and balled his fists until the pain of his
fingernails dug into his palms and distracted him from
lust. "I—I'll try to be gentle."

She unzipped the back of her skirt. "You don't have
to worry." Her chin lifted. "I want to do this." Her words
were brave, but he smelled a slight fear tingeing them.

"You seem nervous."

"I am a little."

"You know I'd never hurt you, right?"

She nodded.

"Then what's making you nervous?"

"Being naked in front of you. It's still daylight."

"Oh, for Pete's sake. I thought we settled that."

"Maybe you're settled with it, but it might take me a
while to catch up."

He sighed. "I guess I can be patient, but you need to
realize that my attraction to you is only partly physical.
I admire you. You're intelligent, strong, and independent. So many women I meet in bars are bimbos. They
think a perfect figure and long blond hair make up for
immaturity and superficiality." He twirled his long
blond hair around his finger and giggled while batting
his eyelashes.

Roz laughed. At last her expression relaxed, and she
let her skirt drop to the floor.

Konrad's eyes widened, and he tore his shirt off.
Buttons popped and clicked against the walls and floor.

She stared at his light furring of chest hair and ran
her fingertips through it. "You're a natural blond, I see."

He chuckled, but it did little to break the tension
mounting. He tried to finish unbuttoning her blouse, but
his hands shook.

"I'll do it."

Konrad turned around and shoved off his black jeans. He didn't dare watch her strip, because if she stripped slowly, trying to tease him, he might lose it.

When he was naked, he set his hands on his hips and asked, "Ready?"

The bedsprings creaked softly. "Ready," she said.

He pivoted and froze. Roz lay atop his fur blanket, playing with a string of pearls around her ivory neck. Other than that, she displayed her luscious curvaceous body in all its naked glory. "You're gorgeous. Why the hell don't you know it?"

A shy smile crossed her face. "Thank you," she said. She gazed over at him, and her mouth fell open. "Oh, my God. I thought you might be um…well endowed, but…you're frickin' huge!"

His natural protector kicked in, and he tamped his urgency. "Don't worry, angel. I'll prepare you to take me." He lay down and scooted beside her.

Her "Thanks" whispered out on a sigh.

He glanced down her body and saw her nipples pebbled tight. He licked his lips. "I'll get you ready. So ready you'll feel as if you'll go mad if you don't get me inside."

"I already feel that way."

It was true. The scent of her sweet arousal filled his nostrils and drove his hunger. He leaned over her, and she tipped her face to meet his kiss.

They shared a stirring passion that grew steadily. His hand trembled, and he pushed it into the mattress to steady himself. It was all he could do to keep from spreading her legs apart and thrusting inside.

Roz couldn't wait to feel his hard length inside her. So what if she'd been feeling needy and desperate ever since her best friend found the love of her life? It was Roz's turn now. She had never jumped into bed with a man so quickly, but it had never felt so right before.

His tongue invaded her mouth, and she welcomed it. The man could kiss! His lips were full and the pressure was just right. When he sucked in a breath ever so slightly, their mouths locked in a sensual vacuum.

Oh, Lord. I could kiss him all day.

"I'm happy to hear that, angel. I have the feeling we might spend a lot of time in this position."

What do you mean by that? She soon forgot to care.

His hand wandered to her breast and cupped it, then he stroked the nipple with his thumb.

Oh, God, that feels good.

He squeezed the globe gently. *"This is just the beginning."*

With his thumb and index finger, he captured the tip and rolled it gently. She moaned into his mouth from the pleasure of it. He broke the kiss and slid downward to suckle her. The mass of his hair fell forward to tickle her skin. She swept it back over his shoulder.

He latched onto her nipple and drew it in, sucking with purpose. A bolt of lust shot straight to her womb, and she arched. She cupped his head and pulled him toward her breast, letting him know she wanted more.

His hand found her mons, and while he continued to suckle, he caressed and stroked her pussy.

The harder he sucked, the more she moaned. The more she moaned, the closer he came to touching her ultimate pleasure point. At last he zeroed in on her clit and rubbed. Overwhelming sensations built quickly as a heady excitement filled her. She was going to come and come hard.

The pleasure drove her to a higher peak than she'd ever experienced before and launched her into space. She shattered. Grabbing his pillow at the last second, she held it hard against her mouth and screamed out her release as she shook and spasmed.

"Oh, God!" Her heart was pounding, pounding so hard she could feel it hammering against her ribs, yet another orgasm was quickly building.

Don't stop. Oh, please don't stop.

"Stopping never entered my mind."

She wanted to laugh. She wanted to cry. It had been so long, and she was greedy. Eyes closed, she concentrated on the intense feelings in her body as he continued to suck and rub. Soon she shot straight to the top of another violent climax. She clamped the pillow down with both hands and screamed herself hoarse. At last she batted his hand away. The pleasure was so intense, she didn't think she could stand another moment without the white hot fire turning to pain.

Eventually when her boneless body quietly vibrated but no longer quaked, she heard, "Are you all right, angel?"

Panting, she communicated weakly. *Yes. But no more. I can't take any more.* Her eyes drifted open, and she saw Konrad propped on his elbow with a satisfied grin on his face.

———м———

"You'll miss the best part if we stop now."

Roz smiled and spread her legs. "Who said anything about stopping?"

"Thank goodness. Even stalling would be hell right now, but I don't want to push you."

"Push me, pull me. At this point, you can do anything you want to me."

He laughed. "I'd rather give you the control until I know your limits."

"*How awesome is he?*"

How awesome is it that I can hear how awesome you think I am?

She giggled and clamped her hands over her mouth as if she'd spilled the beans out loud. He laughed with her then said, "Just think how well this can work. You can tell me what you like and don't like without saying a word."

"I have the feeling you don't need my coaching."

"Think of it as guidance. I want you to enjoy the experience fully."

"I already have, but you haven't."

"Are you ready for me?"

"Why don't you find out?"

He almost growled, but his animal instincts needed to be kept in check. God knows what he might communicate if he wasn't careful. Better stay away from doggy-style too. He might be tempted to mark her as his own with a bite to her neck. It was too soon for that.

Grabbing a condom from his nightstand, he ripped open the packet with his teeth and rolled the latex over his hard cock.

"You're not allergic to latex, are you?"

She shook her head and then her eyes went wide. "Oh, God. What do people do if they are?"

He kneeled between her legs and lowered his face to kiss her neck and shoulder. "As long as neither of us break out in a rash, it's none of my business." He nibbled along the long column of her soft, sensitive flesh. *Roz?*

"Yes?"

Does this feel good?

"Oh, yes."

He worked his way down and stopped to suckle her breast. *And this?*

"You know how good that feels." How convenient that he could ask her for guidance telepathically without breaking the glorious suction.

Konrad let out a telepathic throaty chuckle and continued paying homage to both of her breasts. She arched and moaned her appreciation.

When she seemed thoroughly relaxed, he shifted his position and poised his cock close to her opening. He tested her with two fingers first. She rocked against his fingers as if she were making love to them.

Oh, yeah, she was ready.

"Do you accept me?"

Roz looked up at him with surprise, but eventually whispered, "Yes."

"Do you accept yourself?"

Apparently she couldn't answer that since she turned her face away from him.

Damn. Someday, you will. "Do you at least believe that I accept you?"

She nodded. "Yes."

Konrad smiled and entered her slowly, only an inch at a time. "Are you okay, angel?"

She purred her affirmation.

At last he was fully seated inside her, and she opened her eyes. Smiling up at him, she wrapped her arms around his neck. "Well, are you going to go for it, or what?"

Konrad grinned and moved in and out of her channel slowly. She held his gaze, and something special passed between them, some flicker of golden light.

Could it be love? So soon?

"I'm fine. You can go faster...if you want to."

Whew, apparently she hadn't heard his thought and misinterpreted whatever look crossed his face.

She closed her eyes, and he increased his rhythm. Her hips rose to meet him, thrust for thrust. She opened her mouth occasionally and little mewls of pleasure escaped.

This type of lovemaking was different for Konrad. He was truly more interested in his partner's enjoyment than his own. Correction—his mate's. Holding back from giving into his feral nature had always been difficult, but for some reason he was content to go slow and make sex last with Roz. It occurred to him that he was making love, not just fucking. *So that's the difference!*

"*What's the difference, lover?*"

The familiar pressure began to build at the base of his spine. There was no way he could answer her now. This wasn't the time for a philosophical discussion, especially one that might sound like they were rushing into a serious relationship. He increased his speed again, and Roz rocked faster, staying right with him.

"You're so tight, so wet and hot. So perfect."

Her breaths matched his, sharp, shallow, and quick. He bore down on her pelvis and added a grinding motion, knowing she'd enjoy it as much as he.

She moaned louder. With every thrust he built closer to a fevered peak. At the moment her muscles clenched, he spiraled out of control. His orgasm ripped through him like a hurricane. Roz cried out and buried her face in his pillow again. She shook while her muscles milked him dry. They bucked together, each riding the waves of climax to the very last aftershock.

His instinct to mark her kicked in, but it was too soon. He wanted her to want it. Instead, he kissed the sensitive hollow where her neck and shoulder met.

He lifted his head and saw tears shimmering in her eyes.

Concern slapped him back to reality. "Oh, no. Did I hurt you?"

She shook her head and sighed. "That was beautiful."

Happy that her feelings originated from a deeply emotional place and not pain, he thanked whatever divine power held him back.

———∿∿∿———

"Roz?"

She opened her eyes slowly and realized she had drifted into a contented sleep. Konrad lay beside her, propped on his elbow, and traced a line from her cleavage to her bellybutton. A shiver passed through her, and her nipples pebbled.

"I…I'm sorry. I must have fallen asleep."

"That's okay. You looked peaceful. It was nice watching you."

"You were watching me?"

"Uh-huh. But I'm afraid you have to go now."

"What time is it?"

"I don't know, but the sun is going down."

"Oh!" She sat bolt upright. "I must have been out for hours."

He rested a hand on her thigh. "Don't worry about it. If it weren't tonight…I mean, I have stuff to do."

"That's right. You work nights." She glanced down at her nudity and smiled. Then she whispered, "Thank you."

He smiled, but it quickly faded. "Roz, I want you to know something."

Uh-oh. Here it comes.

"Here what comes?"

"Oh, nothing. Say whatever you were going to say."

He hesitated then surprised her by saying, "It might not always be like that. Gentle, I mean. I can get…well, much stronger. More urgent."

"Oh." *Whew.* "That's fine. I'm really not that fragile. I think I'd like…no, I *know* I'd like having sex with you all kinds of ways. I've never had wild monkey lovin'."

"What I mean is, I can get a little rough."

Her mouth hung open, then she shut it and raised her chin. "I can take it. Hey, who knows, maybe I can get rough too. I've never tried that either."

"This isn't a matter of trying or not trying something. It's who I am." He cocked his head. "What did you think I was going to say?"

"When?"

"When I said I had to tell you something and you responded with, Uh-oh."

She sighed. "Some speech about not getting tied down to one person. Not to expect—"

"Whoa. That's not me. I don't know what kind of guys you've been with, but I'm not the love 'em and leave 'em type. In fact, I assumed we'd be exclusive."

"Already? I mean…yeah!"

"Good. I'm all yours, and you're not seeing anyone but me. Got it?"

"Naturally. That's only fair."

He grinned and rolled out of bed. Extending his hand, Konrad hauled her up. She couldn't get over how comfortable he was in the nude. Of course, if she had a body to die for, like he did, she would walk around in the nude all the time.

"Get dressed, angel. I'll call you tomorrow."

"Promise?"

"Unless I get arrested again." He grinned. "I'd call you because you're my lawyer."

"You'd better be kidding."

The rest of the week passed slowly. Konrad called Roz every night, but didn't want to bug her and come off as desperate. Besides, she had to work, so he bode his time, reading one of the many new novels he'd picked up on his last trip to the bookstore. Now that it was Friday, he figured he'd pop downstairs after she got home from work and see if she'd like to go out to dinner. He dressed casually in one of his many black T-shirts and a pair of jeans.

Konrad heard a knock on his door. Wondering if it might be Roz and she got home early, he strode over and opened it wide. To his surprise and slight disappointment, Morgaine stood there.

"Hi, Konrad. Do you have a minute?"

"Uh, sure. Do you need something moved?"

She chuckled. "No, I don't need your strength this time. I need one of your other skills."

"Really? What's that?"

Morgaine lowered her voice. "I need a thief."

Konrad stiffened and glared at her. When he could speak again, he whispered, "You'd better come inside."

She entered his apartment, and he shut the door carefully to avoid the loud click. He then whispered, "Is Chad here?"

She asked in a normal tone of voice, "Chad, are you in the room?" She waited a bit and shook her head. "Nope."

"Whew. I know he can't blab what he overhears to anyone but you or Gwyneth, but still—"

"I know what you mean." Glancing at the books lining the walls, she said, "Wow, you must really like to read."

"Very much. But right now I'm more interested in what you have to say. Take a seat."

She sat on his brown microfiber couch. "I only know what I overheard a few days ago."

"You're just going by what you heard?" Konrad sat in the adjacent overstuffed armchair. "I mean, you're psychic, aren't you?"

"Yeah, but that doesn't mean I know absolutely everything."

"What *do* you know?"

"Just bits and pieces, and I've learned it's better not to jump to conclusions until I double check the information I'm getting."

"Okay. What do you know, and what do you have to double check?"

"Relax. I know you're a good man, and I'm quite safe sitting here, talking to you. I know you work nights. And yesterday, I overheard that you were arrested. I was hoping you might be able to help me with something in an 'It takes a thief' kind of way."

"I'm not stealing anything for you."

"Oh, no." She laughed. "I didn't mean that."

Konrad shifted uncomfortably in his chair. "Okay, keep talking."

"I need your advice to help me with my first job as a medium. I've been called in to communicate with the ghost haunting the Isabella Stewart Gardner Museum."

"You're kidding. The art museum that was robbed several years ago?"

"Yeah."

"It's haunted?"

"Yup, so there might actually be an eyewitness."

"Excellent! I was severely pissed off when I found out about the theft."

"You and the rest of the world, apparently. But I was down in Maryland then and didn't hear much about it. The cops don't want to tell me anything, either. They say it's so it doesn't affect the questions I ask the ghost, but I think they want me to prove my abilities as a psychic and medium."

"Have you talked to the ghost yet?"

"Yes, Gwyneth went with me, but she couldn't hear

him unless I let him use my vocal cords. He said he was there during the robbery. Unfortunately, he's confusing the hell out of me. What little he tells me doesn't make any sense."

"What has he told you?"

"He says the cops did it."

"That's because the thieves dressed as cops to get in, then overpowered the guards and tied them up."

Morgaine threw her hands in the air. "For Goddess's sake! Why couldn't the police tell me at least that much? I've been going crazy trying to figure out if he was just messing with us."

"What do you know about this ghost?"

"He's been there since the thirties. His name is Reginald. He feels very protective of the place. He won't tell me why. He said he knew the woman who built it."

"Isabella Stewart Gardener."

Morgaine shrugged. "I guess so."

"I know a little bit about her. I can grab a reference book and find more for you, if you like."

"You'd better not. If I sound like an encyclopedia, they'll think I looked her up. But in a CliffsNotes version, tell me what you know."

Konrad sat up straighter. "I love this woman's story. She wasn't accepted by the Boston blue bloods because she didn't live the life of a restrained, Victorian matron. She loved to travel, had a sense of humor, and was vivacious. In other words, she lived large."

"I like her already."

"Yeah, I think you two would have gotten along just fine. Naturally she became the subject of scandals. As far as we know, they were unsubstantiated rumors. She was once quoted as saying, 'Don't spoil a good story by telling the truth.'"

Morgaine laughed. "I'll have to remember that one next time someone accuses Gwyneth and me of being lesbian devil worshippers."

"You're kidding!"

"Yeah, I am. Well, about the devil worship, that is. Dottie and Ralph thought we were lesbians because of the noises we made being phone-sex actresses."

Konrad laughed. "Yeah, I heard about that. You've been quiet lately, though."

"Yeah, she threatened to throw us out if we kept up all the racket, even though it paid the rent."

"Unbelievable."

"Now if I can crack this case, there's a nice reward in it for me."

"I'll bet. How much?"

"The FBI is offering five million dollars for the recovery of all the stolen goods. A portion less, if only part of it is recovered."

Konrad whistled.

"Yeah, so it's a good thing I got this job, and I really want to do it well. I...I have a hard time leaving the apartment building due to my agoraphobia, but a reward like that, and someone going with me...well, it's worth anything I have to do. Anyway, tell me more about this interesting Isabella."

"She loved the Red Sox as well as the symphony and made loads of friends in drastically different circles. She became a major patron of the arts and built the combination home and museum in the Fenway area to house

her growing collection. She wanted to share it with the
average American."

"I saw a portrait of her at the museum."

"Oh, yeah. She displayed the portraits of friends
like John Singer Sargent and James McNeill Whistler,
but also amassed a collection of famous European
painters. It's considered priceless today. She held
concerts too. I went to hear a former student of mine
play piano there."

"What a gorgeous setting for a concert. I don't suppose you're talking about rock and roll, though."

Konrad laughed. "No, it's mostly classical stuff.
Maybe some jazz. I can't picture the calm, serene atmosphere of that atrium being shattered by Aerosmith."

"Me neither."

"Did you see the blank spots on the wall where the
stolen art had been? The curator left it like that."

"Yeah. I was almost sick to my stomach when I realized the theft involved some original Rembrandts."

"The most valuable painting they stole from the
Dutch gallery was the Vermeer. There's only something
like thirty-six of them in the world."

Morgaine leaned forward. "Would you come with
me? Maybe because you know a lot about the museum
and Mrs. Gardener, Reginald will talk to you through
me, and you can make sense of it. Plus, you might know
how they got away with it, because of your…you know."

"My security expertise?"

"Exactly!"

"Sure. I haven't been there for a while. When were
you planning to go?"

"I can go anytime. I just need to call first."

"Don't you need privacy to do your medium thing?"

"They let me upstairs into one of the parlors. That's where Reginald likes to hang out. He's not crazy about the visitors. Especially if they try to touch things."

"Is that how they knew he was there? Did he throw a chair at a tourist's head or something?"

"No. The curator said a couple of people claimed they saw him, and he senses a presence from time to time. That's why the curator avoids the parlor and told me I might find Reginald there."

"It sounds like I'll see the part that's not open to the public if I go with you."

"Yup."

"And we're going to talk to someone who knew Isabella personally?"

"If he'll talk to us."

"If he loved Isabella, he'll talk. Men always like to talk about the women they loved."

Chapter 4

A FEW DAYS LATER, MORGAINE TOOK A SEAT AT THE only table in the room. She sensed it had been for holding canapés and a floral centerpiece at cocktail parties. *So* not her thing. "Okay, remember how we all held hands at the séance when the medium contacted Chad?"

Konrad nodded.

"Well, if Reginald is going to talk to you *through* me instead of just communicating with me through my mind, I'll need all the extra energy I can get. Would you mind?"

"Not at all." Konrad sat opposite Morgaine at the highly polished table and extended his reach.

"Thanks." Morgaine clasped Konrad's hands, closed her eyes, and took several deep breaths to clear her energy. The parlor was illuminated only by natural light and one white candle. She hoped Reginald wouldn't be shy about talking through her to a stranger, but she had prepared him by introducing Konrad as a security expert.

"Reginald, are you willing to speak to my friend through me?" She waited a few moments then sat up ramrod straight, as if a broomstick had been inserted you know where.

"Greetings." The much lower voice of a man spoke through her mouth.

Konrad responded with, "Um, hello. Are you Reginald?"

"Who else would I be?"

THE WEREWOLF UPSTAIRS 55

Konrad sighed.

"Is there a problem?" Reginald asked.

"Oh, nothing. Are all ghosts so snippy and sarcastic?"

"I beg your pardon? Did you just insult me?"

"It's just that you remind me of the only other ghost I know. I need to ask a few questions to help Morgaine. Are you willing to answer them?"

"Ordinarily I'd never speak to a man in such dire need of a haircut, but if you can catch these felons and put them away, I'll do what I can."

"Okay." Under his breath Konrad mumbled, "Talk about insults."

"What was that?" Reginald asked in an angry tone.

"Never mind. What can you tell us about the robbery?"

"As I told the woman with the funny name, I saw the cops come in, hit the guards over their heads, tie them up with duct tape, and rob the place."

"You know those weren't real Boston cops, don't you?"

"How would I know that? Come to think of it, how would you know that? Were you there?"

"No."

"Well, then." A long sigh emitted from Morgaine's mouth. "They took my favorite Degas, *Three Mounted Jockeys*."

"There were three of them?"

"No, you dolt. The name of the painting was *Three Mounted Jockeys*. You know nothing about art, do you?"

"I know more than the average American."

"That's probably true. Ha. I cannot believe how stupid people are in this day and age. Well, back to the matter at hand. There were two robbers."

"Fine. Can you give me descriptions?"

"I'm sure the two guards gave the police their descriptions, but because I'm in a generous mood, I'll try to remember. They were both Caucasian. One was about six feet and the other slightly shorter. They wore fake moustaches and spoke with what passes for a Boston accent these days. Not the eloquent accents of my time, but an uncultured dialect that made them sound ignorant and uncouth. They used foul language too."

"Did you notice anything else? Perhaps the thieves said something to each other after they stashed the guards in the basement?"

"How did you know about that? Perhaps you were in on it!"

"I read it in the newspaper. Why are you so suspicious of me?"

"Oh, no reason. I just don't believe a security expert should have hair longer than the woman he's with."

"Let's get back to the case. Did they say anything about already having a buyer?"

"They mentioned getting the stuff into the automobile and driving to Revere."

"Revere! That's a huge new clue. What else?"

"Well, they had a list."

"It sounds like they knew exactly what their buyer or buyers wanted."

"Yes, and someone knew the value of these items. Like a bronze beaker from the Shang Dynasty. It was at least three thousand years old, possibly four; in other words, priceless."

"Did they take anything *not* on the list?"

"Only a Rembrandt etching that was postage-stamp

size. A self-portrait. I imagine they thought they could hide it pretty easily."

"Probably. They may have tried to fence it themselves. That would be helpful if the piece ever surfaces. It could lead us directly back to the thieves. Then they could tell us where the rest of it went."

"The police and FBI were all over this place, collecting evidence and questioning the staff. I can't believe they haven't caught the hooligans? It's been twenty years."

"I imagine the FBI has done all the right things."

"Maybe they were in on it."

Konrad snorted. "I doubt it."

"But they had police uniforms and guns."

"Those can be bought."

"And the patches that said Boston Police?"

"They may have made or stolen those. My twin brother is a Boston cop. He might be able to ask some of the veterans about it."

"Oh, so that's why you don't want to believe the police are in on it. Your brother is a flatfoot."

Konrad bristled. "Look, most cops are honest, hard-working individuals who put their lives on the— "

Male laughter interrupted Konrad.

His grip tightened, and he growled.

Morgaine let go of his hands, swayed, and leaned over.

Konrad shot to his feet and grabbed her shoulders before she hit the table. "Morgaine, are you all right?"

She took a few panting breaths and opened her eyes.

"Yeah, I'm fine."

"Where did Reginald go?"

"I don't know. I imagine he's still around. I just had to intervene. You two weren't getting along very well."

"No kidding. I have the feeling old Reggie doesn't like cops. Maybe he wasn't squeaky clean himself."

"If we want information, you two have to play nice." Morgaine suddenly sat bolt upright, opened her mouth, and spoke with the formal male voice again. "Don't call me Reggie, and I won't call you Connie. Being a disembodied spirit isn't easy. How would you like to try it, hmmm?"

"Is that a threat?"

"What could I possibly threaten you with? Unless it's withholding information."

"You wouldn't."

A long silence followed, with Morgaine holding her stiff position.

"Oh c'mon. Don't be childish," Konrad said.

"Childish? How dare you. I was born in 1890. I'm well over a hundred years older than you."

"No, you're not. We're barely a generation apart. I was born in 1912."

Loud male laughter exploded from Morgaine's mouth.

"I'll prove it." Konrad stood and stripped.

"Oh, my. You're rather like a work of art yourself. What big muscles you have, my dear."

Konrad grinned, growled, and began to shift. His hair seemed to shrink inside his head and sprout elsewhere on his body. His nose and chin extended, and his back rounded. As he fell forward, his hands and arms became paws and legs.

A long, loud male scream resounded that could have been heard from the sidewalk outside. Konrad shifted back and dressed quickly.

Morgaine felt Reginald practically rip himself out

of her and flee. She wavered a moment and braced her hands on the table. Konrad lowered himself to the chair opposite her as if nothing had happened.

Morgaine crossed her arms and glared at him. "Did you have to do that? I've never seen you change. It even freaked *me* out!"

"Sorry, but I hate being patronized."

"So do I, but you don't see me flying around on a broomstick every time someone pisses me off."

Konrad shrugged. "I figured it was important that he understand that not everyone fits in his narrow view of mankind. Some of us aren't even human and have much longer life spans."

"That's it? That's all you have to say for yourself? This was my first case, and you probably blew it for me."

"I'm sorry. You're right. Maybe if I apologize to Reginald—"

"I doubt he'll ever speak to me again. And he certainly won't speak to you."

"I'm very sorry. Maybe I can think of something to salvage the situation."

The door to the parlor flew open and the curator rushed in. "What happened? I thought I heard a scream."

Morgaine and Konrad rode the subway back to their neighborhood in silence. It was just as well. Konrad couldn't think of much to say in the way of apology. He really couldn't blame Morgaine if she never spoke to him again.

As they strolled toward their building, Morgaine said, "I'm glad you thought fast and said you screamed because you thought you saw the ghost."

"I have a feeling the curator didn't believe me."

"Probably because you don't look like the type of guy to shriek in fear. Besides, Reginald's voice doesn't match the timbre of yours, even coming out of my mouth."

He chuckled. "Yeah, I don't scream like a little girl."

"Well, I almost did when I opened my eyes and saw you changing back."

"You've never seen me change before?" He grabbed the brass door handle but refrained from opening the front door.

"How could I?"

"By looking out your window, although I usually come back before dawn and Sly lets me in. I don't know if you're up that early. Or you could catch me at night, but ever since Jason installed the motion detector, it's bright as hell out there, so I have to find a Dumpster to hide behind, where I can stash my clothes and shift."

"That must be nerve-wracking. What if Jason or Merry pulled into their parking spots just as you were shifting?"

"Yeah, believe me, I worry about that."

"I can cast a spell to shield you from view whenever you shift, if you like."

Konrad almost gasped. "You can?"

"I believe so. I haven't actually tried to put a spell on a werewolf before. I might have to tweak it a bit."

He glanced at the apartment to the right of the front door. "Listen, don't say anything to Roz about me, okay?"

Morgaine placed her hands on her hips and frowned. "You're going to tell her, though."

"Yes, when the time is right." *When the hell that'll be, I don't know.*

She seemed to relax, so he opened the heavy front door and held it for her. Pausing at the bottom of the stairs, she said, "Well, thanks for your…help."

"I'm really sorry."

"No need to apologize. I didn't really know what would happen. I took a chance, and it didn't work out." She sighed. "Back to the drawing board."

"You know who might be able to help you with Reginald more than I can?"

"Who?"

"Roz. She has a way of drawing people out. I've heard her deal with different delicate situations very calmly and non-judgmentally. Plus she knows what kind of evidence is admissible in court. I think she'd be perfect."

"Is she home?"

"Why don't we find out? I told her I'd call on her today anyway. Oh, and just so you know, I'm going to tell her I got fired from my…um, job."

"Why?"

"Because I don't want to do it anymore."

"Why not just say you quit?"

"Because I really don't want to go back to it."

Morgaine laid a hand on his arm. "I admire that. Will she believe you?"

He shrugged. "She has no reason not to."

"Okay. Give it a try." Morgaine waited behind him while Konrad lifted the brass door knocker and rapped on Roz's door.

She opened it and beamed up into his smiling face.

"Good afternoon, ma'am. May I interest you in buying some magazines today?"

"Only if you deliver them in person, naked, holding a bottle of Champagne," she said and gave him a come-hither look. She stepped back and opened the door wider.

Clearing her throat, Morgaine said, "Dottie has rules about public nudity, but it wouldn't bother me."

Roz glanced into the hall and gasped when she realized they weren't alone.

Konrad cringed. "Uh, sorry. I should have said that Morgaine's waiting to ask you something."

"Oops." Roz blushed.

When Morgaine stepped forward, she said, "Don't be embarrassed. I think it's cute when couples flirt."

Roz let out a small giggle and said, "Come in, both of you. Have a seat."

Morgaine sat on Roz's antique-looking couch, while Konrad wandered around and looked at her things. He didn't figure her for an antique buff. An old roll-top desk. A tall wooden cabinet with a glass panel holding thick tomes that he assumed were law books. Lots of fragile-looking furniture he wouldn't dare put his full weight on.

"Can I get you guys anything to drink?"

"No, thanks," Morgaine said.

Roz sat next to her on the sofa. "So…what did you want to ask me?"

"I guess I should start at the beginning. I'm a psychic witch and a medium."

Roz nodded, but her expression didn't change.

Konrad blew out a breath of relief. *Whew. She handled that pretty well*. But then he remembered she knew enough about Morgaine already, like leading a séance with Chad, so the information might not come as a shock.

"I've been hired to work with a new witness who was present during the theft at the Isabella Stewart Gardener Museum."

Roz grew more animated. "Really? There's a new witness? So there might be hope of catching those douche bags who robbed the place, after all?"

"Yes. We've already gained some new information, but we don't know how much of it can be used in court."

"Why is that?"

"Because the new witness is a ghost."

Roz's mouth dropped open. "I…it didn't come home with you, did it?"

It's okay, darling. I'm right here. You're perfectly safe.

"*Are you sure? Ghosts freak me the hell out! Don't you feel uncomfortable around them?*"

No. Even if the room were full of them, they can't hurt you.

"*Ugh, that would be like thinking you're alone in the bathroom while attending a peeping Tom convention.*"

She quickly recovered her neutral demeanor and said, "A ghost? Haunting the museum?"

"Yes, so if we learn anything from Reginald—that's the spirit's name— do you think it could be used to claim the reward? I don't want the court to say it's bunk and cheat me out of my money if I help recover the art."

Roz rose to her feet and paced as she talked. "Has the ghost's presence been substantiated?"

"Well, yeah. I've talked to him."

Konrad spoke up. "So have I. There are two of us who can attest to his being there.

Roz's eyebrows rose as she focused her sharp gaze on Konrad. "You can talk to ghosts too?"

"Oh, no. I didn't mean that. Morgaine did her medium thing while I was there. I heard his voice coming through her mouth."

Roz nodded. "Freaky, but okay…continue."

"Well," Morgaine said, "the curator sensed his presence and admitted a couple of visitors claimed to have seen him."

"I'll have to check precedents, but I imagine we can't use 'sensing a presence.' Even a sighting could be explained away. But I'm curious about your being a medium. Can you prove you have that, um, gift?"

"Sure." She looked to Konrad. "Does she know about Chad?"

"Yes. I asked him not to bother Roz, but I don't know if he listened to me or not."

"Would you mind a demonstration if I can get Chad to cooperate?" Morgaine asked.

Roz sat up straighter. "Actually that sounds fascinating."

"Good. He usually hangs out on the third floor, so I'll run upstairs and see if I can find him."

"Okay." Roz watched as Morgaine left and then crossed the room to where Konrad was leaning against the mantelpiece.

Konrad said, "I was thinking about you all morning, when I wasn't playing ghost busters." He captured her waist and pulled her toward him for a quick peck on the lips and a hug. Her arms around his neck seemed to be shaking.

"Roz, are you all right?"

"Yeah. It's just that…well, there's been a lot to

take in lately. Our strange new way of communicating, Morgaine's a witch and a medium, we have a ghost in the building. What next? Vampires and werewolves?"

Konrad chuckled nervously. "Don't worry, darling. I won't let the boogeyman get you." *Don't think about it, don't think about it…*

"Don't think about what?"

"Uh, nothin'. I got fired today, that's all."

She sucked in a breath. "Really? Is it because you were arrested?"

"Yes. They can't be too careful, you know."

"But you weren't guilty."

He shrugged.

"I don't think they should get away with that. Let me look into grounds for a wrongful termination case." Her lips thinned to a hard line.

"No, don't. I was ready to quit anyway. It just isn't worth the aggravation."

She took his hand. "I'm sorry that happened to you."

"I'm not. Now I can be awake during the day and see more of you." He winked.

"And maybe help Morgaine," Roz added. "Are you sure she's for real?"

"I'm pretty darn sure."

"Look, I believe in certain things I can't explain away with logic. Psychics, for instance. I know the government has been doing psychic research. And it does seem like there's a large portion of our brains that most of us don't use."

He nodded but didn't want to say anything, so she'd continue talking. What else did she believe in?

"Some are charlatans, to be sure. But I guess some

have a certain amount of credibility. Do you believe she's the real deal?"

Konrad squeezed her hand. "I've seen her talk to Chad, and at the museum she seemed to go into a trance, and I heard the voice of someone else come out of her mouth."

"Were you with her the whole time? Had she been there before?"

"That was the second time she'd been there. Gwyneth went with her first. I guess they could have rigged something up before, but if she can demonstrate something here, on the fly, I know I'll be impressed. Do you want to look around to be sure she didn't plant any microphones?"

"Good idea." Roz began to check the couch cushions where Morgaine had been sitting when a knock sounded at the door.

"I'll get it." Konrad opened the door, but no one was there. Then he heard footsteps on the stairs, and Morgaine came into view.

"I guess Chad got here before me."

Konrad stepped back and waited for Morgaine to enter. "Is he here?"

She cocked her head as if listening to someone whisper in her ear. "Yes, he's here. And he wants to know what you're looking for in the sofa cushions."

Konrad shut the door and changed the subject. "Ready?"

"I am, are you?" Morgaine asked, looking at Roz.

She took a deep breath and nodded.

—⁓—

"Chad, you know Konrad and Roz, right?"

"*Know them? That's a stretch. I know who they are. The tall one with long hair who turns into a wolf at the full moon, that's Konrad. The chubby one with glasses and her hair in a bun is Roz. What her deal is, I haven't heard yet. Enlighten me.*"

"Roz is a lawyer," Morgaine said. "I may need her help in the museum case I'm working on."

"*Why? Did you catch the thief?*"

"Not yet."

Konrad and Roz stared alternately at her and at each other. At one point, they both shrugged.

"Okay, I need to demonstrate to Roz and Konrad that you and I are really communicating. What can you tell me about them that I wouldn't know?"

"*Have you been in Roz's apartment before?*"

"I was here when Merry lived here, but this is the first time since Roz moved in."

"*Good. Have you been in her bedroom yet?*"

"No. I've only been out here in the living room. I see what you're getting at. Maybe you can find something in her bedroom that I've never seen. Describe it to me in detail, and I'll tell them what it is."

"*You're pretty smart for a woman who wears black lipstick and nail polish.*"

"I'm not wearing the black lipstick today, in case you didn't notice. I try to be more conservative when I visit the museum."

Chad laughed.

Morgaine rolled her eyes. "Whatever. Get on with it, please."

"*I've already been in there. Tell her she left the top*"

drawer open in her bedside table and there are three things in it: a box of tissues, a book, and a long plastic cylinder. Bright pink."

"Good. That's very specific." Morgaine faced Roz. "He said you left your bedside table drawer open. There's a book, a box of tissues, and some kind of pink plastic cylinder in it."

Roz's jaw dropped and she turned bright red.

"What's wrong?"

"*Oh, and extra batteries. I forgot to mention them.*"

Roz coughed and composed herself. "Nothing. Tell him to look for something else."

Chad was laughing hysterically.

"Chad, what did you do?"

"*Can I help it if she likes to read erotica and keeps a vibrator handy?*"

Morgaine dropped her head in her hands. She straightened, took a deep breath, and tried again. "Chad, cut the shit. Now find something else, and don't embarrass the poor woman."

Konrad smiled.

"*Okay, I'm going into her closet. Never mind. It's dark in there. I'll try the bathroom.*"

Morgaine waited and tapped her foot. Roz folded her hands and bit her lower lip.

"*Here's something. It's behind the shower curtain, so unless you've taken a shower with her—*"

"Of course I haven't. Now tell me what you're seeing."

"*She has about a dozen bath products. One of those natural sponges, a purple washcloth, a set of red plastic bottles with all kinds of perfumey…Aaa-cho.*"

"Goddess bless you."

Roz tipped her head, and the furrow between her brows deepened.

"Okay, he said there's a loofah, a purple washcloth, and a set of bath products in red bottles behind your shower curtain. He seems to be allergic to them."

"Not really, but I was allergic to all kinds of stuff when I was alive. Sneezing is just a force of habit I guess."

Konrad rose. "Roz? Morgaine? Do you want to check his information?"

"No, it sounds pretty accurate," Roz said. "You two can look if you want to."

Konrad smiled. "I'll admit, I'm curious. You wouldn't mind?"

"Be my guest."

Morgaine stayed seated. "I'll wait here just in case there's other stuff in there he can describe."

Roz shrugged. "No need to. I'm satisfied that you're really communicating with a...a—"

"Spirit," Morgaine supplied.

Roz shivered.

Konrad rejoined them. "Well, I'll be damned. It's exactly like he said." Then he strolled over to Roz and bumped her playfully. "No wonder you smell like cinnamon, spice, and everything nice. That's the fragrance in those bottles."

Roz rolled her eyes. "Okay, buddy. I've been embarrassed enough for one day." She turned to Morgaine. "You said you're a medium. Can Chad speak through you?"

"Yes, we've done it. Neither of us likes it very much, but he might be willing to give you a quick demonstration."

"I'd like to see it," she said.

"Chad, are you okay with that?"

"Ugh. If I must. You have no idea how disgusting it is to push myself down through your gray matter so I can use your brain, lungs, and vocal cords."

"It's no picnic for me either."

"Although it might be fun to say things you can't censor…like the juicy sex scene she was reading last night."

Morgaine sighed. "Chad, behave yourself. We don't need to hear about Roz's reading material."

"You know what?" Roz said. "I don't really need to hear him speak. If I go to the museum with you, I'll hear the other ghost talk through you, right?"

Morgaine smiled. "You're a wise woman."

Chapter 5

ROZ AND KONRAD WAITED IN LINE OUTSIDE THE museum while Morgaine was up in the parlor preparing Reginald for another visitor.

Roz stroked Konrad's back. "Why can't you come with me?"

"I really think it's better if I wait downstairs," Konrad said. "I kind of ticked him off. You'll be fine, though."

"What did you do?"

"Oh, nothing. He's a bit…I'm not sure how to put it. He has a superior attitude and gets touchy if you try to prove you're his equal?"

"Insecure?"

Konrad looked thoughtful. "Yeah, that might be part of it. But there's more. He got defensive when I asked how he knew Isabella. He also doesn't like cops. Anyway, I think he just didn't like me, and you'll probably have better luck if I'm not there."

Roz shrugged. "Whatever you say. I guess he can't really do anything to me, right?"

"No, you're quite safe. Morgaine knows when to shut him down, and I don't think he's learned how to use telekinesis to move objects, like Chad can."

"How did Chad learn that?"

"I don't know. Maybe you can ask Morgaine. Oh, look, here she comes."

Morgaine waved them inside.

Konrad dropped a dollar in the voluntary donation box on his way.

"Oh, I should give them some money too," Roz said.

"No. If you can get more information from him and make sure it's admissible in court, you might be able to help the FBI recover the stolen art. That's more valuable than a buck in the box."

She smiled. "That would be so cool. Do you really think—"

Morgaine interrupted by taking Roz's hand and pulling her around the line of tourists waiting to get in. Roz blew Konrad a kiss and followed Morgaine.

How weird is this? Meeting two ghosts when only a few days ago, I didn't think they existed.

Konrad answered telepathically. *"I'm proud of you. Just keep that open mind."*

On her way to the parlor, she asked, "So, how did you learn to be a medium, Morgaine?"

"Chad taught me. Actually, I attended a séance and saw him speak through another, more experienced medium. I've always worked hard to fine-tune my psychic skills, so I was able to hear him when no one else could. It wasn't that big a stretch."

"Ah, so he already wanted to communicate through you to other people?"

"Yeah, he was motivated. He wanted to find out who murdered him, and the only way he could speak to the private detective Jason hired was through a medium."

"He was murdered? In our building?"

"Yeah, but it was a long time ago and in his own apartment...which he still considers *his*. Chad was actually the one who suggested I channel him. It really helps if the spirit trusts you."

"Reginald must trust you too, then."

"Either that or he's motivated to recover the stolen art." Morgaine smiled. "I think he was sweet on Isabella, but he was admiring Konrad too. Maybe he's bisexual."

"So, he wants to do this for her? That's sweet. But if he's bi and admired my boyfriend, why did Konrad say he didn't like him?"

Morgaine looked uncomfortable for a second then relaxed. "Here we are. The curator wants to be present too. Let me find out if Reginald is here and introduce you first, before I go into my trance." She opened the parlor door, and Roz stepped inside.

It was quite a posh suite. Most of the furniture was Victorian. A huge circular velvet ottoman took up the middle of the room, with some ornate chairs by the fireplace. A table was placed on one side of the room and a few more chairs lined the other wall. It seemed like an odd set-up. It might be good for socializing, though. Several people could fit on that ottoman, and facing any direction, there would be someone to talk to.

"Hmm…the curator isn't here. Let's sit in those chairs by the fireplace. All we need to do is move them a little closer to each other."

As they moved the furniture, Morgaine said, "Konrad was able to reach across the table to hold hands, but I don't think you and I have long enough arms to connect comfortably."

"Connect?" Roz wasn't sure she wanted to connect comfortably or any other way to the black-haired, black-clad woman with black-lined eyes and black nail polish. Whatever fashion statement a person wants to make was fine, but this whole goth thing struck her as a little weird.

Morgaine sat in one of the chairs. "I need the energy of another person. It flows through your hands."

"It's not going to drain me, is it? Because Konrad and I have a date tonight." *And you know what that means...I hope. Please, please, please don't ask me to explain.*

"No. You'll have plenty of energy for your...date." Morgaine winked.

Roz wanted to breathe a sigh of relief, but sat quietly in the comfortable chair facing Morgaine.

Morgaine looked up toward the ceiling. "Oh, you *are* here, Reginald. I thought you might have stepped out. Are you ready?" She nodded. "Good. Roz, are you ready?"

"As ready as I'll ever be."

"Okay, hold my hands and close your eyes."

Roz did as she asked. A part of her wanted to keep her eyes open, to be sure there was no funny business going on. No microphones. No man hiding behind her chair, pretending to speak through her. But the logical Roz overcame the suspicious Roz when she couldn't come up with a reason for Morgaine to do those things.

Suddenly Morgaine spoke, but it didn't sound like her. A much lower voice said, "Greetings."

Roz opened one eye briefly. "Um...hello?"

"Are you the lawyer?"

"Yes."

"My, my. They make lovely lawyers these days."

Roz smiled and decided *some* ghosts might not be too bad. "Thank you. As you know, I'm here to ascertain whether or not you might have eyewitness information that could be admissible in court, should your information lead to an arrest. Where would you like to start?"

"Well, first of all, tell me what you just said."

"I'm sorry. Let me start over again. If you saw the thieves again, would you recognize them?"

"Oh, yes. Their faces weren't covered."

"If the police brought in mug shots, would you be willing to look through them?"

"No. Absolutely not. I won't work with the police. You, I don't mind."

Roz cleared her throat. "I see. Why don't you want to talk to the police?"

"Those blasted civil servants are corrupt. You can't convince me that they had nothing to do with it. The thieves walked in wearing police uniforms that fit well. They had all the official-looking patches and accouterments. The thieves might have even borrowed them from real cops for a cut of the profits."

"I hadn't thought of that. You could be right."

"Oh, good. You're willing to believe me. The freak who came earlier seemed to think there's no such thing as a dirty copper, just because his brother is on the force."

"I've noticed that Konrad's very protective of people he cares about. Is that why you didn't like him?"

"Ha. That's not the half of it."

Morgaine shut her mouth hard enough that her teeth clacked together.

She let go of Roz's hands and said in her own voice, "Let's stick to the case. You can investigate Konrad's character some other time."

Roz was taken aback, but nodded. Apparently

Reginald agreed too, because Morgaine reached out and closed her eyes again.

"Continuing my thoughts on the case and a possible trial," Roz said, "do you think you could pick the criminals out of a lineup?"

Morgaine channeled Reginald's voice and said, "Only if you bring them here. I don't leave the building."

Roz thought for a moment and wondered if Chad ever left their apartment building. She heard the door to the salon open, and she and Morgaine opened their eyes. The curator sauntered in.

"Oh, Roz, this is the curator, Mr. Tate."

"It looks like you started without me," he said.

"Yes, and we were doing quite well. Do you mind if we continue on as we were?"

"Please," he said. "Be my guest." He leaned against the door and crossed his arms.

Morgaine held out her hands toward Roz again, and she grasped them. When they had both closed their eyes, Reginald's voice came through Morgaine's mouth loud and clear.

"Hey," he exclaimed, "I think the thief may be in the building right now."

"What?" Roz's surprise almost caused her to drop Morgaine's hands.

"The…person who was here with you before. He's back again. I'll bet he had something to do with it. *That's* why he's hanging around so much. Returning to the scene of the crime. He also seemed to know more about the case than he should have. I had a bad feeling about him. Very bad. Maybe he was the getaway driver."

The curator stiffened. "It makes sense that they'd have one."

Reginald answered, "Absolutely they had one. I saw them dump everything in the trunk, and as soon as they jumped into the passenger doors, the automobile took off."

"Did you see a license plate number, or can you describe the car?" Roz asked, hopefully. That would certainly clear Konrad from any wrongdoing.

"What do I know about automobiles? Nothing. It was wide with four doors and a big trunk. I saw the shadow of a man in the driver's seat. He must have been tall with broad shoulders. He filled the space.

Morgaine clamped her mouth shut and let go of Roz's hands. She opened her eyes and said, "He's gone."

Konrad and Roz stopped at a coffee shop after dropping off Morgaine. A beautiful sunset colored the sky over the Citgo sign, so they found a seat next to the window.

Konrad stirred his coffee and said, "I guess this could be considered our first real date."

Roz's eyebrows rose. "If that's true, then I slept with someone *before* the first date. Oh, my God, that makes me a super slut!"

Konrad laughed. "You're not a slut. Not by any stretch of the imagination."

"Thank goodness. If I had the reputation, I would hope I'd have had the pleasure of earning it."

Konrad tipped his head and feigned a hurt expression. "You didn't enjoy yesterday?"

"Oh my God! That's not what I meant."

He chuckled. "I know that. I was just fishing for compliments."

She blew on her hot coffee. "You don't need to do that, you know. If anything, I'm apt to over-compliment you. It can get downright annoying."

"Go ahead. Annoy me."

"Are you serious?"

"Totally."

She stared at her coffee. "Well, let's see. You're intelligent. Probably the most intelligent guy I've ever dated. You're kind, but I'm used to lawyers, so it's not hard to impress me in that area—"

One side of her mouth curled up in the cute half-smile he recognized as her teasing smirk.

He leaned back and crossed his arms. "All right. I suppose I'll accept that as a compliment. What else do you like about me?"

She grinned and shook her head. "Boy, you're not just fishing, you're trawling with a big net."

He chuckled. "I know, I know. I'm sorry for putting you on the spot. When I told you to annoy me, I didn't think you'd really do it."

"Oh, so you weren't serious?"

"Not really, but thank you."

"Ha! Well, tit for tat, buddy. How about if you give me a few compliments?"

"Easy," he said. *Uh-oh. This could be dangerous. If I'm too superficial, she won't believe me, because of her rotten self-esteem issues.*

"*You never know. I might.*"

"Oh, you heard that?"

"Yup. Go ahead. Be superficial. I dare ya."

"Ha. You know how to get results, don't you?"

"You fish; I dare."

Konrad held up his hands. "Stop. I'll tell you, but first you have to promise to believe everything I say."

"Hmmm. A challenge. Okay, go for it."

"First, you're absolutely beautiful. I love your light-blue eyes and lush lips. Your high cheekbones and the dimple that deepens when you smile." He lowered his voice. "Your soft skin. The way you look at me when we're about to get intimate. Your kisses." He added telepathically, *"The way you scream your lungs out when you come."*

Roz's cheeks flushed, and even though she was staring at her coffee cup again, she was grinning.

"Okay, enough. I believe you, but better not push it."

If only she wasn't a lawyer.

"Why are you worried about my being a lawyer?"

"Oh, you heard me, again." Konrad needed a quick distraction. "I'd really like to find a job I could feel passionate about…almost as passionate as I feel about you. And I thought you said something like that too."

Roz chuckled. "Believe me, I'd like to find another career. I went into law for the wrong reasons."

"What do you mean?"

"My stepfather seemed powerful and untouchable as a lawyer. I wanted to feel that invulnerable too. Now that I look back, I can see exactly how scared I was at the time. Not of him, but all the changes taking place in my life. I was afraid of the unknown."

"That makes sense. You're not scared anymore?"

"Change sounds pretty good about now. But I don't want just some other job. I want to wake up excited to go to work."

"Yeah, I've known a few people who actually loved their jobs. I don't think they're that much different from you or me. They've just found their bliss."

"But how do we discover our bliss?"

Konrad scratched his head. "I guess they try it and fall in love. Just like dating." He snapped his fingers. "That's it. We can try lots of different things, together. Eventually one of us is bound to find something that clicks or something so enjoyable it doesn't even seem like work."

Roz sat back and raised her eyebrows. "That's a brilliant idea. We can make the attempts into dates, if you want to. It sure beats going to the movies or some other time waster, just to have an excuse to be together and have sex afterward."

Konrad's jaw dropped. "We can still have sex after the practical dates, though, right?"

Roz laughed. "What would you do if I said no?"

"Cry, and then ask you to a movie."

They laughed together and wound up grinning.

Konrad reached across the small table and took her hand. They wove their fingers together. A couple of people in the coffee shop glanced their way.

"People are looking," Roz said.

"Let 'em look. They're envious."

"You're not self-conscious?"

He chuckled. "No. Are you?"

She ran her fingers over the hair on the back of his hand. "No. I'm surprised, but not self-conscious. I don't think anyone has ever been envious of me before."

Konrad took her knuckles to his mouth and kissed them. "I'm glad we met." He grinned. "That's an understatement."

"We've made enough people jealous here. Maybe we

should get home before we do something everyone will be talking about for years."

—*~*—

Roz and Konrad barely made it through the door of his apartment in time. They couldn't keep their hands off each other any longer. Kissing and fingers flying, they tore at each other's clothes. Buttons popped and fabric flew in different directions. Konrad was naked in seconds, his cock fully engorged. He trapped Roz against the rolling ladder. Fortunately he'd grabbed a condom from his pocket before he lost his pants.

Roz's heart pounded, and she could have sworn she heard Konrad growl. *At last. The passionate, lust-crazed lover I've always dreamed of!* She grasped his shoulders.

He tore his mouth from hers and gazed down at her with shining eyes. "No matter what happens, Roz, know that I care; that I'll never hurt you."

The warning stopped her. She hooked one high heel on the bottom rung and leaned against the library ladder. Still resting her hands on his shoulders, she drew a deep breath. "Do you think you might possibly get rough?"

He fisted his hands and appeared to shake. "Yes," he hissed through clenched teeth. "It's taking all my self-control not to push you to your knees and take you from behind. Immediately."

Her mouth tried to form a word, but what word that was, she didn't know.

"I want you. Naked. Now. But I won't force you."

"I'm not being forced. I'm here, willingly. Konrad, whatever's happening, talk to me. We'll figure it out."

He turned his head and closed his eyes. *"You wouldn't be here with me if you knew."*

"Knew what? Oh, no! You're not some perv rapist who can't get off without violence, are you?"

"No! Of course not. I just have more of an animal nature than some men." He dragged shaky fingers over his scalp and through his hair. "If you can't take it rough, you'd better go."

"I don't want to go, but, Konrad, you're making me nervous."

He steadied himself against the ladder, trapping her between his rigid biceps, and took a few deep breaths. "I—I'm all right now."

A sigh of relief slipped past her lips. She reached for the zipper at the back of her skirt, unzipped it, and shimmied out of it. At last she wore only her underwear and shoes. She popped the front closure on her bra and let it slip to the floor.

He sniffed the air. With shaking fingers he rolled on the condom.

Her nipples tightened, and she removed her damp panties. "Take me," she said, tossing back her hair.

He was on her in an instant, his mouth on hers, his hands touching and taking. He pushed her back against the ladder, and she felt his cock nudge her belly. Rubbing against him, she urged him on.

His head lifted. His fingers squeezed her nipple, and a bolt of pleasure shot through her. Then his hand slid downward, and his hot, wet mouth was on her breast, sucking, licking, nipping.

His fingers slid into her slick channel, and he stroked her. "You're so wet. I love the way you feel around me. So tight. So hot. I can't wait to fuck you."

Speaking of hot, Roz felt as if she had a fever of a hundred and three. His blunt language got her even hotter, if that were possible.

He touched her clit, and her legs gave way. She would have fallen to the floor, except he caught her and held her trembling hips. She was pinned to the ladder. Her legs spread of their own accord. He dropped to his knees and muttered, "I have to taste you."

His rough tongue rasped against her clit, and a jolt tore through her. He then licked, licked, licked. Her pleasure was so intense, she wanted to scream, but didn't dare. There was no pillow to drown her out. She whimpered.

Her orgasm was building. Her clit throbbed, and she felt energy spiraling though her. "Konrad—"

He pulled away from her, and she wanted to shriek at him, ask him what the hell he thought he was doing by stopping.

He rose, lifted her legs, and wrapped them around his waist.

She grabbed onto a rung and held on for dear life.

"I don't want the whole building to hear you come. That's for me...just for me."

He pushed his cock against her sex. The head of his erection filled her passageway.

"Such a sweet little pussy. So warm and wet."

She squirmed, trying to take more of him inside. She was so close, and if he weren't buried balls deep and pounding into her within a couple of seconds, she was going to slug him.

He growled as if he'd heard her. Maybe he had. A light thrust.

"More," she cried.

Another thrust, deeper this time.

"More, more!"

At last, he thrust deep. Again and again. His cock buried itself in her body and filled her. Finding his rhythm, he pounded against her clit.

Her teeth clenched. *That feels so good.*

"*You're mine. Do you hear me? Mine.*"

I hear you. I want you. You're mine too.

His body slammed into hers again and again. "Come for me."

Ripples of bliss radiated through her core and spread everywhere. Her breathing became shallow and rapid as she built to her peak. At last the contractions began, and she spasmed with glorious release. She let out a choked cry, and he swallowed it, covering her mouth with his.

Still he pumped into her…hard, deep thrusts that rocked her body, and then she felt him shudder. His pelvis jerked and heat flooded her center. He rode her a little longer before he finally stilled and panted.

Roz panted too. She felt completely limp, yet held on with her arms around his neck and her ankles locked around his hips. They stayed that way, with his cock still buried inside her, until their breathing returned to normal.

He carried her easily to the bedroom and lowered her to the mattress. His lashes barely shaded shining blue eyes so expressive she didn't need telepathy. Wordlessly they lay beside each other and slipped into a warm embrace.

"Next time, I'll seduce you, with lots of foreplay. I'll make you beg me to fuck you."

"When?" She giggled.

"As soon as you can take it, honey."

"I'll recover as fast as I can."

Chapter 6

ROZ AND KONRAD SAT AT HER WRITING DESK, NEEDING a brief respite from sex. Her vagina felt well used. She'd never experienced soreness from fucking too much before, but she was pleased to have done so at least once.

She scrawled a heading at the top of a legal pad. *Dates*.

"Shouldn't it be 'hot dates?'" Konrad asked, twirling her hair around his finger.

Roz grinned at him. "I'm sure some of them are bound to be. Now concentrate. We're supposed to be thinking of how we can have fun and discover new ways to make a living at the same time."

"How practical do these ideas have to be?"

She shrugged. "I don't know. Go nuts, I guess. We can always cross things off the list if they're too ridiculous."

"That's true." He leaned over and blew in her ear.

"Cut that out." She couldn't help the grin that contradicted her words. "What's impractical that you were thinking of?"

He shifted and cleared his throat. If she wasn't mistaken, she'd think he was embarrassed.

"Come on, you. Out with it."

"I was thinking…how about dance instructors? You see those shows with celebrities learning to dance in a matter of weeks. Think how good we might get in six months, and it looks like all kinds of fun."

Roz squealed and clapped her hands. "Fantastic idea. I've always wanted to dance like that."

"Okay, then." He smiled, showing lots of teeth. "Let's start the list with that."

"This is a great idea. I think all kids should do this before high school. Maybe more would discover their bliss."

"Yeah, we could call it the Bliss List."

Roz laughed. "One can always hope it leads to finding our bliss…outside the bedroom, that is."

He playfully nipped her ear and growled.

"Don't start, buddy. We need to concentrate on this."

"Okay." He sighed. "How about you? Is there anything else you've been dying to try but never pursued?"

"Like skydiving?"

"Skydiving! You mean you'd jump out of a perfectly good airplane that wasn't going down in flames?"

She chuckled. "I take it you're not into that idea."

"Talk about *dying* to try something."

"I'm sure it's not that dangerous, or we'd hear more about it on the news." She lifted one eyebrow. "You're not scared, are you?"

"Of course not. I was just teasing. Actually it never occurred to me, but I'll try it. I hear some people get really addicted to it."

"Yeah, I've heard that too. Some even compare it to bliss."

"But how would that translate into a job?"

"Maybe we could join some of those fancy dive teams, or we could get certified as instructors after a few hours."

"How few?"

"I don't know, but I'll look into it later. Let's not stop brainstorming while the ideas are flowing."

Konrad paced with his hands in his pockets. "Okay. Let's think of a few more ideas." Suddenly he halted. "I know, cooking school! We could take a couple of cooking classes, and if preparing food is something we feel passionate about, we could go to culinary school and open a restaurant."

"Yeah, the cooking part sounds like fun. I might like to become head chef, but I'll let someone else own and run the place. That sounds like more headaches than bliss."

"Good idea. Let's see if the cooking really turns us on, first. Then if we really like the idea of owning our own place and think the headaches would be worth it, we can follow up after that."

"There's the practical side. I knew you had one."

Konrad raised an eyebrow. "Hey, you were the one who said to dream big. 'Go big or go home,' I believe you said. So should I go home?"

"No. Don't you dare! Here, I'm putting it all on the list." Roz wrote "cooking classes, culinary school, chefs, maybe own restaurant."

Konrad gazed over her shoulder. "Good. All in the right order, too. See how easily a plan springs from a goal?"

"Yup. I see quite well. Now, what else? Do you have any musical talent?"

"Music appreciation is about all I can offer. I don't think that's an occupation."

"Okay, it would probably take too long to learn to play anything but the kazoo, and I'm not willing to practice for years and hope the symphony has an opening someday. What else ya got?"

"I like photography, and I've even fantasized about being a filmmaker from time to time."

Roz narrowed her eyes. "What kind of filmmaker?"

"The legitimate kind. Besides, the only porno I want to make is with you, babe."

She chuckled. "Ugh, no. I'm on board with anything else you want to film. Should I write photography or filmmaker or both?"

"Why not put them both down. We can try one and then the other. If one type doesn't speak to us, the other one might."

"True. Hey, maybe we could try acting or directing."

"Acting is out," Konrad said.

"Why?"

"Look, you'd make a beautiful leading lady, but if you think I'm going to let some other dude play a love scene with you—"

There's that jealous streak again. I can't decide if I love it or hate it. Come to think of it— "I never thought about that. Yeah, I wouldn't like to see you smooching the collagen off some Hollywood starlet, either."

"Good. Maybe we're getting a little unpractical. Let's think of something less lofty."

Roz tapped the paper. "How about bartending? I've heard bartending school is only a two-week course."

"Really? That could work. Tips on a busy weekend night can be tremendous, and if we're working together, who needs to worry about going out to a club or bar on a Saturday night? We're already there."

"And eventually we could own a place where everybody knows our names."

Konrad laughed. "Sounds like our apartment building."

"Yeah, that might be nice, except there are still some residents I haven't met."

"That's right. I've been completely selfish and monopolized all your free time. I should take you around and introduce you."

"Would you? That would be great. I haven't even met my neighbor across the hall yet."

He groaned.

"What?"

"Oh, nothing. Nathan can be a good guy, but he's an acquired taste."

"Well, then, I should start getting used to him, right?"

He nodded, albeit reluctantly. "Okay. Let's do this."

———

Roz put her hand on Konrad's arm and stopped him before he knocked on Nathan's door. "Why did Dottie call him 'Nasty Nathan?'"

"I have no idea. Probably something she imagined."

"Dottie sounds like a piece of work. I wonder what she's going to tell people about me."

"She'll probably like you, as long as I don't make you howl too loud. You live right beneath her, and I live across the hall. She had a problem with the girls on the third floor making sex noises. We'll have to try it in the laundry room." He winked.

"Maybe she isn't getting any."

"That's entirely possible. She's way too uptight. Now, are you ready to meet Nathan?"

Roz took a deep breath. "Sure."

Konrad rapped on the door. They waited a minute and heard several locks clicking on the other side of the door.

Wow, Nathan seems serious about safety.

"He's a little eccentric. Weird sense of humor, but don't let him get to you. He does it for shock value."

The door opened partially, with one last chain remaining between them and the man inside.

"Can I help you?"

Konrad stepped into Nathan's line of sight. "Hi, Nathan. Open up. I want to introduce you to our new neighbor."

"Oh. Just a second."

The door closed, and after some metal rasping against metal, Nathan opened it wide and stepped into the hallway. He wore a black, open-collared shirt and black jeans. Other than jet-black hair and alert black eyes, there was little to distinguish him.

"This is Roz Wells. She moved into Merry's place across the hall."

One side of his mouth turned up. "Roz Wells, huh?"

Roz extended her hand. "Yeah, I'm sure my parents weren't cruel enough to do that to me intentionally."

He took her hand and shook it. "Maybe they did. Easy to remember. Do you believe in aliens?"

That's an odd opening question. Must be part of his eccentric charm. "My experience is too limited for me to voice an opinion."

"Too bad," Nathan said.

Too bad? She glanced at Konrad, and he lifted his shoulders.

"What do you do?" she asked.

"I work in a morgue." He smiled and waited. Probably looking for a reaction, as Konrad had said.

She wouldn't give it to him. "Oh, that must be interesting work."

"Not really. Dead is dead is dead. Not much changes."

"I suppose you're right."

"So what do you do?"

"I'm a lawyer."

Konrad was quick to add, "But she doesn't care for it and wants to find another line of work."

Nathan cocked his head. "There's an opening at the morgue. I don't suppose you see dead people."

"Uh, no. I've watched Morgaine channel a spirit, but that's about it."

"That's good. You'd be perfect to work at a morgue then. You might even pick up some business for your other line of work."

"Excuse me? What do you mean?"

"Ambulance chasing. Oh, but by that time it's too late, isn't it?"

A frown formed before she could stop it, and Nathan laughed.

Damn. He got me, didn't he?

"*Seems like.*"

"Well, it's awfully nice of you to tell me about the job opening, but I think I'll stick to what I'm doing for now."

Nathan smirked. "Suit yourself."

Roz rested her hand against Konrad's bicep. "We should get going. I don't want to be late for my…thing." She gestured in circles.

"Oh yeah, the…thing. I almost forgot." Konrad put an arm around Roz. "Well, I just wanted to introduce you two. I guess my job is done."

"I guess so," Nathan said.

"Nice to meet you, Nathan. I'm sure I'll see you around."

"Maybe," he said and retreated to his apartment. Several clicks indicated he was relocking his door—a lot.

"You were right. He's an odd bird."

Konrad snorted. "You have no idea. Okay, so you've met Nathan from your floor, Dottie and me from the second floor, and Morgaine and Chad. Are you up to meeting the rest of the third floor?"

"Um, I'm not sure. Should I?"

"Why not? Are you nervous?"

"Nervous doesn't exactly cover it. Maybe it's best to take the introductions in small doses."

"Are we 'weirding' you out?"

"It might help to meet someone who's a little more normal…and wears a color other than black. Is there such a person in this building?"

Konrad slapped a big hand over his mouth and looked like he was trying not to burst out laughing.

"What?"

He shook his head. "Oh, sweetheart. If you're looking for normal, you came to the wrong place. The only person like that would be Joe, the private detective, and he, knowingly, has a ghost as a roommate."

"Oh. Ohhhkaaay. It looks like my train stopped at Freak Central Station."

"Maybe we should go back to that list and sign up for some classes," Konrad suggested.

"Probably a good idea. Who needs to know all their neighbors anyway?"

He chuckled, making her more nervous than she already was.

―m―

"I'm so glad we called when we did. One day later, and we'd have missed the deadline to register for these classes," Roz said.

"Yeah, I'm looking forward to gliding around the dance floor with you." Konrad placed a hand on Roz's waist and she placed her hand on his shoulder the way the dance instructors had demonstrated.

"Yeah, and I'm not the most patient man in the world. How long would we have had to wait for the next session? Six weeks?"

They laced the fingers of their free hands together and held them high.

"At least. This is a six-week course, and I don't know if they take a break in between."

Konrad advanced with his right foot a little early, and Roz hesitated. He felt the lump of her toes under his foot just as he was putting his full weight on it.

"Ouch!" Roz cried and hopped away holding her left foot. Her black stiletto teetered on the floor and fell over.

Konrad took a step back. "Oh, God, I'm sorry. Are you all right?"

She drew in a few deep breaths and rubbed her toes. "Yeah...I'm fine."

The female instructor stopped the music and said, "I see we have Cinderella in our class. Where is your other shoe, Cinderella?"

Konrad retrieved her spike-heeled shoe and handed it to her. "It was under my other left foot, I'm afraid."

"Ha! At least the prince admits he has two left feet." The male instructor spoke with a Slavic accent. His female counterpart turned the music back on. "Everyone else, continue to practice. I'll work with these two."

How humiliating.

"*It wasn't your fault, lover. I think I was supposed to get my foot out of your way before you crushed it.*"

"Roz, tell me the truth. Are you hurt? Because we should stop right now if you are."

"No, no. I'm fine. Really. We can't give up that easily."

"I guess you're right. I'm sure all dancers have had their share of injuries."

The male instructor joined them. "It's true. No one learns to dance well without a few spills and missteps along the way. Now take your positions."

Konrad rested his right hand on Roz's waist and took her hand in his left. *I can think of positions I'd rather be in.*

"*We don't have to do this, you know. I mean, if you're not enjoying yourself—*"

No, I didn't mean it like that. He chuckled. *You were just reading my dirty mind.*

The instructor frowned at Konrad. "Is something funny?"

"No, not at all."

"*Pay attention, lover. We'll get to those other positions later.*"

He grinned.

The instructor said, "I'll count one, two, three, go. At that moment, I want you both to move your feet. Sir, your right foot goes forward, and miss, your left foot goes back. Now as soon as you've done that one move, stop. Understood?"

The couple nodded and said, "Understood."

"Okay. One, two, three, go."

They both took the one step they were supposed to take safely.

"Good. Now back to your original position, and do it again."

Now I feel like an idiot.

"Don't. It's no big deal. We can do this."

The instructor repeated his "one, two, three, go" speech twice more, and when they hadn't injured one another, he said, "Good. Now one of you count to three and go, but this time follow with the rest of the steps to the count of three and make the box as we showed you."

Konrad said, "I'll count. Hopefully it'll help my concentration. Are you ready?"

Roz nodded.

"Okay, one, two, three, go." The two of them slid into the first and second steps perfectly, but when it came to Konrad's taking a step back and Roz's stepping forward, his stride was far longer than hers, and he pulled her off balance.

She stumbled, but he caught her before she fell. "Oomph. Damn heels."

The instructor shook his head, slowly.

"Sorry. It wasn't you or your shoes, Roz. I know what I did wrong," Konrad said.

The instructor crossed his arms. "And what was that?"

"I extended my back leg too far."

The instructor cocked his head and frowned. "You have front legs and back legs? No wonder you have two left feet."

Konrad laughed nervously.

"Your partner has much shorter legs than you do. You must always compensate for that," the instructor was saying.

"Okay. Let's try again. I'll take smaller steps."

Roz and Konrad resumed their starting positions, and the instructor said, "I'll count."

After the initial "one, two, three, go," he continued to count the beat of the waltz while the couple made the short steps in the shape of a box.

Are we having fun yet?

Roz laughed, but the break in concentration caused her to miss a step, and Konrad trampled her toes again.

"Oww!" She hopped over to the chairs lining the length of the dance hall, sat on one, removed her shoe, and massaged her toes.

Konrad followed her. "Are you okay?"

"Yeah, I'll live."

"This isn't working out, is it?"

"Let's not give up yet. Someday we'll laugh about this."

The instructor glanced away and mumbled something under his breath.

"I think our teacher is ready to quit."

Roz chuckled. "Well, I'm not." She slipped into her shoe again and stood, taking Konrad's hand. "Come on, let's do this."

They counted and danced, successfully this time, for several turns. The instructor smiled and clapped. That was enough to interrupt their concentration, and the couple went down with a thud, landing in a tangled heap of arms and legs.

Roz gasped and yelled, "Frig!"

"Oh, crap." Konrad rolled off of her quickly. "I hurt you that time, didn't I?"

She breathed deeply through gritted teeth.

Both instructors rushed over. "What happened?"

Roz managed to compose herself enough to say, "I twisted my ankle."

The male instructor extended his hand to help her up. She tried to stand and winced.

Konrad jumped to his feet and picked her up off the floor. "I'm taking you to the emergency room."

"No, I'm sure it's not that bad. Just give me a couple of minutes to rest."

"Your ankle is already swelling."

"No, they're just fat."

Konrad gave her the hairy eyeball and said, "No, they're not. And since one is getting bigger and redder than the other, I'd guess you have a sprain. Now don't argue. I'm taking you to the hospital."

He strode toward the door.

"We should call an ambulance," the female instructor said.

"No need. We're close to the New England Hospital. I can carry her there, if you'll get the door."

"Wait, my purse."

Konrad paused by the chairs they sat in earlier and let her point it out, but he refused to put her down. One of the instructors handed it to her.

"Are you sure you don't want us to call an ambulance?"

"No, I can get her there faster than they can."

"Okay." The male instructor opened the door for them and held it while Konrad carried her down the stairs to the sidewalk.

"Hang on, hon," he said, and as soon as she'd locked her arms around his neck, he sprinted down the street.

Chapter 7

THE EMERGENCY ROOM DOCTOR DELIVERED THE GOOD news as she studied the x-ray. "You're lucky. Nothing's broken. It's just a sprain and should heal in a few days."

"I feel like a complete klutz."

"Roz, it wasn't your fault. It was mine," Konrad said.

"No, it was mine. I tripped you."

Konrad placed his hands on his hips. "Well, clearly dancing isn't our thing."

The ER doctor laughed and finished winding the bandage around Roz's ankle. "There you go, Rosalyn. Now stay off your feet and keep your right ankle elevated. Use ice to bring down the swelling and Tylenol every four hours as needed for pain."

Roz sighed. "Yes, ma'am." *Tylenol. Ice. Nothing really numbing, like Demerol, huh?*

"Do you have any crutches?" the doctor asked.

"No, but I'll buy some."

Konrad patted her back. "I have some you can borrow."

Roz snorted. "Oh, that would be fun to watch. I'll look like a pole vaulter in the Olympics, except with two poles."

The doctor grinned. "I'm sure the crutches are adjustable; most are. Anyway, you're all set to go, but call us if you have any questions or your condition changes. How are you getting home?"

Konrad plucked her off the exam table and cradled her in his arms. "I'll carry her home safely."

The doctor let out a deep sigh. "I wish I had a big, strapping, hottie to—"

Roz raised her eyebrows. *She'd better not be after my guy. I might sprain a wrist punching her, and then who'd patch me up? Probably not the doctor I'd just knocked out.*

The woman cleared her throat and looked away. "Oh, sorry. I guess that wasn't very professional."

Roz finally had a reason to chuckle. "Yeah, well you'll have to get your own. This one's taken." She turned her face to Konrad's for a full-on kiss.

The doctor said, "Hey, get a room. I mean, another room."

Konrad broke the kiss. "I think that's a great idea. Let's go, angel."

"Aw, he even calls you 'angel.' You don't happen to have a brother, do you?"

Konrad grinned. "As a matter of fact, I do. How do you feel about cops?"

"Really?" The doctor's eyes lit up. "Health professionals date cops all the time. Something about serving the public and understanding the need to put the job first, yada, yada, yada."

"Well, give me your number, and I'll pass it on to him."

"Does he look like you?"

"We're twins. Identical."

The doctor fanned herself with the sheet of paper in her hand. "Oh, wow. There *is* a God. Here, I'll write my name and number on your girlfriend's discharge instructions."

She scrawled something on the back before Roz had

a chance to say yea or nay. Roz hoped the good doc wasn't trying to find a subtle way to slip *Konrad* her phone number.

The doctor folded the paper, tucked it into his shirt pocket, and gave it a little pat. "This is my weekend on, so I'm off next weekend. Don't forget to tell your twin to call me." She then hurried off toward the nurse's station.

"Awesome," Roz said, deadpan. "We can double date."

"Not gonna happen. I want you all to myself."

She wound her arms tighter around his neck and kissed his cheek. "Sounds good to me. Let's go home." She'd forgotten to worry about her heaviness until that moment. Putting her full weight in his arms seemed nearly natural.

On the way to their apartment building, Konrad shared the brilliant idea of consulting the witches about what jobs might work for them. Roz wasn't so sure it was brilliant, but couldn't put her finger on why not. They were still discussing the subject when they reached their building.

Roz considered the possibility from different angles, and even though she was open-minded, she wasn't sure she wanted to go to the mysterious women upstairs. "Don't witches predict the future with Tarot cards and stuff? They aren't career counselors." Still in Konrad's arms, she used her outer door key to open the front door. His broad back braced it open as he maneuvered them inside.

"True. But maybe they can look into our futures and tell us what we'll wind up doing. Then we can cut out all the trial and error." He reached her apartment door, and as soon as she unlocked it, they made their way inside.

"Hmm. I'm not sure that's how it works, either. What if we check online? Then if it's not a great way to make this kind of decision and we don't want to take their advice, we won't insult our neighbors."

Konrad set her on the sofa and fluffed up a throw pillow. He carefully placed it under her ankle. "That's not a bad idea. Do you mind if we use your computer? I don't have one."

She pointed and said, "Be my guest. It's in the top of my desk."

As soon as he'd laid the ice pack on her ankle, he strolled to the roll-top desk. Roz admired his strong grace.

"I haven't seen one of these desks for ages." The top clickety-clicked as he opened it. "I always liked them." He took the laptop to Roz and asked, "Are you as into antiques as it seems, from your living room furniture?"

"Kind of. I mean, I like a few nice pieces, but I don't want to clutter my place with dusty old junk."

"No, you have a nice balance between old and… older." He smiled, and she knew he was kidding.

"Thanks." She opened the laptop and turned it on. "Give it a minute to warm up. What keyword should we search?"

Konrad stretched. "I don't know. Why don't you Google *tarot*?"

As soon as the machine was ready, Roz typed in *tarot*. Up came thousands of hits. "Okay, we might have to narrow this down a bit. What should we look for? An online reader?"

"That sounds about right. Try it."

Roz went back to the search function and added *card reader*. "Well, the good news is there are still thousands to choose from."

Konrad looked over her shoulder. "What's the bad news?"

"There are still thousands to choose from."

He rolled his eyes. "We've got to start somewhere. What's the first link?"

"Wikipedia."

"That's not what we want. Find one that says something about giving consultations."

Roz handed him the laptop. "Why don't you pick one and see if you like the website?"

Konrad took a seat on the ottoman, and Roz watched as he clicked and clicked. He seemed comfortable with the laptop, despite his big fingers. She hadn't noticed a typewriter in his apartment, but maybe he kept one hidden away, or maybe he was just used to typing from his former days as a teacher.

"Here's one I like. Tarot by Arwen. Professional, compassionate tarot consultations."

Roz reached for the laptop. "Let me see." She scanned the site, and it seemed well set up and maintained. She looked at a few blog postings from the archives and decided the woman seemed as advertised, "professional and compassionate."

"I like her picture. It looks like a candid of her laughing." Konrad smiled as he said it. "So many psychics seem overly serious, with no sense of humor."

Roz drew in a deep breath. "Okay, let's give Arwen a shot. She even has a handy 'contact Arwen' link." She handed the laptop back to Konrad.

"You want me to contact her?"

"Sure. You seem to know more about it, so why don't you go first?"

"Okay, here goes nothin'."

He clickety-clicked across the keyboard in a rush of words that made her curious.

"Isn't there some kind of form to fill out?"

"No. Just a blank page to give her some basic information and whatever else you want her to know.

"I guess you want her to know everything about you. Hell, even *I* don't know that much."

"Wisenheimer."

"Hey, you talked me into this." She kicked at him and winced. "I shouldn't have done that."

He smirked.

After he typed what seemed to be an extremely long message and sent it, Roz asked, "What was all that about?"

"She needed certain information. Name, date of birth, time and place of birth. Plus I had a bit of explanation I had to include…about the need for a fast track to the new career and how we're trying different things, I mean."

"It sounds as if she's doing astrology, with all the birth info. When is your birthday, anyway?"

He grinned. "It's easy to remember. Twelve, twelve." "*Don't ask the year.*"

"Why don't you want to tell me the year?"

Damn.

"Are you afraid to let me know how old you are?" She crossed her arms.

"I'm older than you; let's leave it at that."

"Not much, judging by your looks." She cocked her head and studied him. "To be honest, you could even be younger. Ah, ha! So that's it. You're younger than I am, and you don't want me to feel old...or worse, like I have the upper hand by being older and wiser."

He rolled his eyes. "Trust me, I'm older. And I like having you on top now and then." He gave her a conspiratorial wink.

"There you go, always thinking about sex."

"Can't help it. You turn me on." He cupped her breast and raked a thumb over the fabric of her blouse.

Her nipple registered the sensation, and she groaned. "Not much we can do about it until this ankle heals."

"Sure we can. We just have to think creatively. Do you have any duct tape or masking tape?"

Roz's eyes rounded. "Du...duct tape? What for? My ankle is already wrapped in an Ace bandage."

Konrad laughed. "I just want to tape the ice pack on."

"Oh." Roz's face heated. "I could probably leave it off. The discharge instructions said to keep it on no more than twenty minutes at a time, and then to leave it off for twenty."

One side of Konrad's mouth hitched up. "I guess we can make twenty minutes count." Then he waggled his eyebrows.

"Wait a minute, cowboy. I haven't even said I *want* to have sex right now."

"Oh." His face fell. "Don't you?"

"Well, yeah. Depending on what your creative position requires."

He chuckled. "I think you can manage it. It's called missionary style."

Roz laughed.

Konrad swooped in for a deep kiss.

A few minutes of making out on the couch later, Roz's laptop pinged, announcing she had email. "Whew, saved by the bell. Would you mind?" She reached in the general direction of the laptop, and he handed it to her.

She opened her email and saw that Arwen had responded. "Wow, that Arwen is fast. She sent payment information and something else. A message for you, I guess."

Konrad practically ripped the laptop out of her hands, looking nervous.

It just said, "I understand. You can trust me." Roz's curiosity was piqued. "What is that about?"

"Oh, I added some personal information…about my strengths and limitations." *"Don't think about it; don't think about it…"*

There he goes again. "I see." Roz eyed him suspiciously. "What is it you don't want me to know?"

He hung his head. "Someday I'll tell you, but right now I just…I just can't, okay? It's a long story."

"You can trust me, you know."

"I know. And even that turns me on."

He stood and abruptly scooped her into his arms. Roz gulped, unable to tear her gaze from his. Konrad's stare grew molten as he carried her to the bedroom and laid her in the middle of the queen-size bed. He unbuttoned her blouse carefully and popped open the front closure of her bra. Then he climbed in beside her.

"You seem to have better control over your rough side this time."

"You're hurt."

His tender treatment of her spoke volumes, and she relaxed, ready for anything he wanted to do with her.

He traced a calloused fingertip across her nipples, and she shivered. He brought the finger to his mouth, wet it, and circled each nipple in turn.

The cool air mingled with her dampened nipples, and they puckered. She wanted to jump him, hurry him, but her injury prevented her from doing anything more than lying next to him, completely at his mercy.

His blond head bent, trailing kisses over her collarbone, licking the dip between her breasts, then, at last, licking one of her nipples. Her breath hitched when he caught the tight bud between his lips and tugged.

Konrad slipped his hand under the other globe and lifted it as if appreciating its weight. His thumb scraped across the nub while he sucked the one next to his mouth. Glorious electricity shot from her nipples to her pussy.

Her heart pounded as he backed away and unsnapped her pants. Placing her weight on her good heel, she arched and lifted her buttocks. Konrad peeled her pants down her legs and carefully pulled them over and off her injured ankle.

Even though she was exposed and vulnerable, she didn't shy away from his piercing stare. She wanted him to finish what he'd begun. *Strip, damn it. I want to admire you too.*

Konrad grinned, and his canines seemed longer.

Must be my imagination.

He pulled his T-shirt over his head, exposing his impressive pectoral muscles and six-pack abs. She'd grown used to his massive biceps, but even they seemed to loom larger than normal. She remembered he'd been carrying her around all evening.

Roz had never been very bold in the bedroom, but this man made her want to try it all. Gentle sex, rough sex, twisted-ankle sex. No one else had ever made her come undone like he did. She could starve to death in bed with Konrad, and for as much as she loved food, that was saying quite a lot.

He lay down beside her and leaned over for a long, languorous kiss. She held him by the shoulders, always worried about accidentally pulling his hair. When their lips finally parted, Konrad planted wet, hot kisses down her abdomen to her navel.

He began to part her thighs by moving her good leg.

"You don't have to do that," Roz said.

"I know I don't *have to*."

"I mean, I love it when you do, but it might be kind of awkward—" Surprise overtook her as he jumped over her good leg, and as she tried to spread her knees, pain stabbed her ankle. "Owww!"

He froze. "I can't do this. I might hurt you."

Roz took some deep breaths until the pain subsided. "I'm sorry. I wish I could—"

"Don't be sorry. There are bound to be times when one of us can't handle having sex." He leaned over and placed a tender kiss on her forehead.

"And you won't dump me for someone less accident prone?"

He laughed. "Not a chance."

Chapter 8

"HERE IT IS, 'TAROT READING BY ARWEN FOR KONRAD Wolfensen.'" Konrad had taken Roz's laptop to her bedroom and stretched out beside her.

Roz, still naked but covered with a sheet, lounged with her foot propped on a pillow. "Read it out loud."

Konrad had stolen a peek before taking it to Roz and made sure nothing incriminating, like his year of birth, 1912, was mentioned. He wasn't ready to explain that werewolves aged at a much slower rate than humans. Hell, he wasn't ready to reveal he was a Lycan at all! Fortunately, Arwen referenced his birthday only as December 12.

Since Roz looked comfortable, reading aloud seemed like the best way to share the information, despite the fascinating pictures of the tarot cards themselves. He set the laptop in front of him so he could read and run his fingers lightly over Roz's arm at the same time. She shivered.

"Sorry. Do you want me to stop doing that?"

"As long as you can read and avoid touching me in those *especially distracting* places, I should be able to handle it."

He grinned. "I'll try to behave myself. Okay, so the first heading says, 'How do you see the people around you?' You don't really want to hear that part, do you?"

"Of course I do! I'm around you, and I'd like to know how you see me."

He laughed. "I think it's more general than that, but here goes. 'People around you represent opportunity. They are your chance to achieve and show off a bit. Sometimes you see what they have and yearn for that.

"'You have an unopened bag of tricks yet. There are things these people still have not seen about you. Things you still have to show them. There is some need to prove yourself to these people.'"

"Hmmm…" Roz interjected. "I wonder what that could be?"

"Yeah, well…who knows? Should I continue?"

"Please."

Konrad cleared his throat. "Okay, just a little left of that category. It says, 'The ships in the harbor represent coming chances with three people. You are focused on one of them, and it is possibly causing you to be a bit off your game. The sandals in the sand indicate that some part of you is ready to put down roots.'"

Roz raised her eyebrows as if asking a question, but didn't verbalize it.

"Here, I'll show you the picture of the card, so you can see the ship and sandals." He turned the screen toward her.

She nodded at it. "Pretty. It kind of looks like a guy is playing limbo on the beach. Maybe it's the Club Med card."

He chuckled, but more to cover his disappointment. Okay, so it didn't seem like she was ready to talk about commitment. He'd have to wait for the right moment. Things like that shouldn't be rushed.

He turned the screen back to where he could read it and scrolled down. "The next category is 'How are you

seen by the people around you?' Ha, now it's my turn."
And my chance to have a little fun.

"Hey, it may not refer to how *I* see you."

"You doubt everyone sees me as gorgeous and great
in bed?"

Roz rolled her eyes.

He leaned over and kissed her. When he returned
to the screen, he feigned surprise and said, "Hey, how
about that? It says, 'You're viewed by others as hand-
some and virile.'"

"It does not."

He grinned, sheepishly. "You saw through that, huh?"

"A little bit. Now go on. Read; I'm enjoying this."

"Okay. 'The Queen of swords is a very mentally focused person. You are seen as driven. Sometimes your
sarcasm comes out wrong.' Hey! I'm not sarcastic."

Roz shrugged. "This is how others see you. Maybe
you're not aware of it."

"Humph. I suppose." He took a deep breath and
continued. "'Those around you may see you as a bit of
a loner as well, because where you live is so different
from where they live, even if it's on the same street.'"

"Now that I can believe," Roz said.

"What do you mean…because our building's full
of weirdoes?"

"Ah ha. That's the sarcasm that doesn't come out
right! *I* live in this building, you weirdo."

"Sorry. Hey, do you want to see the card? It's a
woman on an ice-covered cliff holding a sword, and
a couple of white eagles soaring around the snow-
capped mountains."

"I'll take your word for it. Go ahead. Keep reading."

"'Folks see you as someone with many responsibili-
ties and projects. You seem to have your eye on the prize
always. There is one very close to you who watches and
learns from you.'"

"Well, that's interesting."

"Do you think that has something to do with you?"

Roz smiled shyly and lifted one shoulder. "Maybe.
I'm learning to accept my body. I'm not learning how to
dance, but I *am* learning how to take care of a sprained
ankle, thanks to you."

"Oh, nice. Now who's being sarcastic?"

She grinned. "Never said I wasn't."

"Fine. I'll just continue reading. '"When people come
to you for advice, they know they'll get true Sagittarian
honesty. Low on tact, but high on blunt information.'"

Roz laughed. "I guess you really mean it when you
say you like the extra pounds I'm padded with; otherwise you'd tell me how fat my ass is."

"You see? I'm an honest guy. Now do you believe
me?"

"I guess I'll have to. The cards don't lie."

"No, they're kind of blunt and honest too."

She sat up and wrapped her arms around him. "Don't
worry; they can't say anything that will turn me away
from you. I'm not hearing much to guide you in a career
choice, though."

"The next part might have something. It's titled
'What is your most important goal?'"

"Yeah, that sounds promising. Let's hear it."

"'The nine of swords is an interesting goal. It is about
nightmares and anxieties. It is about feeling as if you
haven't done enough. You carry some past guilt. Your

goal seems to make sure that others are never in this same position. You would move heaven and earth to protect those you consider yours.'"

Konrad stopped reading aloud. This information hit too close to home, and he didn't want to explain to Roz what it meant. He knew the truth, though.

He'd failed his pack. He allowed another Lycan to challenge him for alpha status, knowing the bastard couldn't be trusted. He didn't bother to dispute the lies that Petroski spread, either. He thought his pack knew him well and would never believe that crap.

So what if he did help a vampire who was about to burst into flames from the sun? Watching someone else suffer had never turned him on, unlike his nemesis, who seemed to revel in it. Sly was one of his best friends and had helped him in return, many times. Konrad would never regret their friendship, but apparently enough was said to plant seeds of doubt, and that's all it took. He couldn't blow off the challenge, or he'd be seen as a coward in the eyes of his pack, the very thing Petroski accused him of.

How Petroski found a female in the pack to testify that Konrad had left her vulnerable to attack, he'd never know. One of the foremost werewolf edicts was for all males to protect the pack females, *especially* those who weren't yet mated.

Somehow Petroski got Ella to say she saw Konrad at the top of the hill that led from Newton to Waban. She claimed he ran when a rival pack began closing in. Then she said Petroski came bounding down the hill and saved her.

How could anyone believe such a load of crap? How

could she tell a lie like that? He suspected some kind of bribery but couldn't confirm it at the time. Now he knew his suspicions were well founded, because Petroski took Ella for his mate. *Poor Ella.*

—∾∾—

"Where are you?" Roz asked.

"Huh? Oh, I uh…It's not important."

Not important my ass. "Well then, what was that long pause for?"

"I was…uh, just studying the card. It's kind of creepy."

"Let me see."

He turned the screen toward her, and Roz saw a dark scene. It appeared to be a man weeping in bed with swords all around him.

"Ick, that is kind of macabre. Well, read the rest of it. Maybe there's something positive to counteract the negative."

"Not really. The only thing it says after that is 'This indicates one who failed to protect something or someone and wants to prove to themselves that they are not a failure.'"

"What could that possibly mean?"

His muscles tensed.

She waited, and when he didn't respond, she folded her arms and said, "Okay, I guess you just suck at everything and might as well give up."

He smirked. "You're being sarcastic again, aren't you?"

Roz kissed his shoulder. "You betcha. I doubt this is an exact science. There are bound to be things that don't make sense. Now read."

She may not trust it, but still she wants to hear every

word. Konrad took a deep breath. "'Where do you get your strength from?'"

Roz raised her eyebrows. "Me? Why? Do you think I should be tired?"

"No. That's the name of the next section."

"Oh." She slapped her forehead and chuckled. "Sorry. Didn't mean to interrupt. Read on."

Konrad continued. "'The Ace of Cups shows that you're a very emotional fellow. Your love for others carries and drives you. You gain power from that bond.'"

Roz nodded, but remained silent. *Emotional? Power? Yeah, I've seen him shake with emotion. But is that from love? It seemed more like pent-up desire.*

Unaware of her thoughts, or ignoring them, he read, "'This is about you creating family wherever you go. You may not have your blood family close for the most part, but you adopt people into your world.'" He looked up and smiled.

"What's that for? Are you adopting me?"

He laughed. "That might be kind of awkward at this stage and illegal in several southern states."

"No kidding. Let's hear the rest."

"'You tend to have a pretty good humor about life as well, not a lackadaisical attitude, but definitely a "bring it on, I can take it" style.'"

"That I believe." Roz tickled him.

He flinched. "Don't start. I'm almost at the end."

"Okay, finish it up. I'll wait."

"We're at the last section. It says, 'Why do you want to be remembered?' Maybe there's finally a clue about what I should do for a living."

"Even if there isn't, this has been *verrry* interesting."

"Yeah…for you." He chuckled and then continued. "'The card is the Universe. No little dreams for you. You want to be remembered as someone who carved out their own place. You see the four figures in this card? Each represents a part of you that you are working to bring together. You want to be remembered as the one who created safety for others as well as yourself.'"

"Well, how about that? You're a security expert! It sounds like you should be doing exactly what you used to do."

Konrad's face fell. "Nifty."

Roz's mood deflated as well, understanding how much he really wanted a change. "What does that card look like?"

He turned the screen toward her. A bloated blue woman with big droopy boobs danced in the middle of the card. The four figures in the corners were hardly noticeable compared to that one, but she made out a dolphin, a goat, a lion, and a raven.

"What do you think it means? Who did you fail, and what's all the talk about protection?"

"Nothing. It means nothing. I guess tarot was a bust for career counseling. Back to the drawing board."

Roz didn't believe the irritation in his voice meant nothing, and his earlier pensiveness meant something too. It wouldn't do any good to demand he tell her what was bothering him before he was ready. He'd clammed up before, and he'd just do it again. He had some kind of a secret; that much she was sure of.

"Konrad, I know there's something important you're not telling me. And I can only assume you're not ready to trust me with it yet."

He opened his mouth, but before he had a chance to

respond, she held up her hand and kept talking. "I can understand that. We haven't known each other very long. But I won't let you hide whatever it is from me forever. Eventually you'll need to find a way to let me in."

He hung his head for a moment and then looked up with a teasing expression. "Can't I just distract you with sex for the rest of our lives?"

She sighed. "Nice try, wise guy."

Two weeks and lots of TLC later, Konrad placed his hand on the small of Roz's back as they strolled toward the bartender school. With its location on the second floor of a strip mall, he pictured a bar fight at an Old West saloon with someone thrown out a second-story window.

"I don't know why we didn't think of this sooner," Roz said. "Dancing would have taken months to learn. This bartending course is only two weeks."

"I know. It would be ideal to find a new job in only a couple of weeks. If their placement program is any good, maybe we'll be hired right out of school."

"I'll have to give at least a two-week notice, but you could start right away."

"Yeah, thanks to my getting fired from the security job." *I wonder if I should have told her I just quit. Now she probably thinks I'm a loser.*

"I don't think you're a loser! In fact, you're more of a winner, for telling me the truth."

He stiffened.

Roz glanced up at him. "I got fired once."

"Really? You? I can't imagine you doing anything that wrong."

"You know I'm a klutz, right?"

"Uh-oh. Where did you work? A china shop?"

"Like a bull in the? No, but thanks a lot for the visual."

"I'm sorry. I was trying to make a joke. You know I wouldn't intentionally insult you."

"True."

Konrad changed the subject as they ascended the stairs. "What are the odds of our getting hired by the same bar?"

"Nothing says we have to work together. It might work out better if we don't. I hear that too much togetherness can be hard on relationships."

"Yeah. We could wind up on different shifts if the place is small and they don't need more than one bartender at a time, and then we'd never see each other." He spied the lettering on the first door they came to. "Ah, there it is. Mass Bartending School."

He opened the door for Roz and followed her in.

The place looked exactly like a working bar. A long mirror backed one wall. In front of it sat bottles of every description, holding liquids of every color. The bar itself was made of highly polished wood. He imagined there must be a sink and refrigerator behind it. A few students were already present, sitting on bar stools. He pulled one out for Roz and then seated himself.

"Aw, isn't that cute?" said a thin red-haired girl with several piercings and tattoos. "And they say chivalry is dead."

That one will probably get a job in a biker bar.

"*Looks like she'd fit right in,*" Roz thought loud enough for Konrad to hear.

They gazed at each other and chuckled.

"What's so funny?" the girl asked.

"Oh, nothing. I'm Roz, and this is my boyfriend, Konrad."

The redhead flipped her hair behind her shoulder. "Too bad."

Two other men sat together at the opposite end of the bar. One spoke up. "I'm Glenn, and this is my boyfriend, Bruce."

The redhead rolled her eyes. "Just my friggin' luck. You're *all* taken."

"What's your name?" Konrad asked. *Not that I care a whole lot.*

"I'm Chastity. Yeah, I know. Don't start."

"Don't start what?" Roz tipped her head and looked genuinely puzzled.

Nice acting, sweetheart I know you didn't miss that joke. Maybe if this gig doesn't do it for us, we can try out for some plays.

Chastity waved her away and faced the opposite direction.

A short, chubby guy whose hair looked prematurely gray shuffled in from the back room. He carried an armload of paper and folders.

"Good evening, everyone." Strolling behind the bar, he continued his introduction in a monotone voice. "My name is John Kelly. Welcome to Kelly's Bar."

"I thought this was Mass Bartending School," Chastity said.

"It is. But when I'm instructing, we call it Kelly's Bar. When my partner Ron's instructing, we call it Ron's bar."

Konrad folded his arms. "Ron and John, huh? Don't you have surf shop?"

"Uh…no," he said, sounding bored. Maybe he'd heard that one before.

"Why does Ron use his first name and you use your last?" Glenn asked.

"Because Ron's last name is Dick. He thinks Dick's Bar sounds a little like a gay bar."

Glenn elbowed his partner. "That's what we can name our place."

The other students chuckled.

"Well, let's get started." John passed out the folders first, then each student received a few papers stapled together.

Konrad glanced at the pages of recipes.

John leaned against the bar. "This is what we're going to make tonight, but first I'll talk about the different glasses we'll use." He lined up a few glasses of various shapes and sizes.

—⁓—

Two other guys had joined the class by the time the students started hands-on training. Chastity was happy to learn they weren't together, and Roz noted the one who introduced himself as Bubba seemed just the type that little miss total-body tattoo would go for.

"Okay, so you're about to learn how to pour a shot without measuring," John said. "Pick a highball glass and one of the bottles with a spout."

Everyone grabbed a bottle of colored water. Roz realized their class would cost a whole lot more than

$350.00 if they poured real liquor, but couldn't help being disappointed anyway. *Imagine how fast the three-hour class would fly by if we got to drink our mistakes.*

Konrad chuckled.

You must be reading my mind again.

"Yeah, and I was just thinking the same thing."

"You saw me demonstrate a standard pour a moment ago," John said. "Now I want you all to try it. We'll measure afterward to see how close you've come."

"This guy reminds me of Ben Stein when he talks," Chastity whispered to the guy beside her.

"I'm surprised she knows who that is," Roz whispered.

"*It's probably from commercials. She's not old enough to remember his movies and TV show.*"

While distracted, Roz tipped the heavy bottle upside down, and it slipped out of her grasp. *Crash.* Glass shards and liquid exploded and landed everywhere.

Glenn jumped back, but some of the liquid landed on his gray pants anyway.

"Oh, that's a shame," Bruce said. "That was your favorite pair."

"I'm so sorry," Roz said. "I'll pay for dry cleaning."

The guy named Bubba glanced down at his jeans. "Hey, you got some on me too. Are you gonna pay for my dry cleaning?"

John hung his head and extracted a dustpan and brush from beneath the counter. As soon as he'd handed it to her, he crossed his arms and said, "This is why we don't use real alcohol."

Without a word, Roz cleaned up the glass. Meanwhile, Konrad found a bar towel and sopped up the gold liquid.

"Hey, I mean it," Bubba said, agitated. "I ain't washing these pants."

Konrad straightened. "They're jeans. They'll go through the washing machine just fine. Besides, I don't see anything on them."

"Look here." Bubba pointed out a miniscule drop. The golden color barely showed.

Konrad leaned against the bar. "You're being ridiculous."

Bubba started toward Konrad, and Konrad advanced on Bubba.

Roz slapped a palm against each of their chests. "I'll wash them. No need for bloodshed, okay?"

Konrad stood where he was. "The guy can wash his own pants, Roz."

Bubba glared down at her hand on his T-shirt and snarled, or came as close to it as anyone could. Something about him seemed off.

"Roz, why don't you try that pour again?" Don said.

She picked up another bottle, and when she had the full shot in the glass, Bubba purposely bumped into her, knocking the drink out of her hand. It went crashing to the floor again, except this time it coated her shoes and Konrad's pants. She gasped.

"That's it," Konrad said. "Let's take this outside."

"No!" Getting flustered, Roz tried again to interject herself between the two large, angry men.

Bubba pushed her out of the way, and she fell.

Konrad reacted as if he hadn't thought about the consequences. Before she knew it, he threw a punch that knocked the guy off his feet.

Bubba climbed upright wearing a menacing smile.

He took a swing at Konrad, but her lover's reaction time was too quick, and the guy's fist connected with the bottles. Several more crashed to the floor and shattered.

The other students scurried out of the way.

Bubba grabbed his fist and sucked in a deep breath between his teeth.

John strolled to the phone on the wall and dialed 911 as if he did it every day.

Bubba then shook out his bloody hand.

Konrad said, "We really *should* take this outside, if you insist on fighting."

"Oh, I insist." He ran at Konrad like a football player making a tackle.

Konrad went down with a thud as everyone cleared out from behind the bar. The two fighters rolled back and forth, fists flying.

"Stop!" Roz yelled.

Sirens sounded from far away but were drawing closer.

Konrad finally flipped the guy over and pinned him.

"Now, I don't think you want to get arrested any more than I do. Let's stop this foolishness right now."

"Okay, okay," Bubba said, seeming conciliatory.

As soon as Konrad let him up, Bubba threw a wicked punch, and Roz thought she heard something crunch. She cried out, and Konrad fell like tree. Bubba jumped over the bar and ran down the stairs, disappearing into the night.

Chapter 9

KONRAD RUBBED HIS CHIN AS ROZ JAMMED HER HANDS on her hips and argued with the cop. "It was *not* his fault. You should have seen the other guy; I swear he was psychotic."

The cop jotted something down on a small pad of paper.

Konrad suspected the guy's problem wasn't psychosis, or if it was, could it possibly be due to rabies? Bubba might have recognized a rival pack member. Correction, *former* rival pack member. The idiot's eyes had glowed as if he'd wanted to shift, but resisted, thank God. Konrad figured he was the only one who noticed it.

"Being psychotic doesn't give anyone the right to bust up a bar." The cop faced Konrad. "Are you going to come along quietly, or do I need to call for backup?"

"Call anyone you want. I've already agreed to pay for damages, and an eyewitness who happens to be a lawyer just told you, I was acting in self-defense and averting a threat to her."

The cop turned to Roz. "You're a lawyer?"

"Yes, a defense attorney and a good one. You'd be wasting the court's time, officer."

Fortunately the other eyewitnesses had nothing to say. Konrad was afraid Chastity would open her big mouth and add to the problem.

The cop narrowed his eyes and stared at the rest of the group. "Did anybody else see what happened?"

"We all did," John said.

"Did anyone see something different?"

The other students shook their heads.

John sighed. "The other man was definitely the insti-gator. I have his application in the back and can get you his contact information."

"I doubt he'll go home and wait to be arrested," Konrad said. His jaw still ached, but not nearly as much as it would have hurt a human. Knowing that he'd heal faster, because werewolves do, he'd need to milk it a bit.

The cop continued to talk to John. "Do you want to press charges?"

He shook his head. "I guess not. This man has already offered to replace the bottles and glasses that broke. There isn't much more damage, and I don't want the bad publicity."

He turned back to Konrad and Roz. "What about you two? Do either of you want to press charges?"

Konrad said, "No."

At the same time, Roz said, "Hell, yes."

Konrad rested a hand on Roz's shoulder. "Can I talk to you outside for a moment?"

"Uh, sure."

The cop stuffed his pad of paper and pen back in his pocket. "I'll go with you."

As soon as he and Roz reached the parking lot, Konrad looked at her with such intensity it made her uncomfortable.

"Look, I know how you feel about scumbags getting

off when they're guilty as sin, but I think this will be a waste of time."

Not willing to let him intimidate her, she leaned forward with her hands on her hips. "Why are you suddenly a paper tiger?"

The cop cleared his throat. "I'm still here."

"It's okay," Roz said. "He's not so macho that I can't speak my mind."

"I believe your boyfriend said the guy wouldn't go home and wait to be arrested. He's probably right."

The idea of simply giving up and letting the jerk win rankled her. "The guy may not have gone straight home, but he has to go there eventually."

Konrad gently held her shoulders. "I just don't think it's worth it."

For crying out loud. Is Konrad afraid of him? What about other innocent people? Aren't they worth protecting? "It could have been worse," she said. "Do you want him to pull that somewhere else?"

Konrad's lips thinned.

The cop added, "Look, all you need to do is fill out a complaint. We can take it from there."

"What does that entail?" Konrad asked.

"You fill out a form at the station, and we'll pay him a visit. He'd be told the nature of the complaint, and if, like your girlfriend said, he seems psychotic, we can get him the help he needs."

"Hmm…" Konrad rubbed his chin.

Roz had noticed the same behavior trait whenever he was deep in thought. *Good. At least he's considering it.*

"Will you share with him who made the complaint?" Konrad asked.

"We don't have to, if you'd rather we didn't."

"In that case, go ahead." He turned to Roz. "Since you're the one who wants them to pursue it, would you mind filling out the form? I'd rather not get involved."

"Why are you shying away from this? You don't seem like the type to be easily intimidated."

When he didn't answer her, she figured that either he didn't hear the question or was ignoring her. Either way, she had to make a decision. "Sure, why not? Do I have to come down to the station, officer? Can't I give you the information here?"

"I suppose so. I can take down what you want to say and type it up later. What's more paperwork?"

Sarcastic much?

The cop headed back upstairs toward the school. "I'll go get the guy's contact information. Wait right there."

As soon as he left, Konrad edged toward the street. "If you don't mind, I'd like to get home and put some ice on my jaw and take some aspirin. I can catch the subway from here."

"Oh! Sorry, I didn't realize you were still in pain."

"Yeah, well, you may be able to read my mind, but you can't feel my pain."

I have no idea what's going on in his head right now, and I wish I did. "Yeah, sure. Whatever you need to do," she said.

He jogged across the parking lot, and she called after him, "You may be off the hook as far as the police are concerned, but I still have some questions." *Hmm... not even a kiss goodbye. It's like he couldn't wait to get out of here.*

—◦◦◦—

Konrad was relaxing in his living room, trying to reread one of his favorite books, but noises from the apartment upstairs distracted him.

Thump, thump, thump, thump, thump.

What is that? Sounds like a conga line. "I liked it better when it was just Chad up there. No noise whatsoever." Konrad rose from his chair and stared at the ceiling. "Or maybe that *is* Chad? I wonder if he's trying to get somebody's attention."

If Joe and the witches weren't home, Konrad would probably be the only one to hear him. Or Dottie…*oh crap. If Dottie hears the noise, she'll pitch a fit.*

He sighed. "I'd better get up there and see what's going on."

Konrad took the stairs two at a time. When he arrived at the door to apartment 3A, he knocked loudly. The noise stopped. He waited another moment or two, and when the noise didn't resume, he started down the stairs.

Thump, thump, thump, thump, thump.

"What the?" He jogged back up to the door and banged on it again. "What the hell is going on in there? Chad? Are you trying to communicate with someone?"

The noise stopped again. Konrad sighed. He'd have to come up with some way to talk to Chad. One thump for yes and two for no?

As he was deliberating, the door opened a crack, and Joe peered out at him.

"Oh, hey, Joe. I didn't know you were home. What was that racket? I thought Chad was trying to get someone's attention."

"Uh, no," he said.

A naked Gwyneth came into view. She looked like a redheaded Lady Godiva. "Who is it, Joe, honey?"

"Oh!" Konrad snapped to attention. "I'm sorry, I didn't realize you were…entertaining."

Joe looked over his shoulder at Gwyneth and grinned. "It's Konrad. I guess we were making too much noise."

"Oh, my goodness! If Konrad could hear us, then Dottie probably can, bless her heart. She'll be madder than a bottle full of bees." Gwyneth came to the door, still naked and completely unabashed. "Thanks for lettin' us know, Konrad. I wouldn't want my research to get Joe into trouble."

Konrad scratched his head. "Research? What kind of research?"

"Oh, it's for my book. I'm writin' erotica now."

He raised his eyebrows.

Joe chuckled. "I've never been so happy to be someone's *research* assistant before."

Konrad couldn't hold it in any longer and let out a booming laugh.

Gwyneth frowned and crossed her arms under her pale breasts. "I have to do somethin' to pay the rent. I don't have enough education to get a fancy job."

Joe stepped out from behind the door and put his arm around her. He was wearing boxers, thank goodness. "You're quite well educated in this field, sweetheart. You'll make a fine erotica writer."

"I know it was your idea, and I'm grateful and everything, but I still don't spell worth a hoot."

Joe stroked her shoulder. "You don't need to know how to spell, these days. The computer will correct your spelling automatically. And anything you miss, your editor will catch."

She inhaled. "I guess. At least I'm enjoyin' the research part of it." She giggled and pinched his nipple. "Now can we go back and finish it?"

Konrad stepped away from the door. "Hey, don't let me stop you. I'm going out soon, anyway. Have fun, kids."

"Oh, we will!" Gwyneth said and giggled.

~m~

Chad floated through the witches' kitchen and eventually settled atop their refrigerator.

"*Morgaine, you know I hate to complain, but…*"

Morgaine laughed and continued stirring her soup. Chad had thought it was a potion bubbling in an iron pot on the stove, until she tasted it.

"Yeah, sure, Chad. I can't remember you complaining about anything…in the last five minutes."

"*Oh, c'mon. I'm not that bad.*"

"Whatever you say." She turned off the gas and set the pot on one of the cool burners. "So what are you complaining about?"

"*It's your cousin.*"

Morgaine was reaching into the cabinet for a bowl and hesitated. "Gwyneth? What could she be doing to bother you?"

"*I'm afraid she's going to break my roommate's heart.*"

Morgaine's jaw dropped. "Are you kidding me?"

"*No, she's using him for sex in the name of research. I don't know if he realizes that. I mean she's been honest about it, but—*"

"Wait a minute. You actually care about the feelings of someone else?"

"*Huh? I didn't mean that.*" Chad floated over to the table and hovered by the chair Gwyneth usually used. "*I'm afraid she'll hurt him, and then he'll move out, and no one will be working on my murder case anymore.*"

Morgaine smirked. "That's more like it. I was about to look out the window to see if I woke up in some alternate universe this morning." She set her bowl of soup opposite him and made herself comfortable. She started eating, apparently not at all bothered about the disaster waiting to happen.

"*Morgaine!*"

She flinched. "What?"

"*Aren't you going to do something about it? Isn't this against the Witch's Rede or something?*"

She shook her head. "The Rede says, 'and it harm none, do what ye will.'"

"*What the hell does that mean?*"

She sighed deeply. "It means that if you're not hurting anybody, you're in the clear. Do whatever you want."

"*Well, what if she is hurting someone?*"

"Like who?"

"*Me.*"

Morgaine shook her head and muttered, "So predictable."

"*Look, you may not want to take this seriously, but it could easily happen. She's a beautiful young woman. He's a horny old dude. Eventually she'll find someone who really turns her on, and she'll leave him.*"

Morgaine ate her soup as if nothing could interest her less.

"*Well? Are you going to talk to her about it?*"

"No."

"*Why not?*"

"I have better things to think about. I'm trying to solve a cold case using my skills as a medium."

Chad levitated and crossed his arms. "*The skill I taught you?*"

She bit her lip. "Uh, yeah."

"*What's the case? Maybe I can help.*"

"I doubt it. I'm working with a ghost at the Isabella Stewart Gardener Museum. You don't like to leave the building. Neither do I, for that matter. But do you think you could make it to the Fenway?"

"*Weather permitting.*"

"I wouldn't want you to talk to Reginald, anyway."

"*Why not? I get along fine with other ghosts. Harold across the street and I would never have been friends in life, but now that we have something in common, we talk all the time.*"

"Really? I didn't know you two were so chummy."

"*Well, I wouldn't say we're best buds. We're more like two dudes in the same life raft.*" He chuckled. "*I guess life isn't the right word, but we're both adrift.*"

"What's his story?"

"*He just died in his sleep. Borrring. Not like my cool story of murder and intrigue.*"

Morgaine rolled her eyes.

"*What?*"

"I've been meaning to ask you, why haven't you gone into the light, now that your unfinished business is finished."

"*But it's not.*"

"Yes it is."

"*Look, all I know is—*" Chad floated over her head

toward the door. *"Crap, the jig's up. To be honest, I'd go if a beam of light appeared someday, but it hasn't. I don't think they want me on the other side."*

"Awww...I'm sorry. I know what it's like to feel excluded."

"I'll bet you do. Just the way you present yourself would scare off most people. Are you trying to protect yourself? Were you traumatized at some point in your life?"

"What a crazy question! Of course I'm not trying to scare people, and I've never been t-traumatized."

"You can't fool me, Morgaine. How long have I known you? How many times have you left the apartment?"

"It's the business. I have to be here to answer the phones."

"Bullshit. You always send Gwyneth to do your shopping. I don't think you've even left to see a dentist or a doctor."

"I'm a witch. I can heal myself."

"So you're saying you've never thought about dating? That you can't go out and meet real people, because you have to answer the phone if a horny dude calls?"

"No, I'm not saying that at all. I just...well, guys don't find me attractive, that's all."

"Then give up the '90s gothic look, already! Get a makeover. What are you, thirty?"

Morgaine crossed her arms and frowned. "You're one to talk. You're stuck in the '60s! Complete with bell bottom pants and love beads."

"I'm dead. What's your excuse?"

Chad waited for her to speak, but she remained silent.

"*Oh, don't pout.*"

"I wasn't pouting. I was trying to think of a spell to shut you up."

"*The truth hurts, doesn't it?*"

"Goddess, please take pity on the spirit of Chad and help him pass over to the other side. If for the good of all, so mote it be."

She waited a moment and then glanced around the apartment. "Chad?" She smiled. "Not very creative, but it *might* have worked."

Hmm. Should I mess with her head by leaving her apartment without saying a word? He chuckled to himself. *Hell, yes!*

Roz heard a knock on her door and hurried over to it. *It must be Konrad.* They had to talk. For one thing, she didn't want him fighting to protect her. Filing the complaint was the least aggressive way to go, and he didn't want anything to do with it. Even before that, he had reacted badly before they'd exhausted diplomacy. What was going on with him?

She threw open the door and was surprised to see Morgaine standing there.

"Morgaine! What's up?"

"Well, not me. Do you have a minute?"

"Sure. Come in." Roz stood aside and let a hunched Morgaine amble over to the couch and flop onto it. "What's the matter? Did something happen?"

"Yeah. Chad happened. I usually ignore his little digs, but I think he's right this time."

Roz sat beside her. "Oh? What did he say?"

"He said I'm stuck in the '90s, and I need a make-over. I've noticed you have a good sense of style. I was wondering if you'd give me some ideas."

Roz bolted upright. "Did you say a makeover? What fun! Sure, I'd love to help! When can we start?"

Morgaine chuckled. "I didn't realize it was an emergency."

Roz patted Morgaine's hand. "Oh, I didn't mean it like that. I'm just excited about the idea of a little girl time. Merry's been in Florida, and I've missed doing the things we used to do together, like shopping."

"In that case, we can go anytime you're free. My schedule is flexible."

"Are you getting anywhere with the art museum case?"

Morgaine shrugged one shoulder. "I have a feeling there's more Reginald wants to tell me, but he would rather talk to me alone. The only problem with that is not having a witness. And I'm not sure he trusts me completely yet. Now that Chad said something, I think my clothes and makeup might have intimidated him."

"It's possible."

Morgaine hesitated. It seemed as if she wanted to tell her something else, so Roz gave her the time to put her thoughts into words.

"Yeah. It's more than that. I…I have a mild case of agoraphobia. I hate to leave the building alone. At least if someone I trust is with me and I have a panic attack, I'm sure they'll help."

"Of course I'll help! I had no idea."

"No, I'm pretty sure nobody does, except Gwyneth, of course. She does all our errands. If we need something she can't find locally, I order it online."

"That must be inconvenient at times. I have a car. If you ever need a ride somewhere…"

Morgaine gave her a grateful smile. "That's sweet of you. I have to really, really need something badly to accept a ride anywhere. My grandmother died last year and my uncle had to come all the way up from Maryland to drive me to the funeral."

"I understand." She didn't really know much about agoraphobia, but she'd look it up on Wikipedia later. Roz took a deep breath and smelled something earthy and sweet. "What's that scent you're wearing?"

"Patchouli."

"What is that? Some kind of Italian designer perfume?"

Morgaine laughed. "No. It's an essential oil. Witches wear it to attract money, and I need some. Our phone-sex business is drying up, since Dottie put the kibosh on loud noises. Some of the guys like us to sound like we're, um, enjoying ourselves too."

"Then you need to solve the art museum case."

"Exactly. If I can help recover the stolen artwork, I could make millions. I'd be set for life."

Roz understood the stakes a little better. "So you think your gothic style is interfering with your mediumship? Reginald's from a different era. Does he seem easily intimidated?"

"Judging from his reaction to Konrad, I'd say he has limits."

"What reaction to Konrad?"

"Oh, he hasn't told you yet?"

"Told me what?"

Morgaine covered her mouth and stood. "I'm sorry. I've said too much. I should go."

"Wait. What are you saying? What didn't Konrad tell me?

Morgaine started toward the door.

"No, don't leave yet." *Maybe I can get it out of her during our girl time.*

"No, I really, really have to go. I'll talk to you later."

Roz looked at her askance. "Promise?"

"I promise. It's not like we live miles apart."

Roz rose and walked Morgaine to the door. "Okay. I think I understand. Whatever it is would be better coming from him, right?"

Morgaine let out a deep breath and looked relieved. "Yes. I'll just be upstairs if you need me."

Need her? What's he going to do? Break my heart?

———— ᴥ ————

"What aren't you telling me?" Roz demanded, standing opposite Konrad in the hallway outside his door.

He pulled on his jacket and wondered who had told her. "It's nothing, Roz. Well, let me amend that. Yes, there's something I have to tell you. It's just that now's not the time."

"Are you married?"

"No."

"Do you have any illegitimate kids?"

"No."

"Insanity in the family?"

"Not per se, but some might argue that point."

"Why can't you tell me? I don't have to go to work for another hour, and you're not working at all right now."

"An hour isn't enough time. That is, unless we do something else and save the talk for later." He grinned and hoped she'd catch his drift without his having to wiggle his eyebrows.

"Oh, no, you don't. No sleazing out of it with sex."

"Sex isn't sleazy between consenting adults who care for each other."

"That's something we need to talk about. It's fine if you care *about* me, but you don't have to *take* care *of* me. It's very sweet of you to want to, but I'm a grown woman, and I can take care of myself."

Konrad cupped her cheek. "I wasn't talking about taking care of you. I was talking about loving you."

Roz's eyes rounded, and Konrad watched as she experienced a suspended moment in stunned silence. At last she was able to respond. "Oh!"

He expected her to say something more, and he waited and waited. "Roz? Did you hear what I said?"

"Yeah," she murmured, seeming completely distracted.

Maybe she needed it spelled out a little more. He cupped both her cheeks and waited until she was gazing into his eyes. "I'm telling you I love you, Roz."

"I...I love you too. I think."

"You think?" Konrad dropped his hands and took a step back.

"It's just that I know there's something you're not telling me. I need to know what it is, or at least why you can't tell me right now." She stepped forward and rested her hands against his chest. His arms automatically extended to her waist while she continued. "Before, we hadn't known each other very long at all, but we've been on several dates now, and...I should know what the big secret is before we go any further."

He heaved a heavy sigh. "Trust me, there's a right

time and place to talk about this, and I'll do my best to find them."

She narrowed her eyes and scrutinized him. "Soon?"

"As soon as I can."

Eventually she sighed. "Okay." She stepped into his space and raised her face to his for a kiss.

Thank God. He kissed her tenderly at first and then the inevitable fire sprang up and so did part of his anatomy.

After kissing her thoroughly, he asked, "Are you sure you're not in the mood for a quickie?"

She rested her head against his chest and mumbled, "You're incorrigible."

"But you love me."

"I think…"

Konrad gazed at the ceiling and asked for strength. Now wasn't the time to push for a commitment, either.

He kissed the top of her head. "At least you know I love you. I'm glad I said it."

She tipped her face up, and her eyes sparkled. "I'm glad you did too."

Chapter 10

KONRAD RETURNED TO THE GARDNER MUSEUM TO think. The place was ideal for that. Not only was it an art museum, but also the whole building surrounded a courtyard rich with verdant plants and flowering shrubs. Gray stone benches had been strategically placed throughout the courtyard to allow visitors to appreciate the subtly fresh-scented air and quiet surroundings.

Too preoccupied to appreciate the beauty all around him, he paced and obsessed about his impossible predicament. Now that he'd told Roz he was in love with her and knew she was in love with him too, despite reservations, he had to tell her the truth. Trust was an important ingredient in a mature, loving relationship.

But how do you tell the woman you love you're a werewolf and you want to be mated for life? How do you admit you lied to your lawyer and committed the crime you were accused of? How do you keep pretending you're unemployed and expect to pay the rent?

Konrad sank onto a bench and slumped over with his head in his hands. The last thing he expected was for anybody to come over and talk to him about it. People in the city didn't talk to strangers. If you were on fire, they might stop to put you out, but they might also walk right past you, glaring at you for having the nerve to disrupt their thoughts. That's why he jumped, startled, when he felt a touch on the back of his head. As he whipped around to see who was standing behind him, he felt a sharp prick of pain in his scalp. A few of his hairs had been yanked out by a toddler.

The child's mother rushed over, pushing an empty stroller. "Oh, I'm so sorry! I thought it was safe to let him walk off a little energy here."

Konrad smiled, relieved that no one wanted to chat his ear off and simply wanted to pull his hair. The boy clutched a few long strands of blond hair in his chubby fist.

"Oh, he got some of your hair!"

"Don't worry. It's no big deal." He patted the little tyke on his head.

The boy drew the strands toward his mouth. The woman yanked his fist away and worked the hair out of his hand. She dropped the strands on the path and said, "No, dirty." She shook her head vigorously and enunciated, "Dirrr-tcy."

I washed my hair this morning. Even as much as he understood a toddler needed simple explanations, Konrad couldn't help being slightly offended.

The woman didn't say another word. She simply plucked the boy up off the ground before he went after the fallen hair and wrestled him into his stroller while he squirmed and whined. Eventually she pushed the screaming child away.

So much for peace and quiet to think.

--~~--

Finally I have some of this freak's DNA, and I know right where to put it, Reginald said to himself later that evening.

The long strands of hair appeared to float on an invisible wind, through the dark gallery and down to the basement.

They didn't have that type of testing back in my day. They didn't even fully understand fingerprinting back then. Of course, they did in the '90s, but the real thieves wore gloves, so they didn't leave any prints.

As the hairs disappeared behind some shelving, they attached themselves to a piece of duct tape that had been left behind when one of the bound security guards was cut loose after the robbery.

Konrad strolled along the wide sidewalk with his twin brother, Nick. Their broad shoulders seemed to span the whole width, and a passerby walked into the gutter to avoid the two men.

"Now that you've ignored my advice and gotten involved with this human lawyer, you want my advice again? Isn't that a little ironic, bro?"

Nick hadn't used the concept of irony properly, but Konrad wasn't about to correct him. He needed his compassion, and Nick was sensitive to criticism, no matter how well intended.

"How should I tell her?"

Nick shrugged. "Don't ask me. I've never had to fess up to a woman before. I just love 'em and leave 'em. It's what we do."

"I've never liked that part."

"Yeah? Well, you should try it. Much less messy."

"How would you know that?"

Nick gave his brother a sidelong glance. "Because it is. Look at you. You're a wreck. I've never seen you this insecure!"

"She's worth whatever pain I have to go through."

"You mean, 'It's better to have loved and lost,' and all that?"

"Maybe, but I'm hoping not to lose her at all. How can I manage that? I mean the stakes are ridiculous. I just don't know if she trusts me enough, yet."

"You should have stuck to our own kind. They know the ropes. Speaking of ropes, you could test her trust."

Konrad raised his brows. "How?"

"Ask if she'll let you tie her up."

He laughed. "I guess letting me do that might be a sign of trust. Or how kinky she is."

Nick looked over at him. "By the way, that doctor you sent my way? What a freak!"

"Oh, shit. Sorry, bro. I didn't realize."

Nick laughed again. "I mean *freaky* in a good way! She was all over me like an octopus on caffeine."

Konrad laughed out loud with his booming voice. "Must have been a fun night."

"The best."

"Aren't you tempted to call her again?"

"Nope."

"So, that's it? You're just going to dump her and let her wonder why?"

Nick raised an eyebrow. "What would you suggest? Date her for a month, have lots more great sex, fall head over heels in love, and then tell her I'm a werewolf? Oh, no wait. That's what *you'd* do."

Konrad let out a long sigh. "It's more than that." Taking a deep breath, he told his twin the rest. "Rosalyn is my soul mate."

Nick stopped walking. "Your what?"

"My mate. The one. The love of my life."

"Shit, how do you know that?"

"We're able to communicate telepathically."

Nick's jaw dropped. "Get the fuck out. Did you just say you can hear her thoughts? And worse…she can hear yours?"

"Yeah. It's been a challenge, believe me."

"How the hell…" Nick clasped his brother's shoulder. "I hate to say this, big guy, but you are so fucked."

"Thanks, Nick. You've been a big help."

―――⁂―――

Sly stretched out on Konrad's sofa. His long arms spanned the back of it. He crossed one ankle over his knee.

"What's so urgent?" he asked.

"Nothing's urgent." Konrad settled into the adjacent chair. "Can't I just want to spend some time with my buddy?"

Sly lifted one eyebrow.

"Okay, okay. I have a dilemma. I thought you might be able to give me some advice, since you went through it recently."

Sly cocked his head. "I did? What are you talking about?"

Konrad smiled. "I know you told Merry about your being a vampire. Now I have to tell her best friend I'm a werewolf."

"And then, if I weren't her father and she weren't married, we could double date?" Sly mocked.

Konrad reeled. "What the? Incestuous visual aside, that's…oh, you're kidding again."

Sly laughed. "Of course I am. I just couldn't resist

yanking your chain. You sound like an adolescent talking to his older, more experienced friend about girls."

Konrad's lips thinned.

"I'm sorry. You had a dilemma. I shouldn't have poked fun, but you have to admit, it broke the ice."

Konrad leaned against the back of the chair and blew out a long breath as he stared at the ceiling.

Sly said, "Come on. Give me a break. It's not an easy subject to discuss. I tend to joke around instead of getting overly serious."

Konrad bent forward with his elbows on his knees. "Tell me about it."

Sly's voice softened. "Naturally I was afraid of what she'd say. Or do. But Merry's not like other girls. She has the heart of a lion, but the compassion of Mother Teresa. And she's open-minded. I know she had doubts, even so."

"I think because you and I had saved her from that rapist, she was predisposed to trusting you."

"That probably didn't hurt. She *did* feel indebted to both of us. But when I expressed my concern about her relationship with Falco, she showed me what she was made of." Sly shook his head wistfully. "Just like her mother."

"How did you tell her?"

"I didn't. Nathan did. All I had to do was tell her he was right and try to dispel the myths."

"Shit. I'm not about to let Nathan tell Roz for me. He'd scare her to death and laugh about it."

"No, I wouldn't recommend that. I didn't ask him to tell Merry. He just blurted it out. Apparently she wanted to bake a dessert to thank us for coming to her rescue.

When she asked Nathan where I lived, he couldn't resist telling her my lair was in the basement and I was on an all-liquid diet."

Konrad chuckled. "Sorry, man. I can just imagine what she must have thought."

"Yeah, she thought Nathan was psycho, not me. Not that he isn't…"

Konrad shook his head. "Man, that must have been bizarre for poor Merry."

"I'm sure it was. I'm glad she didn't take his word for it and came to me instead."

"Yeah, but you had to tell her it was true. What did she do then?"

Sly shrugged. "She listened. I think she might have been too stunned to speak, so I took advantage of the silence and poured out my whole story."

"And she believed you? Just like that?"

Sly shook his head. "Not 'just like that.' I had to give her details no one but her biological father would know, and then she added things up. My strength, her birth surname being the same as mine, my watching over her… But her ability to smell blood a mile away was what finally made a believer out of her. She'd never been able to explain that, except to say it predisposed her to becoming a nurse."

"I see, so you actually had to persuade her of two things. Not just your vampirism, but also your being her only living—let me amend that—her only blood relative."

Sly smiled. "Yeah." He adjusted himself in his seat. "I'm afraid I don't know your Roz at all. I've seen her, but we've never met. I don't know what she's like or what you should do. I'm sorry."

Konrad sighed. "It seems like a recurring theme. I'm the one who knows her, and I have to decide how to tell her. I get that. The only problem is she's the type who needs proof. She wants to see or experience everything herself."

Sly shook his head. "I don't envy you. Do it wrong, and you're screwed, man…*so* screwed."

—⁓—

Roz dragged herself home from work the next afternoon, completely fried. Some of the sociopaths she had to defend were extremely intelligent, fooling even the savviest judge, and some, like the idiot she got today, were stupid enough to shoot themselves in the foot, literally.

The guy then had the nerve to say it wasn't his gun. He was "holding it for a friend" when it went off in the convenience store. She had told him not to open his mouth. So, why didn't the dumbass just sit dumbly and let her do the talking?

She fiddled with her keys and let out a huge sigh when the door opened in front of her. Nathan was exiting the building and held the door open for her.

"Thanks. I don't know if I would have had the strength to open the damn thing if you hadn't come along."

He stared at her. "Were you hit by a truck?"

She chuckled. "No, I just feel like I was."

"You look like you were, too."

Oh, nice. "Thanks, Nathan."

"Where are you coming from?

"Work." Anxious to get rid of him, she said, "Well, you have a good evening."

"Yeah, I will. My job must be a lot easier than yours, and sometimes I come home dead tired."

She didn't care what he meant by that comment. She slogged past him to her apartment door, still looking for her keys. Before she had the key in the lock, she remembered scheduling her girl time with Morgaine for that evening.

"Aw, crap." All she wanted to do was fall face first on her bed and sleep until morning. But when she thought about it, a nice massage and some aromatherapy might do her a lot of good.

Once in the door, she dropped her purse on the sideboard and hung up her coat, keeping her keys in her hand. She'd ride the elevator to the third floor today, even though ordinarily she'd walk the three flights of stairs and call it exercise.

Heavy footsteps sounded on the stairs. She no sooner relocked her door and spun around than Konrad came into view. First his thick, muscled thighs, then his taut black T-shirt that showed off his abs and pecs, and then his—"What the..."

Konrad's long, blond hair was gone! His chest and shoulders were no longer covered with a curtain of gold. Instead he sported a tousled style, still longer than most men wore, along with his always present facial scruff.

*Holy heck...*Roz had never seen him looking so good. Ugh. She must look all the worse because of it.

"Roz!"

Oh no. He spotted me. No chance to duck back in and close the door quietly so he'd never know I was here.

"How's the ankle?"

"Oh, uh...much better. Thanks."

"Why do you look so nervous? Is everything all right?"

"You cut your hair. I almost didn't recognize you."

He grinned. "Yeah, you like?" He turned his head left and right so she could take in the whole thing. The sides were swept back, but it was hard to say where the rest was going. It certainly wasn't parted anywhere.

"I love it. When and why did you cut it?"

"A couple hours ago. I was just in the mood for something different."

"I hope you sent the rest off to Locks of Love. They makes wigs for children with cancer. I'd hate to think of all that gorgeous hair just going into the trash."

"Actually I have it upstairs. I figured I'd donate it, but I didn't know where to send it."

"Morgaine and I were about to go to a day spa and salon. I'll ask if the people there know. Maybe we can send yours and Morgaine's at the same time."

His eyes widened. "Morgaine's cutting her hair too?"

"Maybe. She's getting a whole makeover and asked me to go with her. I can't wait!"

"Oh." His face fell.

"What's wrong? We weren't planning to go out until tomorrow morning's date, skydiving, right?"

"Yeah, but I thought maybe I'd see if you were free tonight."

Her heart leapt. He couldn't wait until tomorrow to see her? Suddenly it occurred to her why, and she gasped. "Were you going to tell me your secret? Is that why you cleaned up?"

He smiled. "It's no big deal. Go have your fun, and I'll see you tomorrow. You still want to try jumping out of a perfectly good airplane?"

Roz bit her lower lip, but smiled. "I committed, so I'll see it through. I mean, it would be too easy to chicken out, right?"

"Right. Well then, give me a kiss, and I'll see you in the morning."

"I could come up tonight after I'm all relaxed and cleaned up. I figured I'd get some pampering while Morgaine is going through her transformation. Then maybe I'll look as good as you do."

He laughed. "You look fine, but I'd love to see you." He framed her face with his big hands. "I've missed you."

"But it's only been a couple of days."

"Really? It feels like a couple of weeks."

"Awww…"

He slanted his mouth over hers and lowered his lips for a warm kiss. When he pulled back, he whispered, "I love you."

She smiled, but still didn't know what to say, knowing he was keeping a secret. "We need to resolve this, if for no other reason than to feel comfortable saying it back…or not."

He pulled her into his arms and held her. "It's enough to know you want to."

"Are you two at it again?"

Morgaine came up behind them, and Roz hadn't even heard her approach. *I guess that's how distracted I am when this man kisses me.*

"Hi, Morgaine." Konrad stepped away.

Morgaine folded her arms. "I hardly recognized you without your hair. If I didn't know better, I'd have thought Roz was kissing another guy."

"Ha. She'd better not."

That was a little presumptuous.

"*I just meant that you'd break my heart.*"

Oh, you heard that?

"*Yup.*" Konrad faced Morgaine. "I understand you're going out for some pampering?"

He may have been changing the subject, but the girls had to get going anyway. She could talk to him about it later. It seemed like they had *a lot* to talk about later.

"Yes, I made an appointment at a beauty school. It's cheaper, since the students get a chance to practice on real volunteers."

"In other words, you're guinea pigs?" Konrad scrunched his eyes shut. "Sorry. That didn't come out right."

Roz and Morgaine laughed.

"Don't worry." Roz patted his arm. "I knew what you meant. It'll be okay, though. Their instructors are right there, so they can't screw up. Besides, I can't look much worse."

"Hey, cut that out. You're always beautiful."

"You don't have to pretend. I know I'm a little bedraggled. Nathan told me I looked like I'd been hit by a truck."

"Sounds like something he'd say. What's going on? Bad day at the courtroom?"

"Yeah, but I'd rather just put that behind me and get to my massage."

"If all you wanted was a massage…"

Roz held up her hand. "Too much information! Quick, let's go, Morgaine, before he says something I'll regret."

———~~~———

Later that evening, Konrad lay in bed reading. He was
using his clip-on reading light so his apartment would
appear dark. He hated to deceive Roz and avoid her, but
he still didn't know how to tell her what she deserved to
know. *She's dating a werewolf.*

He hoped she'd still be dating him after he dropped
his bombshell, but something else had him worried.
What if she didn't believe him? How could he prove it
to her?

She had laughed at the possibility of vampires and
werewolves. *But legends don't evolve out of nothing.*

He could shift, but that would scare her to death.
Hell, it scared him the first several times he witnessed it.
Maybe he could demonstrate his super-human strength.
But what if she didn't know werewolves had that kind of
strength? She might only think he was freakishly strong,
and *that* would reopen the memory of his arrest. If he
was capable of, say, lifting his upright piano by himself,
perhaps she'd realize he could also lift a freezer.

A knock at the door snapped him into high alert.

"Konrad?"

Roz's voice seemed excited…expectant.

He froze, not daring to move a muscle. A few seconds ticked by.

Maybe she'd gotten all dolled up just for him. How
could he leave her standing out there?

She knocked again. "Konrad? Are you home?"

Crap. He couldn't ignore her.

"Hang on a minute," he called out. Jumping out of
bed, he messed up his already tousled hair as if he'd been
asleep. Then he tossed on his velour robe and plodded to
the door. As he opened it, he stretched and yawned.

"Oh, I must have woken you up. I'm sorry. I thought you were expecting me."

"I was…I mean, I am. I must have dozed off. Come in."

She walked past him, and Konrad did a double take.

"You look different."

"Yeah, while Morgaine was getting her makeover, I had my hair highlighted." She turned side to side so he could admire the results.

He almost growled his approval, and his robe began tenting. "It looks good. What's Morgaine look like now?"

"She's a blonde."

Konrad took a step back. "You're kidding! How the heck did they take her from black to blonde?"

"It was quite an ordeal. They had to strip out all the color, put in one overall color, then add highlights and lowlights. That's what took so long. The instructors were thrilled to get such a challenge, and the students did a really great job."

Konrad laughed. "I'll have to see it to believe it."

"They left it long and just trimmed the ends. After all the chemicals, I was afraid her hair might fall out. I found out how to send yours to Locks of Love. It has to be at least ten inches long."

"Mmm. I have ten inches for you."

She laughed. "Are we still talking about hair?"

He reached out and touched her hair. "I'm glad you left yours long."

"You call this long?"

"Longish." He slid his hand behind her neck and leaned down to kiss her.

She wrapped her arms around his neck and kissed him back. *Good*. Maybe she'd decided to love him regardless of his secret. Could he have been given a reprieve by some giant miracle?

Without waiting to find out, he tossed her over his shoulder and hastened to the bedroom as she laughed. He remembered her ankle, so he gently placed her on his unmade bed and asked, "Are you sure your ankle is healed enough for some bedroom aerobics?"

She shot him an impish grin. "We can always try it and see what happens."

That time he did growl, but it was low and came from the back of his throat. He crawled over her like the predator he was. Her grin suggested she wasn't afraid of him one whit. Thank God. He wanted her to trust him as much or more than he wanted to have sex with her. Almost.

Bending down, he kissed her deep and slow. He held himself up with one hand and unbuttoned her blouse with the other. Roz's cooperation had calmed the urgency he experienced in the beginning of their sexual relationship. Knowing he would be rewarded in the end made going slower tolerable.

She threaded her fingers through his hair. Now that she could do that without getting caught in a snarl along the way, he was glad he cut it. The scalp massage felt incredibly pleasant.

He popped open her bra, captured her plump breast in his hand, and squeezed it gently. She moaned.

Konrad backed down the bed until his mouth was level with her breast, and suckled. She arched and moaned some more. Her responsiveness turned him on every bit as much as her beauty.

I can't believe how much I love her. Why do I have to tell her what I really am? I don't want this to end.

Roz suddenly retracted her fingers from his hair. "What do you mean?"

Konrad looked up into her expectant eyes. Something like fear brewed behind them.

"Tell me what you heard."

"Why? Can't you just tell me what this big secret is?"

He hung his head. Realizing he'd have to tell her something, he decided to divulge the less frightening of the secrets he'd been keeping. She'd probably be angry, but he'd prefer anger to her being frightened of him.

He scooted up beside her and pulled her into his arms. "You're apt to be disappointed with me. Are you sure you want to know?"

After a long pause, she finally said, "Yes." He'd hoped she might change her mind, at least until after they'd made love. Oh well. It seemed like that ship had sailed for the moment. He hoped it was only temporary.

"Roz, I don't know how to say this without…well, hear me out before you get angry, all right?"

She took a deep breath. "I'll try."

She broke out of his embrace and sat up, leaning against the headboard. The loss of her warmth made his job that much harder, but she was expecting an explanation, so he had to press on.

"Okay, you know I have a brother, right?"

"Yes, your twin."

"Nicholas." He sat up and scooted next to her.

She nodded.

"We tried to start our own business together, selling alarm systems."

"Tried to? I thought you still did."

"Yes, we do. But it's a tough time for any small business, and unless people feel security is absolutely necessary, they won't pay for an expensive alarm system." He dragged a hand over his face.

She nodded. "Go on."

"You could say my job was to drum up business."

She frowned and shook her head. "I don't understand."

He took a deep breath. "I'm a thief, Roz. Well, not a real thief. I don't actually steal anything of value. I just jimmy a lock or break a window, something to make business owners realize they need to be better protected. In a way I'm doing them a service."

She snorted. "Is that what you tell yourself so you can sleep at night?"

He hung his head. "Kind of, yeah."

"So that night you were arrested, you weren't just taking a walk, were you?"

"No. I—"

"Shhh." She hurriedly put her finger against his lips. "Don't say any more."

He figured she might have to turn him in. There might be some kind of lawyer's pledge or something, but he was willing to go to jail if she did. By stopping him, maybe she didn't want to hear the details and wouldn't have to take any action.

"Are you still…taking late night walks?" she asked.

"No. I haven't taken any walks like that since, and I don't plan to. I really do want to…change my career."

She remained quiet.

"You're not upset?"

"I didn't say that. Look…" She sighed. "I understand desperation. The cost of living in this city is one of the highest in the country. Plenty of people I defend are pushed to do things they wouldn't have attempted ordinarily."

"But you're disappointed."

"Sad, disappointed, but not angry. I get it. You probably left teaching to make more money, and as soon as you started your business, the economy tanked."

He nodded. He didn't exactly leave teaching. He was the dean of students—and a disgraced alpha, run out of town.

Roz was right. He would never have started down his path otherwise, but when business had started to flounder, he and Nick had to resort to desperate measures.

"Was your brother a cop all along? Or did he get into it as a result of the business failing?"

"The latter. He knew a couple of guys on the force, and they thought he might be well suited to the job."

"How about you? Did you ever think about going into law enforcement?"

"No, that's not for me. Or, as my brother would say, I'm too much of a softie."

Roz stroked his erection and said, "You don't feel very soft to me." She finally smiled and reached for him.

He practically dove into her arms and held her tight. "Do you forgive me?"

"As long as it's all in the past…"

"It is. I swear on every book in my library."

She grinned. "That's a lot of swearing."

He let out a deep breath. "I can't tell you how relieved I am."

"I guess I am too. When I heard you telepathically worrying about telling me what you really *were*…well,

I didn't know what to think, but I assumed it was something really terrible."

Before they went too far down that road, he tackled her and set out to finish what they'd started.

Chapter 11

Roz was glad he'd finally told her his secret, without exactly telling her. She still had her values to maintain. Was associating with a known thief a problem? She hadn't witnessed him stealing anything, right?

Konrad nibbled her ear, and she moaned.

Problem? What problem? Had she just been puzzled about something?

He swirled his tongue in her ear and whispered, "I love you so much. I love you more than my life. I mean it, Roz. You're everything to me."

The combination of his hot breath and tender words made her quiver.

He kissed her neck, nipped her jaw, and licked her collarbone. "Can you say it back yet?"

"Yes," she murmured. "I love you too."

"You don't know how much I've wanted to hear that."

He stopped to deliver a masterful kiss. Deep and meaningful. When he drew away, he kissed her forehead, her cheeks, her nose, and her chin.

He makes me feel like he cherishes every inch of me.

"*I do.*" He slid down and cupped her breast. "Do you trust me now?" He found her nipple and sucked.

"I…ohhh." She arched as the pleasurable sensation shot straight to her womb.

He suckled the other breast thoroughly then asked, "Well?"

"What?" *What did he say?* "Did you ask me something?"

"I asked if you trusted me." He kissed his way down her middle and swirled his tongue in her belly button.

"Y-yes, I trust you."

"Good. Because there's something I'd like to try."

"What's that?"

"You'll see." He made quick work of her skirt and underwear and flung them across the room. Sliding down, he licked her slit, and then he slid his tongue down over one ridge and up the other.

"Ohhh…" She moaned. "But you've already done that. Why would you need to ask if I trust you?"

"Because of this…" He jumped out of bed and stripped out of his clothes quickly, crossed to his closet, and came back with two neckties.

Roz blinked. "What exactly do you plan to do with those?"

"Bind you to my bedposts, so I can do whatever I want to you."

Holy moly. "I see where the trust comes in."

He sat beside her on the bed. "So can you allow me to do that?"

She bit her bottom lip and thought it over. "Can I ask *why* you want to? Will it turn you on to know I'm helpless?"

"Of course not. I thought it might turn *you* on, though." He grinned at her. "I'll untie you the minute you ask me to."

"I…I wouldn't be here if I didn't trust you, Konrad. I don't have to prove it to you, do I?"

He tipped his head toward the ceiling and slapped his forehead. "Damn! I forgot about your history. Of course you don't. I'm sorry."

"It's not that. I'm not sure I ever want to be that vulnerable. I mean, what if you had a heart attack and died?"

"Just keep yelling until Dottie busts the door down and tells you to shut up."

Roz laughed. "You're probably right. Her crazy rules about noise pollution might come in handy."

"For once." Konrad tossed the neckties on the floor and said, "Now, where were we?"

"You were going to tie me up." She chuckled.

He straightened and looked surprised. "I thought you didn't want me to."

"Hey, as long as we're not all alone at a cabin in the wilderness with no one to hear for miles…"

"Let's skip it. It's enough to know you trust me that much. But if we do try it sometime, I want you to know you're perfectly safe with me. Always."

Roz nodded and gave him an evil grin. "I know that, but are you safe with *me*?" She tried to flip him over, but couldn't.

He clambered down between her legs, where his mouth found her pussy and teased her folds. She moaned softly. His fingers glided down her thighs and sensitized her everywhere he touched. Every now and then, it tickled, and she couldn't help giggling. Eventually two of his fingers entered her wet quim.

When his tongue found her clit, she let out a yelp and an "Oh…oh," but she quieted on a gasp, followed by a trembling moan. She arched, and no matter how she tried to be quiet, her moans grew louder and more frequent as he continued to pleasure her.

His fingers moved faster, insistent, and he latched onto her clit, sucking and flicking it with his tongue mercilessly, until she shattered. She cried out in ecstasy. Concentric circles of bliss radiated though her. Her thighs shook in spasms.

"Stop. I can't take any more!"

He raised his head and grinned at her.

She reached for him. "I want you inside me."

He sprang onto his knees, his engorged erection sticking straight out. "Oh, yeah. We'll get to that, but not just yet."

She groaned.

He inserted two long fingers, pushed them in deep, and reached for her G-spot as she writhed. He dipped his head, took her puckered nipple in his mouth, and suckled. His thumb stroked her clit while he fingered her sensitive G-spot inside, and he didn't stop until she came in an earth-shattering, fevered, screaming release. The sound echoed all through the room, magnifying. She clamped a hand over her mouth and smothered what was left of her cries.

He looked down at her.

"Sorry," she whispered.

"Hmmm. You don't look sorry."

----❦----

She was glowing pink, so ready, so primed, he couldn't be upset with her for the noise. It was his fault anyway. He should have saved that move for another time, when they knew Dottie wasn't around. Without saying a word, he reached for a condom from his bedside drawer and rolled it on. Konrad paused in front of her opening and smiled.

She looked up at him and nodded.

He penetrated deep.

She sucked in a breath, clasped the mattress, and arched into him.

"Are you all right?"

"God, yes!" she whimpered. "Fuck me like there's no tomorrow!"

Hearing her use that word surprised him and turned him on even more. He found his rhythm quickly and thrust in and out, riding her hard. She reached around and clutched his glutes, mating with him intuitively, undulating as if to the beat of drums only the two of them could hear.

Her moans rose in a crescendo until, at last, she bit his shoulder, squeaked, and shook like she was lying on the epicenter of an earthquake.

Surprised, Konrad followed her over the edge and welcomed the blissful sensation, the surge shooting through him, letting go, then finally enjoying each precious ripple and aftershock. Holding one another and panting heavily, neither one moved to uncouple.

Konrad had no desire to jump up and hint that it was time for her to leave, as he often did after having sex with a willing but less significant woman. Making love to Roz was more exhilarating than he could have anticipated. He'd be willing to bet she felt the same way.

Before long, he eased off of her, aware that his weight on her chest might be uncomfortable.

When their breathing finally returned to normal, she let out a long sigh. "I'm sorry about the noise."

He kissed the warm space between her neck and shoulder. He eyed the spot, and his mouth watered. He knew that someday he'd have to mark her as his, which meant biting her right there. It was ironic that she'd gripped him with her teeth in that same place, as if by instinct.

"I don't want you to worry. I love it when you really let go."

"What if someone thinks I'm being attacked?"

"We'll let Dottie know that if the screams come from anywhere but my apartment or yours, you *are* being attacked, and I *want* her to call the police." He gave her earlobe a playful nip.

———

Dottie stormed across the hall and pounded on the door to Konrad's apartment. When no one answered, she bludgeoned it until she heard him call out, "I'm coming!" She thought she heard some snickers.

He threw open the door and stood in his bathrobe, blocking the entrance with his broad shoulders. He had the audacity to smile as if nothing had happened.

"What the hell is going on in there? Are you murdering some poor women?"

"No, I assure you, she's quite all right."

"It sounded like the Boston chainsaw massacre over here. I'd like to see for myself that she's alive and well. Please let me in…if you have nothing to hide."

"Leave her alone. She's embarrassed enough."

"Oh, you'd like me to take your word for it, wouldn't you? I'm not going anywhere."

Konrad grumbled and then called over his shoulder, "Roz, honey? Can you say something to Dottie so she knows you're all right?"

"I'm fine, Dottie," a high voice called from within the apartment.

"She could be bleeding to death and afraid you'd hurt her more if she said any—"

"Jesus, Dottie, will you quit worrying?"

The higher voice from the other side of the apartment called, "Be right there."

Konrad didn't step aside.

"Well? Can I come in, or what? It's late. I don't want to disturb the other residents by discussing this in the hall."

"She'll be out in a second, and there's nothing much to discuss."

"Nothing to discuss? Are you serious?"

Konrad crossed his arms as if daring her to walk past.

Momentarily Roz scurried out to meet them, wearing a sheet wrapped around her, toga style. Her hair fanned out in various directions, thanks to static electricity. "See? I'm perfectly fine." A blush colored her cheeks.

"Other than the humiliation, that is," Konrad said scornfully.

"Making sure there isn't a domestic disturbance going on is more important than anyone's feelings."

Konrad leaned forward.

Roz held up one hand as if anticipating a defensive response. "You're quite right, Dottie. My shouting must have alarmed you, but it had nothing to do with being mistreated. I'm sorry for disturbing you."

"Well, see that it doesn't happen again."

Konrad frowned. "You never want me to satisfy my lover again?"

Roz gasped and her hands flew up to cover her mouth.

Dottie's eyebrows shot up. "You call that satisfying your lover? It sounded like she was dying in there."

"That's why the French call it *la petite morte*."

"It figures the French would have something to say about it." Pulling Roz aside, Dottie whispered to her, "I warned you about him, didn't I?"

"Yes, you did. And I'm glad I didn't listen."

———⁂———

The following morning, Roz gripped Konrad's hand, hard, yet he barely noticed it. He was busy trying to still his nerves and keep from shaking, and they were only watching the training video.

The virtual plane had already taken off and was ascending to the required twelve thousand, five hundred feet. Wolves didn't belong in the air. He liked his paws firmly on the ground, yet how much of a wuss would he be if he told his girlfriend he was afraid to skydive? The big bad werewolf scared shitless? No way.

"When in doubt, whip it out." The instructor's voiceover caught Konrad's attention and dragged him back to the moment. *What the hell is he talking about?*

"*The reserve chute,*" Roz answered telepathically.

Fear must be amplifying his thoughts. He'd have to be careful.

The video droned on.

"Many jumpers faced with minor problems such as a broken line or minor canopy damage choose to jettison the questionable parachute and go to their more reliable reserve. So long as the jettison and reserve activation are initiated at a safe altitude, which is a minimum of 1,600 feet, this practice is considered to be very conservative. It's called a 'break-away' or 'cut-away.'"

Conservative? Cutting your number of parachutes

from two to one with no spare? That didn't sound very conservative to him.

"...the benefits ranging from peace of mind, to avoiding sprains or broken bones incurred when a damaged canopy lands you too fast or too hard, to actually saving your life."

Saving your life is a benefit? He thought it was a given. Konrad squirmed in his seat.

"Jettisoning an unreliable chute causes it no damage, and it can be instantly reattached later. Most jettisoned canopies are recovered, but with prices for new canopies starting at around $1,500, one lost canopy can be quite a setback for instructors."

"And I need to know this, why?" he whispered.

"Shh."

"Once the reserve has been deployed, an FAA-certified parachute rigger must inspect and re-pack it. This service can cost around fifty to seventy-five dollars, sometimes more, and cannot always be performed immediately. It's not uncommon to see a skydiver moping around the drop zone after a reserve deployment, frustrated because his 'reserve ride' has left him grounded, possibly for the rest of the day, while he searches for lost gear and waits while his reserve parachute gets its inspection and repack, called 'I and R.'

"It's for that reason that instructors are sometimes reluctant to employ the break-away technique."

Crap! I sure didn't need to know that. And did they have to *pay* for all of that, if the primary chute fails? Konrad knew skydiving was expensive; after all, they'd paid two hundred fifty dollars to jump this once. He hoped they wouldn't fall in love with it.

Konrad's finances were already suffering badly.

Hearing a loud bellow, rather than actually seeing Konrad, she just knew he had jumped out right behind her. Was he supposed to?

Fighting for breath crowded out thoughts of Konrad. When she finally had her breathing under control, she tried to look over her shoulder. He was right behind them, and his instructor appeared to be praying, his cocky expression replaced by a serious one, and his eyes were closed.

Her own instructor looked back, and even under his goggles, she saw his eyes pop. Something told her Konrad wasn't supposed to have jumped when he did. Now what? If she opened her chute, it would hit the jumpers behind her.

"Holy shit," her instructor yelled. He veered off to one side, trying to clear a path for the other two. Apparently both Konrad and his instructor were afraid. Roz could barely see Konrad's face anymore, but he looked terrified, and his instructor was still praying, his head resting against Konrad's back.

Something was wrong. They were tumbling. Was his instructor that much of a wise guy that he'd *try* to scare Konrad?

Roz waited in uncertainty until her instructor tapped her arm and yelled, "Pull!"

She pulled and waited an anxious couple of seconds for the sail to billow and the wind to fill it. The chute yanked them out of their high-speed descent, and she glided more gently. But where the heck were Konrad and his highly religious instructor?

She peered down. Her heart was in her throat when she finally spotted them, *way* below. Their chute finally opened. Thank God! Wait until she got her hands on that instructor. She'd give him a piece of her mind he wouldn't forget.

At last, out of freefall, and with Konrad out of danger, she could relax and enjoy the view. She looked down at her feet hanging in midair and then at the earth below. She saw a far-off lake and mountains, smaller ponds, and trees. As she descended further, the air strip, parking lot, building, and cars grew larger and more distinct.

The ground came closer and closer. She'd lost track of where Konrad was. The other two must have wound up behind them.

At last her feet touched down, and she bent her knees to absorb the impact. Her instructor landed at the same time in the same way, so she didn't even fall over. If she hadn't been so worried about Konrad, the ride might have been fun. She grinned, but mostly because it was over.

She noticed the few people waiting on the ground were ignoring them and shading their eyes, staring with open mouths at something off to the right.

Following their gaze, she spotted the other two jumpers, but it looked like their chute had collapsed, and they were in the trees.

Roz gasped, then let out a scream so loud she barely recognized her own voice.

Chapter 12

OUCH, OH, OUCH, OW, OW, OH...KONRAD HIT PINE TREE branches, taking the impact to his face and body as he tried to protect the poor guy strapped to his back. He was fairly sure he could survive a hard fall. He didn't know if his instructor could.

At last they stopped falling and bounced, suspended, above the ground. As soon as Konrad caught his breath, he called out, "Hey, are you all right back there?"

An eerie silence answered him.

"Shit." He squirmed despite his pain, trying to pull himself loose from the harness so he could turn around and examine his instructor. "Damn trees," he muttered.

Konrad knew their descent wasn't normal. He just didn't know what to do about it. His instructor yelled something like, "Don't!" as Konrad dragged him out the door. He hadn't heard him speak since.

But Roz had screamed in fear. He had to be sure she was all right and reassure her, and himself.

People ran toward them shouting. He groaned and didn't know if he should call out that they were okay or not. He was cut and bruised, but breathing. He couldn't speak for the man strapped to his back.

When the first two guys got to them, they called out, "Are you all right?"

Konrad answered, "Yes, I think so" and waited an anxious moment.

At last a shaky voice behind him said, "Fuck. What the hell—?"

"Curtis!" yelled a guy from the ground. "Are you okay? What happened?

The guy behind him spoke in exhaled breaths. "Student panicked…Bailed too soon…Hit my head… Managed to…pull the drogue…before I…passed out… Came to…just now."

Roz and her instructor were among the last to arrive. She looked up at them with wild eyes. "Help them," she cried.

One of the onlookers said, "They've got to be fifty feet up. It would take anyone a while to climb, even a professional tree climber. Hey guys, if I throw you a knife, can you cut your way out?"

"I'll give it a shot," Konrad called down to them. He felt blood trickle down his face.

"They might fall!" Roz cried. "Wait, they're not far in. Maybe the fire department can reach them."

Konrad's hearing was so acute, he could understand what people were saying on the ground, even when they were whispering among themselves.

Roz's instructor nodded. "Good idea. Besides, it's against protocol to climb down from a tree landing."

Roz looked around at the small crowd that had gathered and asked, "Can someone call 911 and ask them to bring a ladder truck?"

"I will," one of the female employees said. She pulled a cell phone from her vest pocket.

Roz turned to the woman and said, "Have them bring a couple of ambulances too. They could have internal injuries."

"No ambulance for me," Konrad yelled. "I'm fine." The moon was almost full again, and he'd heal fast. Besides, he couldn't afford an ambulance ride and hospital bill. He swiveled his head. "You okay, buddy?"

"My head hurts and feels like it's about the size of Mount Rushmore."

"There are four heads on Mount Rushmore."

"Exactly." He groaned.

Roz turned to the woman with the cell phone and whispered, "Don't listen to my boyfriend. He's in shock."

She just nodded and walked a few steps away while she spoke to the dispatcher.

"I'm not in shock, Roz. I'm fine, really. One ambulance will do it."

She looked startled.

Oh yeah. He wasn't supposed to be able to hear her whisper from so far away. He'd have a hard time explaining that, unless…He sent a message to her telepathically. *You're upset, darling. I know that. I can hear it and sense it. Please don't worry. I'm all right. Really. The tree broke my fall.*

"*And you broke your instructor's fall, but he sounds like he's badly hurt. You might not feel it right now because of the adrenaline, but you have to get checked out.*" She crossed her arms and tried to look tough. "*I mean it!*"

Unfortunately she only looked more adorable, and he couldn't say no. He sighed deeply. *Okay. You win.*

A hint of a smile curved her lips. "*I guess sky diving's off the list.*"

You are so right.

—⁓—

His instructor was being kept overnight for observation, yet Konrad had broken his fall. The hospital reluctantly discharged her stubborn boyfriend, even after he had refused an MRI to check for internal bleeding. Roz had tried everything she could think of to reason with him and make him stay, but he just kept saying he was fine.

He sure as hell didn't look fine. His denim jacket sleeves had been shredded, he was cut and bruised all over his face, and yet he wouldn't let anyone lay a hand on him. He wouldn't even let the doctor stitch the gash on the side of his temple. Once it stopped bleeding, and it seemed to stop quickly, a few butterfly bandages kept it from starting again. Roz hoped that was a good sign.

By the time they had been seen, processed, and spit out, it was evening. Konrad promised to go straight to bed.

She knew it was late, but to leave Konrad alone in his apartment was wrong. He was proud and stubborn, but she shouldn't have left, even when he insisted. What if he was unaware of some kind of internal injury and died in his sleep? She'd never forgive herself.

She made a big pot of chicken soup and carried it carefully up the stairs. When she reached the landing, his door opened, and he stepped out of his apartment... naked! *What the?* There wasn't a scratch on him. No blood, no bruises, no Band-Aids. He was as naked and perfect as the day he was born.

His gaze snapped in her direction. "Roz!"

"Konrad, why are you—? How did you—?" As she stammered, he stared at her as if *she* were the one standing there naked.

"I can explain," he said.

She waited, but no explanation followed.

What the hell could he tell her? He was a fast-healing nudist? He wore a bruise suit earlier, but he took it off in favor of his birthday suit?

The full moon was approaching, and he could feel the urge to change. This fiasco couldn't have happened at a worse time.

"Roz, can the explanation possibly wait until tomorrow?"

Her jaw dropped. "You've got to be out of your ever-loving mind! No, it can't wait."

Down below, Nathan exited his apartment with his bicycle. He froze when he saw Roz on the landing above. "Oh!" He looked quite surprised to see her, and then he spotted Konrad. "Shit."

Now what? Nathan was the one who let Konrad out on his way to work in the evening, and Sly let him in just before dawn. Konrad had tried stashing his clothes in the alley behind the Dumpsters, but a couple of times they were gone in the morning. Although rare, some thorough city worker probably made sure everything hit the dumpster. In that case he had to wait until he could shift back, knock on Sly's window, because his keys had gone missing with his clothes, and traipse naked through the hallway and up the stairs. *Crap.*

Quickly assessing his options, he realized there were only two things he could do. Get back into his apartment, *fast,* or change right in front of her. *Not* shifting into his wolf form during the full moon wasn't an option. That decision had been made for him when he was bitten long ago.

He could feel his body vibrate, the first sign of an impending change. He fled into the relative safety of his apartment and hoped Roz wouldn't follow and catch him in mid-shift. She'd be horrified. He had to leave the door unlocked and open a crack to get back out.

Could he manipulate the doorknob with his paws? Perhaps. But if he couldn't, the wolf in him would likely panic and try to claw his way out. A wolf had to run.

Not this time. If she saw him change it would be more traumatizing than to think he had a pet wolf scratching and howling at the door, so he retreated and slammed the door.

Nathan, still gazing at the top of the stairs, said, "Uh-oh."

Roz snapped her attention to him. "What the hell is going on?"

He shook his head and said, "Oh, boy."

Roz set the pot of soup beside Konrad's door and scurried back down the stairs for an "in your face" interrogation, which she'd occasionally done with the most tight-lipped criminals. "Nathan, you know something about this, don't you?"

Nathan didn't lose his cool. He cocked his head and answered, "I'm not known for my discretion, but in this case, I'm going to forget what I saw, and I suggest you do the same."

"Forget what I saw?" Her voice rose. "Forget? How can I? I'm not just concerned about his coming out of his apartment stark naked. A few hours ago, he was badly bruised, cut, and bleeding. Now there's not a mark on him. What the hell is that about?"

He shrugged. "What can I say? Some of us are fast healers." He started to wheel his bicycle past her, but she grabbed his collar.

"Oh, no you don't."

He pried her fingers off and calmly said, "I'm afraid I can't stay and chat. I'll be late for work."

A tiny bit of sanity returned. She couldn't keep him there against his will. With a deep sigh, she stepped back and let him go. He opened the door, but stopped to fiddle with something on his bike.

Now, about Konrad. She heard some type of faint grinding noise coming from upstairs and then a whimper.

She dashed back up the steps and tried his door. To her surprise, it opened. Sitting in front of her was a big dog. It looked like some kind of scruffy German shepherd, but the biggest one she'd ever seen. She'd have been afraid, except that with his tongue hanging out, he looked like he had a big goofy grin on his face.

"Huh? Who are you, boy?" Should she pat this strange dog or not? His eyes looked friendly, but his jaw appeared powerful enough to snap her arm like a twig.

The door across the hall opened, and Dottie came into view. "What's all the racket out here?" she demanded.

Roz turned toward her and stammered, "Oh, I uh…" She was trying to think of what to say, when the big dog ran around her legs and bounded down the stairs.

Dottie threw her hands in the air. "Darn it. I told Konrad to get rid of that wolf months ago. What the heck is it doing back here?"

Nathan called up the stairs, "I'll get rid of him,

Mrs. F." He opened the door, and the dog—or wolf or whatever—ran off. Nathan followed him out and let the door slam.

Puzzled, Roz turned back to Dottie. "Wolf? That was a wolf?"

Dottie didn't answer. She marched across the hall and banged on the doorjamb, because the door was already open. "Konrad! Come out here."

They waited. No answer.

Roz said, "Should I go in?"

Dottie raised her eyebrows, smiled, and said in a syrupy way, "I suppose you'd be welcome any time, since he's your boyfriend. Go ahead. I'll wait right here."

Roz remembered that he was naked and said, "No need to wait. I'll talk to him about his…um, pet. He'll probably want to know it ran away."

"Thank God," Dottie mumbled.

To Roz's relief, Dottie returned to her apartment and shut the door.

She crept in and called out, "Konrad?" Still no answer. What could he be doing? Was he hiding from her? The more she thought about his mysteriousness, the angrier she got. "Where the hell are you?"

She took a deep breath and marched to his bedroom. She threw open the door, half expecting to find him hiding under the covers. He wasn't there, and his bed was made. Okay, he must be in the bathroom. The door was open, so she poked her head in. It was empty.

Where could he have gone? He must be hiding in a closet. Now she was pissed. She opened each closet and pantry door and found no one.

"What the fuck?" It was as if he'd disappeared into

thin air. She jammed her hands on her hips. "Well, that does it."

She found a sticky-note pad and a pen and scribbled, "Your disappearing act and deceit have me at a loss. There's more you're not telling me, and I won't stand for lies. I'm afraid we're through." As she reread it, tears formed in her eyes. Was she being rash?

The more she thought about it, the more she realized the words were right. She'd been patient, *more* than patient, yet her belief in him had only led to more lies and disappointment.

She slammed the door on her way out and returned to her apartment for a good cry.

―――― ∿ ――――

"Roz, open the door." Konrad pounded so hard he was afraid he'd splinter the solid oak if he didn't calm down. He took a couple of steps back and raked his fingers through his hair. Dottie would be down in seconds, if he kept that up. Tough. *Nothing can drag me away; certainly not some ninety-eight-pound busybody*. He could hear someone inside Roz's apartment, and he would not leave until she opened the door.

Wait a minute… He didn't have to wait for her to open the door. All he had to do was open his mind to her.

Roz, please give me a chance. I'll tell you everything.

"*You'll tell me more lies. Go away.*"

I won't. I swear! I'll tell you the truth, the whole truth, and nothing but the truth…so help me, God.

"*God is probably the only one who can help you, because if you lie to me again, you're beyond redemption.*"

I'm not evil, Roz.

"Says you."

Open the door. Please, please, please open the door!

She didn't answer him, and the door didn't open. His nerves were getting the best of him, and he tried pacing off the pent-up energy.

Okay, I'm going to have to tell you everything like this. I had hoped to be with you to reassure you, hold you, and show you how gentle I can be. But if this is how you want it, so be it. I'm not going to lie to you anymore.

He heard a long, resigned sigh on the other side.

This is going to sound preposterous, but I swear it's true, and I can prove it.

My brother and I were about ten when we decided to run away from home. We were making our way through the woods by the light of the full moon, when we came upon a sight so bizarre, we couldn't believe our eyes. A group of human beings changed into a pack of wolves.

He waited for some reaction. There was a barely audible thump, as if she'd plopped into a chair or dropped something on the floor.

Are you all right?

"That's a trick question, right? Continue."

At least she hadn't fainted.

Okay. We tried to run but were overtaken by the wolves and pinned down. I thought we were done for. Apparently they were waiting for their leader, the alpha wolf, to decide our fate.

For some reason I couldn't scream or cry. I simply waited for the inevitable. Nicholas whimpered, and it spurred me into action. It was bad enough that I was about to be eaten; if I could spare my brother…Well, I punched and kicked and fought as hard as I could to get to him. Yes, I was bitten, but I didn't know at the time that Nick would take his cue from me and try to fight too.

We were both bitten and clawed and thus infected with the same Lupine toxin that had infected the rest of the pack.

He paused, half expecting her to laugh. When all he heard was her rapid breathing, he continued.

We were bitten by werewolves. Before you dismiss this as insane, think about some of the things you've seen with your own eyes. I healed in hours from a fall that might have killed anyone else. I have superhuman strength. Last night, you saw my wolf form moments after you saw me disappear into my apartment, naked.

He heard something and waited. He hoped she was getting up to open the door. He heard her footsteps, but instead of coming closer, they sounded like they were going farther way and picking up speed. At last he heard a thud and creak as if she'd thrown herself on her bed, followed by the unmistakable sound of weeping.

"Merry?" Roz knew her voice was shaking and hoped she didn't sound like a scared little girl, despite feeling like one. At least over the telephone, her best friend couldn't see her face, red and blotchy from crying.

"Roz! I'm so excited to hear from you. How's everything going?"

Roz sat on her bed and examined her Egyptian cotton sheets. Mascara stained her pillowcase. "Not good."

"Oh, my God. What happened?"

"I'm sorry. Before we get into my troubles, how's married life?"

Merry chuckled. "It's awesome. Really great. But it sounds like you need to talk more than I do."

"Yeah, big time." Roz sighed. "Are you busy right now?"

"Nope. I was about to make dinner, but I can ask Jason to go grab takeout, then we'll have complete privacy."

"You don't have to do that. In fact, you might like to have Jason nearby when I tell you this."

"Oh, no. What happened? It sounds horrible."

"No." Roz shook her head. "I didn't mean to alarm you. It's not a disaster…at least not to anyone but me… and maybe Konrad."

"Konrad? The Konrad who lives in my building?"

"*Our* building. I moved into your old apartment."

She heard Merry gasp, then squeal.

"That's fantastic! I can't wait to get home and welcome you with a big hug."

"Yeah, I was going to save it for a surprise, but now I—" Her voice broke, and she couldn't continue. Sobs rose to the back of her throat and threatened to burst out.

"Roz, what is it?"

She coughed. "We fell in love. I was so happy. Then—" Her throat clogged again. *How the hell do I tell her the love of my life is a werewolf?*

Merry made a soft, sympathetic sound. "Oh, honey. Whatever happened, I'm on your side. You know that, right?"

"There are no sides. It's not like that. I—" She sniffed. Somehow she had to find the courage to tell her. The only person who *might* understand this was

Merry. "Do you remember when you told me about Jason's secret?"

"God, yes. I'll never forget it. You were so brave and understanding. I thought you'd call the men in white coats on me, but instead you just listened. I can't tell you how much that meant."

"Well, maybe now you can return the favor. Konrad was holding something back, and I knew it. I didn't want to push him because he's—" She was going to say, *the best thing that's ever happened to me,* but knew she'd choke up if she said the words. "I'm sorry. This is hard."

"I know," Merry said softly.

A quiet moment of understanding passed between them, and Roz steeled herself, calling on courage she didn't feel at the moment.

"Merry, apparently Jason isn't the only shapeshifter in the building."

"I know. There's his uncle Ralph and Nathan too."

Roz sat up straight. "Nathan?"

"Yeah, he's able to shift into a raven. He even battled off Morgaine's pet owl that Jason was up against in falcon form. He would have been toast if Nathan hadn't intervened. I didn't tell you about them, because I didn't think it mattered. It was enough to accept that my husband was a shapeshifter, and I didn't know you were going to move into the building. I'm not sure I'd have let you, if I'd known."

Roz chuckled. "That's why I didn't tell you."

Merry joined in the brief moment of humor and said, "What does Konrad have to do with this?"

"Konrad's a shifter too."

"Really?" Merry sounded not only surprised, but pleased.

"Yeah. Don't get excited, though. He's not a pretty bird like your husband or Nathan. He's a werewolf."

"A…a what?"

"You heard me right. A *werewolf*. A big, furry doggie with huge teeth and supernatural strength. Not the kind you'd want to sit on your lap."

Merry's side of the line went eerily quiet. At last she said, "That explains how he and Sly managed to save my life the night I was attacked."

"He what? Saved your life? What attack?"

"I didn't tell you because I didn't want it getting back to my father, and the fewer people who knew, the better. It happened the day after I moved in. I had just returned home from work, exhausted, and wasn't paying much attention when I walked from my car to the back door of the building. Somebody jumped me, and Konrad and Sly rescued me from a would-be rapist. He had a knife to my throat. They tossed him off me like he was a sock puppet."

"Dear God! Why didn't you tell me?"

"As I said, I couldn't risk my father finding out about it. He'd have dragged my ass back to Rhode Island faster than Jason can throw a baseball."

"How did they save you?"

"I thought it was Sly who did it, but now that I know about Konrad…well, it could have been either of them. One of them picked up the guy by the belt and flung him several feet away, like he was a big blow-up doll. Well, maybe that's not the best description, but you get what I mean, right?"

"Yeah. I do. Konrad's lifted and carried me like *I* was a blow-up doll. And come to think of it, that's a very apt description." At last she was able to chuckle, remembering how his strong arms cradled her or tossed her over his shoulder, and the phenomenal sex they'd had. The sadness descended again. "I…I don't know how I'll ever replace him, Merry. He was so kind and gentle. And he made me feel almost petite. It's the first time a guy has ever made me feel so…so feminine. Oh, damn." The tears broke through, and she let them flow. Eventually she sobbed from deep in her gut.

"Roz, it's okay. Let it out. I'm here."

Merry's quiet voice crooned words that were meant to be accepting and comforting through the sobs, but Roz felt no better. She wanted nothing more than to run up the stairs and throw herself into her lover's arms, wolf or no wolf, yet the rational part of her wouldn't allow it. She knew nothing about what he was. And if everything he said was true, what about that—what had he called it? Toxin? Had he exposed her to something? Was it sexually transmitted?

"I have so many questions, Merry. But I don't dare ask him about any of it. I don't know if I'm safe with him."

"I've always felt safe with him. Has he done anything to make you feel unsafe?"

"No. In fact he made me feel very safe. Completely protected, loved…even treasured."

"Well, there you go. You probably are all those things. How would you feel about leaving a child in his care?"

"Before I knew? I'd absolutely, totally trust him with a child. I even saw him run into traffic, risking his own life to save a toddler."

"That's the Konrad I knew. What's changed? Other than your knowing his secret. Anything?"

"I know he lied to me. I don't know if I can believe anything he tells me now."

"How did he lie?"

"The first time he was arrested for attempted theft, I represented him. He allegedly lifted a one-ton freezer full of frozen meat, carried it out of a restaurant, and dropped it onto the sidewalk. We got the case dismissed by saying it wasn't humanly possible to do what he was accused of doing."

"That's probably true, Roz. But if he's a werewolf—"

"Then either he lied or he's not human. I don't like either of those explanations."

Merry took a deep breath and let it out slowly. "Roz, there are all kinds of things in this world I never knew existed until I moved to Boston, specifically to our building. Welcome to wacko central. Now that you live there too, you should probably know all of it."

Roz gulped. "There's more?"

"I'm afraid so. You're sitting down, I hope."

"Yes."

"Where are you, exactly?"

"In my bedroom, on my bed."

"Good. You might want to lie down in case you faint."

"Merry! What the hell?"

Merry chuckled, but it sounded like a nervous laugh. "I'm sorry. I didn't mean to make it worse than it is. Just take a few deep breaths and try to relax."

Roz did, and it helped. "Okay, I'm ready. Lay it on me."

"Okay, here's the thing. Even though we live in a building full of paranormals, I feel safe, maybe even safer, than I would in a building full of human strangers. How well does anyone know their neighbors, anyway?"

"Apparently not that well."

"Right. But I've gotten to know everyone in our building *very* well. You, Dottie, Joe Murphy, and I are the only so-called normal people there."

Roz took in the information and ticked off the names of the other residents out loud. Okay, I know about Jason, Nathan, and Konrad, so Ralph?"

"Another falcon."

"Gwyneth and Morgaine?"

"Witches."

"What do you mean? They're not supernatural, just regular women who practice Wicca, right?"

"I guess so, although I'm not totally sure. Sly asked Morgaine to put a spell on the newspaper ad I answered, advertising the apartment. He said the spell made the ad visible to me and my family, but no one else could see it. That ensured I'd be the only one to answer the ad."

"By Sly you mean the guy who turned out to be your biological father, right?"

"Right. Sylvestro Flores is his real name, but he likes to be called Sly. He's in the building too."

"He lives here? I didn't know that? Which apartment?"

"None. He's in the basement."

"The basement? There's no apartment in the basement, just a laundry room and a dark, dirty storage area and utility room."

"Uh, yeah. Sly doesn't have a lot of stuff, and he doesn't need fancy digs, although I'd love to see some kind of fixed-up space for him. He is my father, after all."

"Of course. Let me get this right. If you, Dottie, Joe, and I are the only guaranteed humans—"

Merry interrupted. "No guarantees."

Roz groaned, but continued her inventory. "And Gwyneth and Morgaine are witches, and Jason and Ralph are shapeshifting falcons, and Nathan's a shapeshifting raven and Konrad's a werewolf, that would mean Sly is a—"

"Vampire."

Roz froze in shock. Her throat constricted, or she would have yelled, "A *what*?" Merry must have interpreted her silence, though.

"He's a vampire. Don't worry. He doesn't feed on the neighbors."

Roz's head spun. Finally, she understood why Merry wanted her to lie down.

Chapter 13

ROZ HAD INVITED MORGAINE TO HER APARTMENT FOR a cup of tea, hoping to get a little perspective on the wolf-man in apartment 2A.

She carried an antique silver tray to the living room and set it on the coffee table. Two bone china cups filled with Constant Comment tea steamed and scented the air with a fragrant orange aroma.

"What a beautiful tea set," Morgaine commented.

"It was my grandmother's. I'm happy to finally have a use for it. No one has fancy teas anymore."

"Well, I'm glad you brought it out. I hope you didn't go to too much trouble." Morgaine lifted her cup and blew on the hot liquid.

"No, don't worry. I'm not the kind to make water-cress finger sandwiches." Roz stuck her pinkie finger out as if to make the point.

Morgaine chuckled. "No, I'm not either."

Roz couldn't get over the change in her friend since her makeover. "Are you getting used to your new look?"

Morgaine took a sip of her tea and smiled. "Sort of. I'm used to getting negative attention for the goth stuff. Now, because I'm a blonde, I'm getting the opposite kind of attention. It's weird."

"Oh, really? Sounds like a good thing to me. Maybe I should have gone even lighter."

Morgaine grinned. "How did Konrad like the highlights?"

Just the mention of his name sent a knife through Roz's heart. She set down her teacup. "He…um…he liked them, but we're not…" She took a deep breath and forced the words past her lips. "We're not seeing each other anymore."

Morgaine gasped. "What? My Goddess! What happened?"

Roz was unprepared for such a strong reaction. "Morgaine, I had to call it off. He lied to me."

Morgaine stared at her, open-mouthed. When she finally spoke, she didn't ask what he lied about, as if she already knew. "Well, of course he did!"

Roz blinked. "What do you know about it…and how?"

"Duh, psychic, remember?"

Roz had to chuckle. "Okay, so if you know what he is, maybe you know what I should do about it."

Morgaine reached over and squeezed Roz's hand. "Put yourself in his shoes. If you had the kind of secret he has, would you blab it to everyone you knew right off the bat?"

That thought stopped Roz for a moment. "I'm not just anyone, Morgaine. I'm his…I mean, I *was* his girlfriend."

Morgaine shook her head. "You were a lot more than that, sweetheart. You were his mate."

There was that word again. "He'd said that a couple of times. Well, not when he thought I could hear him. It…confused me."

Morgaine's lips thinned, and anger brewed in her eyes. Her expression made Roz uncomfortable.

"If he'd chosen me for his mate, I'd be damn grateful.

He's one of the few men who never judged me. Instead, he picked *you*. And it sounds like you've judged and condemned him and tossed away any hope he ever had of a happy life."

"What?" Roz frowned. "What are you talking about?"

"Wolves mate for life. Or didn't you know that?"

"N…no. I didn't," she said in a small voice.

Morgaine placed her hand on her hip. "Well, at least you know he's monogamous."

Roz straightened. *Merry had said the same thing about falcons. Would knowing that information have made a difference?* "But there's still the physical danger, isn't there?"

"Clearly you know nothing about wolves. They don't attack humans unless they're protecting themselves or their families. Tell me what you *do* know," she demanded.

"I…uh, well—"

"That's what I thought. You didn't bother to find out, did you?"

"It…it was such a shock. How often does a girl hear that she's been dating a werewolf?"

Morgaine took a deep breath, as if finally remembering Roz's point of view. "Look, it couldn't have been easy, but I pushed him to tell you. I don't know how he went about it, but I guess he wasn't all that tactful. What did he say?"

Roz felt tears forming. Yes, she had jumped to conclusions. No she didn't know the first thing about it, but a werewolf? What was there to know?

"Well?"

"Huh?" Roz looked up and realized Morgaine had

asked her something. What was it? Oh yeah. She wanted to know how he'd told her.

"We went skydiving, and his parachute failed to open properly. He came down in the trees so hard, I thought he was dead. Honestly, my heart was in my throat. He was bruised and bloody, but thank God he was alive. Only a few hours later, I caught him naked in the hallway without a mark on him."

Morgaine leaned toward her. "And that's bad, because—?"

"Well, because he lied to me. He pretended to be a normal guy."

"So it would have been better if he'd crashed and died."

"No! Look, I'm more confused than ever. I don't know what to believe anymore. Does he turn into a monster at the full moon? Am I in danger? What if we had kids? Would they be normal? Would they be in danger if he shifted?"

Morgaine's look was cold. "And you never bothered to ask him about any of that, did you?"

A sudden ruckus in the hall alerted them to trouble. Roz stood, but didn't know if she should get involved or not.

Morgaine strode to the door and opened it wide. Two cops had Konrad in handcuffs and were wrestling him down the stairs as he tried to explain some kind of mistake.

"Look, I don't know what kind of evidence you think you have, but I'm innocent, and I can prove it."

"Tell it to the judge, buddy," one of the cops said.

"I don't want it to get that far. There's got to be something I can do to convince you I didn't do it."

Roz stepped into the hall. "What are you accusing him of, officers?"

"Look lady, it's none of your business."

Konrad froze and stared at Roz. The cops couldn't budge him another inch. "It *might* be her business. Roz, is…er, *was* my lawyer."

"Great, you saved a phone call," the other cop said.

Roz tried to stay calm. "What are the charges?"

Konrad didn't wait for the cops to provide details. "They're accusing me of the 1991 Gardener Museum heist, Roz."

Her head jerked. "What?"

Morgaine stepped into the hall behind Roz. "That's impossible. He's been helping me *solve* the case."

"So?" One of the cops said as he tried to push Konrad toward the door. "Ever heard about criminals returning to the scene of the crime?"

Morgaine grabbed Roz's arm and shook her slightly. "*Do* something. I *know* he didn't do it. I'd have picked up on that in a heartbeat."

Roz shook her head. "There's nothing I can do if they have a warrant."

The first cop said, "We have a warrant, all right, and if your client doesn't come with us right now, I'll add resisting arrest to the charges."

Konrad's gaze dropped to the floor. He could probably break out of the handcuffs and toss the officers aside easily, but he wasn't even trying to do that.

"Okay, I'll go, but you're making a mistake."

"*Roz, for the love of God, if I ever meant anything to you at all—*"

Even though she still had plenty of unanswered

questions, she could answer one of them easily. Yes, he meant something to her. She might wish he didn't, but she'd be lying.

"I'll meet you at the station," she said softly.

Konrad hung his head and rested his clasped hands on the small table in front of him. It seemed like he'd been waiting an eternity for his lawyer to show up. Had she decided not to represent him and had to find someone else? If so, could he blame her?

At last the door opened, and Roz walked in. She wore her professional gray suit, tortoise-shell glasses, and her pretty highlighted hair was gathered in a bun. Their gazes met briefly, but she quickly shifted it to the papers in her hands as she sat down.

"Mr. Wolfensen, we're looking at a high-profile grand-jury case. More seasoned lawyers may offer to represent you. Are you sure you want a public defender?"

"I want *you* to represent me. I need someone I can trust."

"Then I'll need to ask you a few questions."

"Of course." *Do we have to be so formal?*

She shuffled the papers, as if trying to organize them. "*Konrad, don't respond to my telepathy out loud. As you can imagine, we're being watched.*"

She folded her hands and raked her stare over him as if sizing him up. "*I think I may have an idea about what happened. I'll have to get you out on bail so we can talk privately with each other and with Morgaine.*"

He sat quietly, trying not to react.

"According to this, the Gardener Museum's curator was made aware of some new evidence. Upon following

that lead, you were named as a suspect, or at least someone who might be complicit in the robbery."

"I'm curious what that evidence could be."

"Where were you at the time of the robbery?"

"Newton, Massachusetts, I suppose. I lived and
worked there. I was probably sleeping in my apartment."

"That's still close enough to have been involved."
"*Damn. I wish you'd said Australia*." "Do you have an
alibi for that night? Was anyone with you?"

"I…I'm not sure. That was a long time ago. Why
would anyone suspect me out of the blue?"

"I need to know more about this so-called evidence
before I answer that. The state wants to obtain some of
your DNA. I'd like you to refuse that for now."

Konrad cocked his head. "But wouldn't that make
me look guilty?"

"*I need to stall for time.*" She licked her lips. "Right
now, all that needs to happen is your arraignment and
a bail hearing. In one month there will be a pre-trial
conference where the prosecution and defense will
compare notes, and I'll have a better idea of what we're
dealing with."

"Bail, huh? How much will that be?"

She shrugged. "I don't know. We'll find out tomorrow."

"So I'll have to stay locked up tonight?"

She nodded. "What can you afford, so I can get bail
reduced to something you can manage?"

Shit. He couldn't afford much. He had only a few
thousand left in his savings and stock portfolio. "Well,
I've had a lot of unexpected expenditures recently. If I
liquidated every investment I have, I might be able to
scrape together fifty thousand dollars."

She jotted down the number and rose. "I'll see you in the morning, then."

"Wait!"

She turned to him, eyebrows raised. *"Whatever you do, don't say anything that might connect us as lovers."*

He looked down at his hands. "Never mind."

"Yes, well, if there's nothing else, I need to make some calls."

She paused with her hand on the doorknob. "I'll do my best for you, Mr. Wolfensen."

I know you will. He looked up at her anxiously. "What are my chances?" *Is there any chance at all for us, angel?*

She smiled sadly as she passed through the doorway. "I'll have to get back to you on that. We have a lot of work to do."

Work? Did she mean on their relationship or on the case? It didn't matter. He'd work his nuts off to make things right in both areas.

Roz opened the door to her Smart Car and smirked as Konrad folded himself to fit inside.

"How did you get me out with bail set so high?"

"I called in a few favors, and found an anonymous donor." She had been saving that money for a down payment on a condo, damn it. "This is a high-profile case. I had to agree to include a team of publicity-seeking lawyers." She started the car and pulled into traffic. "That's not a bad thing, though. The more power players sitting on our side of the aisle, the better."

Konrad swallowed. "As long as you're the one

doing the talking, I guess it'll be all right. Do you think Reginald has something to do with this?"

"That's a theory I intend to look into. I asked Morgaine to expect us to drop by."

"What a schmuck. I'd like to ring his virtual neck."

"You need to stay the hell away from that museum…and every other art museum. Remember, I vouched for you."

"Yes, ma'am."

"I'm serious. And even though you're not considered a flight risk, you'd better curb your nocturnal activities for a while too."

"The full moon is going to happen, like it or not. As long as I can shift before I leave the building, no one should suspect a thing."

"If I'm really safe with you in wolf form, I'll let you out…doggie."

Konrad laughed. "Thank God your sense of humor is returning."

After a short silence, he asked, "Why didn't Morgaine warn us if she was the one interpreting for Reginald? "

"Either she didn't realize what he was up to or she was sworn to secrecy."

"Yeah, and she really lives by that witch's-oath thing. It's one of the reasons I admired her. Now I'm not so sure I like it."

"Maybe we can use it to our advantage. What is it exactly?"

"I think it goes something like, 'If it doesn't hurt anybody, do what you want.'"

"Hmm…if she refuses to divulge what she knows, it could be considered harmful to you. We'll find out anyway at discovery, but I'd like as much advance warning as possible."

"Yeah, maybe we can get Chad to talk to him, ghost to ghost."

"Do you think Morgaine can persuade him to do that?"

Konrad sighed. "We can ask."

---w---

As much as Morgaine doubted Chad would be willing to travel to the Gardener Museum, she said she'd ask him to help. She confirmed that Reginald had reported new evidence, but wouldn't tell them what it was until she double checked the legality of doing so with an independent legal expert.

Konrad and Roz had done all they could do for the case and decided to continue following their bliss list for a while. Culinary classes were next up. It would take their minds off the case, Roz had said. Konrad hoped it would accomplish more than that.

At her apartment, picking her up for their cooking date, he said, "Thanks for agreeing to another date, Roz. I don't know what changed your mind, but I'm not going to look a gift horse in the mouth."

"Are you calling me a horse?"

"No!" *Oh crap.*

Roz laughed. "I knew that. I was just teasing."

Konrad gulped. "Don't do that. I feel like I'm walking on thin ice with you as it is."

"You are." She looked down pensively. "But I talked to a couple of friends. They seemed to think I was being a jerk."

"You were scared, not a jerk. I would have been frightened too."

"Yeah, and it didn't help that you were hiding things from me."

"I know. I'm sorry. I wanted to tell you earlier, but I couldn't figure out how to do it without alarming you. I know your need for proof. I guess I was scared, too... of losing you."

"So you waited until I fell for you, and then you gave me the good news, 'Guess what, Roz? You're dating a werewolf!' How was I supposed to deal with that?"

He eyed her sadly. "I know. I should have prepared you for it, somehow. I just couldn't come up with the right words."

"I'm not sure there are any *right* words."

"Now that you're willing to listen, you can ask me anything and talk to me about your feelings. I promise not to hide the truth anymore."

"Really? You promise?"

"It's hard to hide anything from each other now that we have the dubious gift of telepathy."

She chuckled. "By the way, did you ever find out what that weird ability is all about?"

He took a deep breath. "As far as Nick and I know, it only happens between true mates."

"And are werewolves like regular wolves, in that they mate for life?"

He leaned over and rested his forehead against hers. Looking right into her eyes, he said, "Yes. You're the one, Roz. I'll never look elsewhere."

She spoke under her breath. "I'm so confused."

"What did you say?"

She moved so she could look up into his eyes. "I don't know what to say."

"Say you forgive me."

"I forgive you."

He lifted her off her feet and kissed her.

"Whoa! Put me down."

"Still don't think I'm strong enough to carry you?" He held her a few inches off the ground.

She chuckled. "No, I just prefer to feel the floor under my feet."

He set her down. "Want to skip the class and—" He nodded toward the bedroom.

"Maybe later. We paid for the class, and I really *do* want to find another career. Roz Wells can't take many more strange cases. Besides, I think I'd enjoy the culinary arts."

"Even though my case might make you a famous lawyer?"

"Especially so. I hope it will be my last case, Konrad. The public will be rooting for the prosecution. They want a fall guy, someone to punish. If I succeed in getting you off, and I intend to, I won't be popular."

"Crap. I'm sorry."

"I'm not. I really want and need another job." She looked at her watch. "We'd better get going. Maybe I'll become a famous chef instead. That I could live with."

"And after, maybe we can cook up something spicy in the bedroom. That *I* could live with."

Roz smirked. "Horndog."

―∾∾―

Even though Roz still wondered about her sanity, being with Konrad felt right. All the way to the class, Konrad had spanned the short distance between them in Roz's car to stroke her thigh or touch her hair. Each time she glanced over at him, he was smiling, and his eyes seemed sincere.

In class she tried to concentrate on what the chef was saying, which was not an easy task, when fifteen of them stood arm against arm along the crowded prep counter. She remembered how Konrad's warmth seeped into her when they first met. If anything, she was even more aware of it now.

The chef was French, arrogant, and short. Didn't matter. She'd brave anyone, even a jerk with a Napoleonic complex, for the chance to change her profession.

"Sweetheart," Konrad whispered.

She gazed up at him and lost herself in his eyes. "Yes?"

"All these knife techniques are great, but I'm barely able to concentrate. All I can think about is you. I'm afraid I'll chop my fingers off."

She stifled a chuckle. "Pay attention, then," she whispered back. "We need your fingers."

He grinned and slipped an arm around her waist. When he pulled her close and kissed her on the forehead, the instructor looked over at them.

"*Excusez moi*, am I interrupting you?" he asked with obvious sarcasm.

Konrad cleared his throat. "Um, no. Sorry."

Roz elbowed him playfully and pulled her attention back to the matter at hand. Yes, chopping veggies without chopping off one's digits, always a good idea.

"Now, everyone, take the vegetables in front of you. Use the proper knife to seed and chop them. I'll come around and watch each of you."

Roz picked up the small paring knife and cut open a green pepper. She glanced over at Konrad and noticed he was using the huge butcher knife for the same job. Yup, one of them hadn't been paying attention.

"The gentleman with the blond hair, what is your name?"

Konrad stopped struggling with the pepper. "Konrad."

"Well, Konrad, are you inventing new ways to seed a pepper? Perhaps you can explain your reason for using the largest knife in front of you?"

"Yeah, I have big hands."

The class tittered. Roz grimaced.

"We pick our instruments based on the size and texture of the ingredients, not our thick, meaty hands."

"Oh. I guess I'm not very good at this."

The chef frowned. "All you need to do is watch and repeat the technique I use, exactly."

"Okay, I'll try to do better."

The annoying man sighed and moved on to the other students. "Very good. I'm glad some of you managed to watch and learn. When you all have your vegetables prepared, we'll move on to meat."

At last everything they needed for the recipe was ready, and they were instructed to split into pairs and find a stove. Next they had to add olive oil to a large frying pan and turn on the gas.

Konrad sneaked over to Roz and copped a feel as he poured the oil. She squirmed and giggled. Finally she slapped his hand away. When he lit the burner, a huge flame shot up, setting off the fire detectors, and Roz's hair began to blaze.

"Crap! I must have missed the pan."

Roz ran to the sink to fill a pan with water, not realizing her hair was burning. Konrad tackled her and patted out the fire with his bare hands.

The chef yelled, "Stop! Turn off the gas. I'll get the fire extinguisher."

Roz bolted back to the stove and shut off the gas, but the flame continued to burn. The chef charged toward them with the extinguisher and sprayed foam all over their stove, covering their meat and vegetables.

He set the fire extinguisher down and crossed his arms. "I'm afraid you two must leave. When you can pay greater attention to food preparation than to each other, you can come back."

"Damn," Konrad muttered. "I'm sorry. Are you sure we can't have another chance?"

"Another chance to burn down my kitchen? I think not." The chef tipped his nose in the air and waited for them to gather their things and go.

As they entered Roz's apartment, Konrad said sheepishly, "Roz, can you forgive me for ruining the cooking class…and your hair? I'll cook dinner for you and pay a hairdresser to make up for it."

"You don't have to do that."

"I want to. I feel really awful about it. It seemed like you were getting more out of the class than I was."

She set her purse down. "I'll get over it. Since all I learned to do was chop stuff, if we stay together you'll probably get nicely cut up meals. I can't guarantee their taste, though."

"That's fine. When I'm old and have no teeth, I'll appreciate bite-sized pieces." He grinned. "But at the moment, the only thing I want to eat is your pretty pussy."

She rolled her eyes. "You're incorrigible."

"But consistent."

It had been hard to look at him and *try* not to want him. Roz felt her panties dampen. *Can he smell my arousal? If he's part wolf and a canine's sense of smell is so much better than a human's—*

"Yes, I can," he said.

"Oh damn. You heard me?"

"Heard, smelled, and noticed a few other signs. You're ready to mate, sweetheart, and I can't wait much longer."

"Fuck. I'm ready to fuck. I don't know about mating yet. You'll have to convince me." *I'm not going to respect myself in the morning, but who cares?*

He stepped into her space and pulled her close. "I intend to."

Roz's nipples hardened and brushed against her blouse. He lifted her and tossed her over his shoulder. She squealed as he headed to her bedroom.

He dropped her onto the bed and crawled over her. "I'm in love with you, Roz, and now that you know what I am, I want to take you the way a wolf takes his mate."

She shivered inside but tried not to let him see her need. "And exactly what does that mean?"

"Doggie style."

"Appropriately named."

He laughed as he began unbuttoning her blouse, but his hands shook. Was he nervous? Afraid of rejection? If what Morgaine had told her was true, he had a lot at stake.

"Here, let me. It'll save time."

He jumped off the bed and stripped out of his jeans and T-shirt before she reached the last button.

"You seem as eager as you did when we first made love," she noted.

"I am. It's been a while, sweetheart, and I can hardly wait. I've missed you."

She nodded at his huge erection. "I can see that."

At last her blouse was unbuttoned, and she sat up so she could remove it. Everything was taking too long in Konrad's estimation. As soon as it was off, he reached behind her, popped open her bra, and flung it across the room. He pushed her onto her back and began to suckle her breast as he tugged open the zipper of her slacks.

She moaned her pleasure, and he stripped her in seconds.

"Well, I thought it would save time if I did it myself. Clearly I was wrong about that."

He leaned back to take in the view of Roz's naked body. "Dear lord, I've missed seeing you like this."

"Like what? Nude?"

"Nude, ready, and primed, waiting for me to take you and make love to you as my own."

He moved to her other breast and suckled harder. She arched and moaned some more. His hand slid over her abdomen, reminding her that he didn't mind the extra flesh there. His hand kept traveling downward until he kneaded her thighs. There was a bit more flesh than she liked there too.

Eventually his fingers slipped into the crevice at her apex, and she shuddered at the sensation. *Oh, how I've missed this.*

"Me too, sweetheart."

Would she ever get used to the intrusion on her thoughts? At least they weren't able to hear every little nuance that traveled through each other's brains, but when a strong thought voiced itself to one of them, it was as if the thought occurred in the other one's head too.

What had he said that was about? True mates? Didn't she have a choice in this?

He crawled down her body and replaced his fingers with his tongue. She lost all train of thought as he teased her nether regions. He feathered light licks and kisses over her mons at first, then zeroed in on her clit.

By the time he lapped her bud, she was so sensitized she yelped and her body bucked involuntarily. She grasped the pillow and stuffed it over her face in hopes of stifling the scream she knew was coming.

He flicked his tongue over her mercilessly, until she was vibrating inside and gripping the sheet with her other hand. Sooner than expected, she came apart.

He held her tight and continued his assault on her clit while her thighs shook violently. The pillow barely contained her muffled screams. Blissful release blasted from her core and radiated over, through, and beyond her body.

At last, when she settled down and removed the pillow, her hair, except for the back, flew out in soft, straight strands from the static electricity. She peered up at Konrad. He was grinning.

"Pretty proud of yourself, aren't you, stud?"

He chuckled. "If I accomplished my goal of giving you the best sex of your life, then yes. I'm darn proud. Of course, we're not finished yet."

He nudged her legs open with one knee and crawled up between them. "Are you ready for me, angel?"

She could have offered to give him some oral too, but not only was she still spent, she also *wanted* to let him show her the best sex of her life. Hey, that was his goal, after all. Who was she to get in the way of a man's goal?

She bent her knees so she could lift her hips to meet him and then remembered something. "Didn't you want to take me doggie style?"

"You look tired." He cocked his head, "Of course I could let you lie back and relax while I make love to you now and then flip you onto your knees and do it all over again later."

She giggled. "Pretty sure of your endurance, aren't you?"

He hung his head. "Yeah, maybe I'm being overconfident. It's been quite a while, and I can't wait to get inside you."

"Then don't."

His gaze shot to her eyes. "What? Don't? What do you mean, *don't?*"

"I meant don't wait. Fuck me now."

He exhaled audibly. "Thank God."

Without waiting for anything to happen that might change her mind, Konrad positioned himself at her entrance, and in one smooth motion, plunged inside her. He let out a low moan of satisfaction and stayed fully seated, as if savoring the moment.

Roz welcomed his heat as he stretched and filled her. How she'd missed him. The long hiatus between lovers in the past hadn't bothered her nearly as much as how she'd been longing for Konrad.

He'd said it to her first. *You're the one, Roz. I'll never look elsewhere.* Could she say it to him too? She felt it. She'd felt it ever since they'd confessed their love for each other. She wanted no one else…just him, for the rest of her life.

Konrad began his slow, rhythmic thrusts. She answered each one. Their building desire increased the tempo naturally. Her heart knew the truth and her head could no longer deny it, so she let herself go and threw herself into the moment. Before long he was hammering into her, and she clung desperately to his neck while she welcomed each lunge.

A subtle sensation began building, but there was something different about it. The only direct pressure reaching inside of her apex was Konrad's cock. He must have been stimulating her G-spot. While she concentrated on the sensation, waves of heat flowed into her face and perspiration broke out on her forehead; meanwhile, something else yielded inside her. Somehow deeper, richer, a new feeling shook her to the core. Tears filled her eyes, yet she didn't know why.

Konrad let out a soft grunt, and the pistoning gave way to a few jerky motions. At last, he stilled and collapsed.

"Oh, God," he groaned.

When she didn't answer, he levered himself up on his elbows and gazed at her face. Shock registered in his eyes. "What's wrong, angel?"

"Nothing." She sniffed. "Not a damn thing. Everything's right...except you're a werewolf."

He inhaled deeply. "We're back to that again, are we?"

She chuckled, realizing that she must be confusing the hell out of him. "No, it's not like that. I just... I don't know. Maybe you could call it a breakthrough or something. I just realized that...well, like you said to me before. You're the one, Konrad. I won't look elsewhere."

He dove for her mouth, kissing her deeply. When she thought she was going die if she didn't take a breath, she pushed against his chest lightly, and he broke the kiss.

"Whew," she said and panted.

He smiled. "I know."

She ran her fingers through his hair. "God knows how we wound up together…the werewolf and the human."

"The lawyer and the thief…"

"But we belong together."

"Thank God." He laid his head next to hers and whispered, "You'll never regret loving me. I'll be good to you. I promise."

Chapter 14

Roz walked through the purple door of the beauty school and salon where she and Morgaine had gone before. Beverly, the head instructor, stood next to a student working on a haircut and glanced over her shoulder.

"Back again so soon? Is there a problem with your color?"

Roz said, "Not the color. Look." She turned around to show off her singed ends.

The woman in the student's chair gasped.

"Oh, no! That damage isn't from the student," Beverly was quick to point out. She rushed over. "What happened?"

"Uh, it was a cooking accident."

"Holy smokes!"

Roz chuckled. "You can say that again. Is there any way it can be fixed?"

"We'll have to try. My best student is just finishing up. Caroline, are you happy with your hair?"

"Very, considering I didn't come out looking like that." She pointed to Roz.

"I don't want to bump any of your scheduled clients. I just wanted to show it to you, first to see if you can fix it, and second, so you could figure out how much time you'll need."

"I can't let you walk out of here looking like that. I trust the girls to finish what they're doing without my hovering over them. I'll take care of you myself." She spoke to the student. "Anna, take your client to the front desk, please."

"Okay, but as soon as I do that, can I watch what you're doing?"

"Sure, fixing things like this would be good for you to see. In fact, all my students should see it. Do you mind, Roz?"

"I guess not." *Hmmm…I'm a guinea pig after all.*

The client got out of the chair and gestured to it. "Here. You need this more than I do."

Roz thanked the tactless woman and got comfortable in the black leather chair. Beverly walked around the salon and gathered students who weren't in the middle of anything time sensitive.

Anna walked her client to the front desk and returned. "That's a shame. You're lucky it was in the back, though. You could have singed off your eyebrows."

"Yeah, and have to draw them on again every morning." *At least I still look all right lying on my back. I'm glad Konrad can wait for doggie style a little longer.*

"You're right. It could be worse."

"You know, you could always go for the Victoria Beckham look. It's very chic."

"That would be great, if my hair will cooperate."

Beverly chimed in as she made her way back with three more students. "I was just thinking of doing that. A wedge in the back and longer in front. Anything shorter, and you'd look like a boy."

Roz sat up straight and raised her eyebrows.

"Oh, no. I didn't mean that you're not feminine. You're beautiful! Really."

Okay, she still earns a tip.

"So, what happened?" Anna asked.

Roz smiled despite herself. "I was taking a cooking class with my boyfriend. If we'd been paying nearly as much attention to the stove as we were to each other, this wouldn't have happened."

The girls laughed.

"Love," said Beverly. "It can' be hazardous to your health."

Despite her embarrassment, Roz liked the idea of helping students learn, which is why she'd come to the school instead of an upscale Newbury Street salon in the first place. Well, that and the three-hundred-dollar difference.

"Okay, girls. For singed hair like this, what do you think you should do? Dry cut it, or wash and cut?"

The students sounded as if they were split about evenly on the answer.

"Well, I'd cut it dry first, just to get the hair all of the same integrity, then wash it and cut it again."

I'm bound to be here all day. The girls looked so interested, though. Roz decided, *What the heck.* "Go for it."

Beverly looked excited too. She probably hadn't had the chance to show off her skills for a while. She combed out the parts that weren't burned first, blunt cut the extra length off, and then pulled the back of the hair out straight.

"Ugh, what a mess," one of the students said.

Roz saw Beverly squint at her in the mirror. "Is that the way to talk to clients?"

"No, ma'am."

She's right. My hair is ugly.

Beverly continued teaching, "If you were going to do

a layered look, you'd start from here and work toward here, but in this case—"

Roz tuned her out for a while. All she knew was she wanted to come out looking good. Good for Konrad? Good for court? She was happy when she realized she just wanted to look good for herself. She was ready for a change. "It must be fulfilling to take someone from icky to beautiful."

"Oh, it is," Beverly said. "When you know someone leaves your chair ten times happier than they came in, it's the best feeling in the world. Isn't it, girls?"

They all nodded and murmured agreement.

Roz had an epiphany. "How long does it take to complete a hairdressing course?"

"It depends. Most programs are under a year, and then you have to pass an exam to get your license. For young beginners, I recommend a vocational school or junior college for formal training. Some with experience can go to an advanced program and learn salon ownership and management.

"This is a good time to get into hairdressing, especially in the city. Predictions are for steady employment growth, especially in upscale urban salons."

"Seriously? So what if I wanted to wind up in one of those really high-end salons on Newbury Street? What training would you suggest for someone like me?" *How cool would that be? Konrad and I could own a trendy salon, and I wouldn't have to worry about women hitting on him, because they'd all assume he was gay. Wait a minute, I don't have to worry about that anyway, because he's monogamous.*

"You? I thought you were a lawyer."

"Yeah, but I'm tired of cutting people off at the knees. I think I might like cutting their hair and making them feel better instead of worse."

Beverly grinned. "I'd like to recommend this school, but if you can afford it, there are a couple of places with names you'd recognize."

"Like?"

Beverly glanced at her students. "I'll write down the information for you later."

―――

Morgaine explained to Roz that she couldn't just drive Chad to the museum. Spirit energy wasn't like occupying a corporeal body. If he sat in the backseat, as soon as Roz rolled out of the alley and onto the street, the car would take off, and Chad wouldn't. Apparently it made Roz picture an episode of *Casper the Friendly Ghost* in her brain, and she laughed. Chad wasn't amused.

The trio strolled up Brookline Avenue with the intention of walking Chad to the Gardner Museum. It was only a couple of miles, but for Morgaine it was a big deal. Agoraphobia meant fear of open spaces. Riding in a car could still be problematic, but walking outside, in public, made her chest tighten and her pulse race. *Remember,* she told herself, *millions of dollars in reward money.*

After that, their plans were fuzzy. Morgaine would try to summon Reginald and let the two spirits communicate while she listened in.

"Morgaine, thanks for speaking to Chad. Is he still with us?"

"Chad?"

"*I'm here,*" he communicated halfheartedly.

"Don't sulk. You agreed to help Konrad, remember?"

"*I'm not sulking. I'm looking at that big-ass bridge over the highway.*"

Morgaine came to a halt. "B…bridge?"

Roz's hand covered her mouth. "Oh, no. I read about agoraphobia. Fear of bridges was mentioned specifically."

"Yeah. I feel pretty exposed on bridges. But I think Chad sounded nervous about it too. She took a deep breath and grounded herself. "Are you saying you might have trouble crossing the bridge, Chad?"

"*It's the wind.*"

"What wind?"

"*From the traffic below. If it kicks up at the wrong moment, I'll be blown halfway to Brighton. If memory serves, the turnpike is always busy, so this bridge is almost always windy. It's been nice knowin' ya.*"

Her jaw dropped. "Why didn't you tell me this before?"

Roz cocked her head. "What's wrong?"

A young woman wearing jeans and a sweater approached from the other side of the bridge. Her long, sandy hair suddenly lifted in the wind and wrapped around her face. She grasped it, twirled it into a ponytail, and knotted it behind her head.

Morgaine whispered furiously behind her hand to Roz. "Even if I manage to cross this thing, Chad says he could be blown off course by the wind from the highway below."

Morgaine and Roz turned to each other and at the same time uttered a worried, "Oh, no."

Roz looked crestfallen. "How are we going to manage this?"

Morgaine wrung her hands. "I guess it wasn't such a good idea."

"Hey, kids. Don't give up so easily. I can try to use the two of you as a shield. If that doesn't work, I'll simply make my way back as soon as I can."

Morgaine waited for the woman to pass them before she answered. The woman hung her head and didn't make eye contact, so there was no need to say hello. When it was just the two—or three—of them again, Morgaine said, "Chad, that's really decent of you. I didn't realize you cared about Konrad so much."

"I don't, but you said something that made me think."

"Really? What was that?"

"You said he'd do the same for me. And you were right. In fact, recently, Joe and Gwyneth were making whoopee over his head, and something made him think the noise was me trying to get someone's attention. He actually got off his butt and came upstairs to see if there was anything he could do."

"Even though he can't communicate with you?"

"What's he saying?" Roz asked.

"He said he realized Konrad would do the same for him. Come to think of it, Konrad's the one guy in the building *everyone* counts on for help if they need it."

Roz smiled. "That's my guy...or werewolf or... whatever." Her expression turned serious again. "Are you sure I'm not going to be in danger if he shifts when he's with me?"

"What did he tell you?"

"He said he'd never attack me, that a werewolf will protect the pack, especially his mate and pups, over all others." She shook her head. "I still can't get used to the idea of calling children *pups*!"

Morgaine raised her eyebrows. "Are you saying you might give birth to a litter of wolves?"

Roz let out a howl of laughter. "No. He was human until about age ten, when he was bitten, and unless the children are turned, they'll stay human."

"Whew! That must be a relief."

"Yeah, somehow we'll make this work...if I can keep him out of jail."

"Then we need to talk to Reginald and get him to admit to planting false evidence. I'm still not sure how we're going to get Chad to the museum."

"Okay, let's figure out a way."

"Chad said we might be able to shield him from the wind. What if we make sort of a 'bat wing' thing," Morgaine suggested. "If we wrap our arms around each other's waists and hold our coats open on either side, we should be able to create a fairly wide shield. If I can close my eyes and let you lead, it might help me, too."

"*It figures you'd think of bat wings,*" Chad said. "*Let's try it.*"

The two women put their arms around each other's waists and shimmied sideways across the bridge.

Roz glanced over at Morgaine. Her eyes were squeezed shut.

"I feel pretty foolish doing this, don't you?"

Roz laughed. "Not really. There's an art school on the other side of this bridge. You wouldn't believe some of the strange things I've seen happen here."

"Like what?"

Roz grinned. "Streaking, bed races, rainbow parades that had nothing to do with gay rights..."

The two women chuckled and continued to shuffle

across the bridge side by side. "Are you still with us, Chad?" Morgaine asked.

"*I'm here. Oh, shit. Here comes a truck, stay as close together as you possibly—*"

Morgaine stopped.

Roz took a step without her. "What's wrong?"

Morgaine paused. "Chad?" When he didn't answer, she called out louder. "Chad?"

Roz stared at her wide-eyed. "Oh, no. Is he—?"

Morgaine let out one final cry, "Chad? Where are you, God damn it? If you're playing some kind of game—"

Silence.

"Shit. We lost him." Morgaine wailed and tossed her free hand in the air. "Now what?"

"Let's keep going."

Morgaine swallowed hard. Roz was right. She couldn't stay there. "Hopefully Chad will meet us at the museum, and if not, I'll try to talk to Reginald myself. I just don't know if I can persuade him to change his story."

Morgaine and Roz resumed a more natural pose, as long as Roz's arm around Morgaine's waist was considered natural. With Morgaine's eyes closed, the two women walked next to each other over the rest of the bridge. Morgaine opened her eyes and continued along the sidewalk toward the Fenway.

"What made Chad think he could get the other ghost to recant?"

"You know what karma is, don't you?"

Roz nodded.

"It exists on the other side too. Chad thinks he's improved his karma since he stopped driving tenants out of the building. He hopes to transcend this plane and go to a higher one as soon as the powers that be notice."

"And he thinks Reginald will want to do that too?"

"He claims that without someone to talk to, being trapped on this plane is sheer torture. He used to amuse himself with pranks on the residents, but we figured out that his behavior was probably the thing holding him back.

"Joe Murphy solved his murder case, so his unfinished business was finally finished. Unfortunately he still didn't see any beam of light or porthole or anything to indicate he was welcome to transcend, so he made an excuse to stay around, saying he wanted to know how karma paid back his murderers. The truth is, it's his own karma that's in trouble. He can't transcend, even though he wants to."

"That's terrible. So he's cleaning up his act?"

"He's trying to. He's been such a smartass for so long, I don't expect miracles overnight."

Roz kept walking. "At least he has you to talk to. If Reginald hasn't had anyone to communicate with for all these years, he's probably losing it."

"That's what Chad thought. I mentioned there was something 'off' about his energy and that he reminded me of Chad when I first moved into the building, before we discovered we could talk to each other."

"So Chad was losing it before he had you to talk to?"

"Yeah. He was going stark, raving bananas. You'd think Reginald would be nicer to me when I show up to talk to him, but maybe he knows it won't last."

"That could make him feel even worse, having a taste of companionship but knowing it will end as soon as the case is closed. Now it makes sense that he'd give false clues. Anything to keep you there."

"I know. If only I could find someone to talk to him on a regular basis."

"Why not you?"

Morgaine waved away the question. "If it weren't for the money…I have to make a living. Something tells me the museum won't hire me to chat up its disgruntled ghost."

Roz made a "Hmmm" noise as if thinking of a plan.

Morgaine remained quiet. Maybe the smart lawyer could come up with a solution if she let her mull it over.

"Reginald, please listen to me. I'm a lawyer, and seeing justice done is my job."

Reginald regarded the two women while one tried to reason with him and the other acted as his mouthpiece.

He had nothing to lose. What if he *did* plant the hairs and lie about it? The police couldn't lock him up for falsifying evidence or perjury. He was already in his prison and had been there for decades. The curvy young woman with the brown and blonde strange hair could go pound sand.

"*I've done nothing of the kind. I merely reported what I saw.*" Hearing his words come from a woman's mouth was still bizarre, but at least he finally had a voice.

"You saw Konrad take the guards to the basement and duct tape them almost twenty years ago?"

"*No, I didn't say that. I said they missed a piece of evidence, and I told Morgaine where to find it.*"

The lawyer shook her head and looked disgusted.

"Morgaine told me what our friend, Chad, was going to tell you before he got—uh, waylaid."

"*Yes, about that. What detained your ghost? Why didn't he come with you?*"

"I'll let him explain when he gets here," Roz said. "Meanwhile your testimony, which can only be considered hearsay, is causing an innocent man major problems. I think you should recant."

"*And I think you should lose a few pounds.*"

Roz balled her fists and her face turned red, but before she came up with a retort, Reginald sensed another presence.

"*Is someone else here?*"

"*Yeah, hello, bonehead. My name is Chad, and I have a message for you.*"

"Bonehead?"

"*It's a modern expression meaning idiot, moron, a person who's stupid beyond belief.*"

"*Oh?*" Reginald was highly offended, but decided to play it cool. Perhaps the fellow was trying to get him so riled that he'd blurt out the truth. Well, he wouldn't let that happen.

The medium continued to speak for him, but apparently the other spirit preferred she didn't.

He said, "*Morgaine, do you think you could give us a few minutes of silence to speak ghost to ghost?*"

Morgaine nodded, opened her eyes, and came out of her trance.

"*Yeah, listen up dude. Konrad is kind and decent. He hasn't done anything to deserve this frame job. And you're an ass for not only trying to ruin his life, but your afterlife too.*"

"What are you talking about? What more can happen to me?" Was it possible this other spirit knew something about the afterlife? Reginald had been stuck for eighty-something years, and no heaven or hell had opened its gates to claim him. At this point, he didn't care which. Any change would be welcome.

The other spirit sighed. Reginald didn't know why he couldn't see him. He wished he could. It would be nice to know what kind of man he was dealing with.

Chad continued. *"Do you know what karma is? I doubt you do, or you'd realize how messed up yours is."*

"Karma is a term I'm familiar with, although it has to do with an Eastern religion, and I fail to see what difference—"

"That's because you're a dumb ass."

All this name-calling was getting ugly. Reginald liked having someone to talk to, and he'd thought communicating with another spirit would be a special treat, but not this one. *"Now see here—"*

"No, you see. You'll never get to the other side if you keep pulling this kind of crap."

"What other side? What do you know about it, and if that's where we're supposed to be, why are you still here?"

"I thought it was because of unfinished business, but once my murder had been solved and I still didn't move on, I realized it had to be more than that."

"And have you deduced what that additional criterion might be?"

"I knew enough to realize I was losing my shit. I had gone a little nuts from being alone so long. I took it out on the residents of my building, simply because I was bored."

"*How so?*"

"*I learned to move objects with my mind. It's called telekinesis. I had an obnoxious sense of humor and redirected moving objects to hit someone in the eye or set up an obstacle course so I could laugh my ass off when they tripped. And then Morgaine talked to me, and I slowly came to realize what I had been doing.*"

"*What? Enjoying yourself?*"

"*That's what I used to think. Now I know I had been lengthening my time here in purgatory.*"

Reginald snapped to attention. "*Purgatory? This is purgatory?*"

"*Either that or limbo. Whatever you call it, we ain't here, and we ain't there. We're trapped because we can't go back, and we're not welcome wherever we were headed, yet.*"

"*I see.*" The rude spirit made sense. "*And if I continue along this path, I'll stay here forever?*"

"*I guess so. I don't know if there's someplace worse you could go or not. Looking around, I can see you have some pretty groovy digs. You might not want to downgrade.*"

"*Hmmm…I'll have to think about whatever you just said.*"

"*I said—*"

"*Never mind, I understood you well enough.*"

"*So you'll give the ladies a statement of retraction?*"

"*Certainly not. I said what I said because I saw what I saw and heard what I heard.*"

"*You're a friggin' piece of work, you know that?*"

"*I know nothing of the kind. And I imagine you know nothing about the afterlife. Unless you've been there and back, everything you say is just theory.*"

Chad blew out a deep breath of exasperation. *"I can't think of a better explanation, can you?"*

"I'll admit I've been puzzled about why I'm still here, but I don't have the answer, and I'm sorry to say this, but neither do you."

―――――

Konrad sat on his sofa with Roz and played with her cute new haircut. "You couldn't get Reginald to admit he lied?"

"I'm afraid not," Roz said. Her shoulders sagged. "Chad is staying for a while, hoping to wear him down."

"That's surprisingly decent of him." He stretched. "I have a little good news. I was able to rebook our photography class date. We can start this week."

"Oh, by the way, I thought of another career that might be fun. It's not something we can try on a date, though."

"Really? What is it?"

"Hairstylist. I spoke to the instructor at the school where I got my hair cut, and she said training was less than a year and the job prospects in urban areas look good."

"It might be fun for you, but I can't see these big meaty hands of mine doing something that requires that much dexterity."

"Hmm…I guess you have a point. But maybe I could go for hairdressing, you could go for management, and then we could buy a trendy salon."

"With what?"

Roz grimaced. "Oh, yeah. I forgot about the hefty down payment on a mortgage like that."

"So are you still interested in the photography classes?"

"Maybe. Just don't take any pictures of me, okay?"

He looked her up and down. "Are you back to the body issue again?"

"Well, yeah. I hate having my picture taken. I either blink or have some goofy look on my face. And then it's there for all eternity."

"Not with digital cameras. These days if you don't like a picture, you can delete it."

"I guess."

"Maybe it will help distract us until either the case comes to trial or Chad persuades Reginald to fess up to whatever he did."

"Yeah, about that. I'm afraid the circumstantial evidence might be hard to disprove."

"You're kidding. What the hell is it? I still can't figure out why they'd want my DNA."

"Because a couple strands of hair were stuck to a tiny piece of duct tape left when they cut the guards loose. Since the thieves wore Boston cops uniforms, the police checked the hair against their DNA. Your twin brother's DNA is a 99.9 percent match. Since twins DNA are so similar, it could be yours."

"Shit, I never saw that coming. Wait! The second time I went to the museum recently, when I was trying to think of how to tell you about my, um, condition, a toddler pulled out some of my hair."

"Of course! That's how Reginald got it. He must have been watching."

"Goddamn filthy, lying ghost. He framed me for something I didn't do!" Konrad leaned over, dropped his head in his hands, and groaned. "What now, Roz?"

———m———

A few days passed before Chad was able to make his way back to the building and talk to Morgaine. When he said Reginald refused to back down, Roz's hopes for a retraction were dashed. She had conferred with colleagues, and the best they could hope for was that Konrad's alibi would hold up or the prosecution's case would fall apart.

Roz decided that to be thorough, she should get ghost hunters to investigate the existence of Reginald; not that she didn't believe Morgaine, but she knew the woman needed money. Anyone could claim mediumship powers and fake a channeled spirit, right? Konrad refused to believe that Morgaine would do such a thing, so he stayed out of the next part of Roz's research.

She stood in an Airstream trailer in Hyde Park, the makeshift office of B.A.S.H. (Boston Area Spirit Hunters), talking to the lead investigator, Shawn. She had already explained the basics.

He rose from his chair. "You said over the phone that this is for a court case. Would we be required to testify?"

"Not unless we can prove that the ghost doesn't exist."

"It would be easier to prove rather than disprove the existence of a spirit with our infrared equipment." He pulled out a chair on the client side of his metal desk.

Roz took a seat on the hard folding chair. "What do you mean?"

"If we don't see anything, it doesn't prove he isn't there, because he might be hiding from us. If we capture an image, it could *confirm* his existence."

"At least in some minds," Roz said. "I might luck out and get a jury who disbelieves everything supernatural, but I read studies that claim at least sixty percent of Americans have had firsthand encounters with some sort of spirit activity, so that's unlikely."

Shawn scratched his head. "And yet at least ninety percent of the calls we investigate turn up nothing. You said this is a cognizant spirit, right?"

"Yes, if the medium is genuine, and she probably is, then she channeled a ghost named Reginald who died in the 1930s. He seemed quite aware of who was in the room, what we looked like, and what we wanted to know."

"If you believe the medium is genuine, why do you need us?"

"My natural skepticism demands it."

Shawn nodded. "I understand, but if you hire us and we confirm his existence, then you might prefer you hadn't been so thorough."

Roz paused and considered it. "No," she said eventually. "I need to know the truth, at least for myself. Is there any way of doing this surreptitiously?"

"You mean without the medium knowing, or without the museum's knowledge and permission?"

"Both, preferably."

Shawn leaned back in his chair and looked like he was considering the implications carefully. "It's not the ideal situation. We generally like to go into places when it's dark, in order to use our infrared cameras, and we'd need to gain access to off-limits areas. Spirits who want to hide—and that's most of the harmless, cognizant ones trapped on this plane without an agenda—will avoid the public. We can still use thermal imaging, but it might attract attention."

"Damn." She should have thought this over more carefully or asked more questions over the telephone.

"We could always bring in our own sensitive."

"Your own what?"

"Sensitive. It's what psychics and mediums like to be called these days. I have a few I trust completely. They've worked with us while we're using our equipment, and usually the sensitive's contacts validate the electronic findings and vice versa."

"I see, so I assume you'd charge less for the sensitive only, since you wouldn't need to use your fancy cameras and thermal equipment."

"I'm sure we can work something out."

After breaking everything down, Roz negotiated a fair price and signed the contract hiring B.A.S.H. if, for no other reason, than to put her own mind at ease. She didn't have to tell Konrad about it, did she? After all her fuss about honesty, she felt a little conflicted, but the less he knew about certain things, the better. He'd be bound by oath to answer all questions truthfully.

Would she have to verify the haunting of the Gardener Museum in court? *Not unless they place me on the witness stand. Very unlikely.* And even then, she could word her answers like a good lawyer and commit to nothing.

When Roz returned to her apartment, she found an envelope addressed to her taped on the front door. She recognized the handwriting. Immediately, she ripped it open.

"Oh, no."

Konrad's door slammed, and when Roz glanced up, he was jogging down the stairs.

"What's wrong, angel?"

"How did you know something was wrong?"

"I was coming down to see if you were home any-way, and I smelled fear." He nodded at the paper in her hand. "Is there something in that note that upset you?"

"It's nothing." She glanced away and tried to act ca-sual. "You can smell fear?"

He folded his arms and frowned. "Yes. Now you want complete honesty from me, so I think I should expect the same from you."

She stepped back. "Yeah, you're right, but I can handle this."

"And by *this*, you mean—"

"My stepfather's in town and wants to see me."

Konrad's eyes popped. "The perv?"

"It's okay. He just heard I have a high-profile case and said he wants to 'help.'" Roz made finger quotes in the air.

"That's right, he's a lawyer too."

"Yeah, and what he really means is he wants a piece of the publicity."

"I'd like to be present when you talk to him."

"No!" She bit her lower lip. "I mean, I don't think that's a great idea, considering you're the defendant… unless you want the benefit of his expertise."

"Hell, no. I don't want anything from him. I just want to be sure you're safe."

"I will be. Don't worry."

"That's like telling me not to get furry under the full moon. It isn't something I can control. At least let me hide nearby so you can call me telepathically if you need me."

She thought it over. "I guess it would make me more

comfortable knowing you were handy, just in case. You're not the only one who can smell fear. Seasoned lawyers are good at that too." She quickly added, "But *I* want to be the one to stand up to him."

"Noted. When and where are you seeing him?"

"He said he was going to lunch with a client and he'd check back here after that."

"Okay, so we'll wait for him in your apartment. When he knocks, I'll lock myself in your bedroom."

"There's no lock on my bedroom door."

"Then I like the idea of being in there even better."

She folded her arms. "It's not like he's going to try anything…again."

"He'd better not."

Roz jumped when she heard a knock on her door. Konrad, sitting next to her on the couch, pulled her close and whispered, "If you need anything, anything at all, I'll be right in the next room." He gave her a quick kiss and retreated to the bedroom.

She rose, steeled herself for facing her stepfather, and hoped the meeting wasn't as awkward as she anticipated. She crossed to the door warily and opened it a crack. There he stood, hands in his pressed pants pockets, looking as nervous as she felt.

"Hello, Roz."

She crossed her arms. "Hello, jerk. What do you want?"

He smiled the smarmy smile she remembered. "Oh, for heaven's sake, Roz. Water under the bridge. Can't we be friends after all this time?"

"Not really."

He held up both hands. "Well, I came in peace. In fact, I thought I could help you. I understand you have a difficult case coming up."

"I have all the help I need, thank you."

He hung his head. "Please don't be like that, Roz. We haven't talked in so long, and you never know, I might have some insight. If you're uncomfortable inviting me into your apartment, perhaps I can take you out for a cup of coffee."

She wasn't fooled by his contrite act. He'd never admitted doing anything wrong, and she knew he never would. "No thanks, Stan. I have coffee here."

He tossed his hands in the air and paced, but he didn't leave. She knew him well enough to know he wouldn't, even—or maybe especially—when he looked exasperated and was getting nowhere.

At last he whirled on her and took his authoritative stance. "There's no reason in the world you should treat me this way. I have nothing but your success in mind. Surely you can't believe I'd be fool enough to come here with any motive other than professional. Look at you. It's not like you're irresistibly attractive. You've put on at least twenty pounds."

The fine hairs on the back of her neck prickled. Roz's nostrils flared, and she clamped her lips together tight so she wouldn't say anything to make her sound like the hurt little girl he was trying to manipulate her into becoming.

"Roz, I'm coming out."

No! I can handle this. Stay right where you are.

"Then end the conversation. One more comment like he just made, and I'll punch him in the face."

Roz stepped back and began to close the door.

"What's the matter? I just spoke the truth to ease your mind and put the past behind us."

She mustered an even tone and said, "The past is part of me now. Maybe that's the extra weight you're looking at."

"Oh, now don't try to blame—"

The loud bang as the door slammed drowned out the rest of Stan's sentence. She turned the dead bolt and ignored his demands to open the door.

Konrad came barreling out of the bedroom. She placed herself between him and the door and pushed on his solid chest, stopping him.

"Are you all right?" he asked.

She took a deep breath and exhaled in an effort to steady her nerves. "I'm fine...or I will be."

"Roz, please, let me escort him to the sidewalk...by the seat of his pants."

"No, it's better if he doesn't see you. Just...just hold me."

He grasped her in a tight embrace.

She felt his heart pounding and imagined adrenaline rushing through his veins. *He really does love me, enough to fight for me. Yet he's willing to listen and respect my wishes. It's a damn good thing, since I'm ninety-nine percent sure that jerk-face will be in the courtroom for the trial.*

"Take me to the bedroom," she whispered. "I need to lie down."

He swooped her into his arms and carried her to her bed. Gently he placed her in the center of the bed and crawled in next to her.

Propped up on his elbow, he asked, "Is there anything else I can do? Can I call Dottie and sic her on him?"

Roz laughed. "You don't have to protect me from everything, Konrad. I appreciate your being here for me, but honestly, sometimes all I need is your moral support.

"You've got it." He bent over and kissed her tenderly. "But just in case I need to know whom I'm punching out sometime, what's his name?"

Roz chuckled. "Stanley Addison."

"Well, if he upsets you again, he'll be Mr. Subtract-a-son."

Chapter 15

"MORGAINE?"

Morgaine was whipping up a batch of something brown and gooey. It could be an earth-based spell-infused poultice, a mud mask, or brownies. Chad was never sure what the witches were concocting.

She didn't respond, stop stirring, or even act as if she'd heard him.

"Earth to Morgaine…or maybe I should say air to Morgaine. Chad here. Knock, knock. Come in, Morgaine."

She set down the bowl with a thump. "What the hell do you want, Chad?"

"Well, excuuuuse me. Did I just interrupt some kind of George Clooney daydream or something?"

"For your information, I was visualizing the manifestation of my intentions and stirring the energy into…oh, never mind. You don't really care."

Chad hovered above the stove, since it was warmer there. *"No, I don't. But now that I've broken your concentration anyway, can you help me talk to my roommate?"*

"Can't you see I'm busy? Get Gwyneth to do it. She's probably over there anyway."

"I can't. It's her I want to talk to him about."

"Huh? If you have a problem with Gwyneth, why don't you just talk to Gwyneth?"

"I did. She doesn't care."

"Doesn't care about what?"

"Whether or not she breaks my roommate's heart." Chad rubbed his spirit hands together, trying to warm up.

Morgaine put her hand on her hip and grinned. "Why Chad Robinson, I can't believe you're worried about your roommate's happiness. As far as I know, you've never cared about anyone but yourself."

"That's true. And I'm not really looking out for him now, either. I'm worried that if she dumps him, he'll fall apart and move out rather than having to face her every day."

"And how is that *not* looking out for him?"

"I'm looking out for myself. I don't want to listen to a broken down blubbering middle-aged man who'll never get a nice piece of tail like Gwyneth again."

"Hey; that's my cousin you're talking about."

"Well forgive me for having eyes. Er, you know what I mean."

Morgaine relented. "Yes, it's true. Gwyneth is stunning. Most guys can't resist her, but she wouldn't break up with Joe without a good reason."

"Yes, she would. She told me she was just using him to research her erotica novel."

"Are you nuts?"

"Completely, but I'm not a liar."

Morgaine paused, pensively. "But I thought her novel was about a coal miner in West Virginia. Joe is a private investigator in Boston."

"It is. That's not the part she needs help with. She's using his body to better describe her sex scenes."

Morgaine burst out laughing. When she was able to talk again, she said, "I thought you were a guy, Chad. I doubt Joe minds helping her research her sex scenes."

"You wouldn't laugh if you saw the way he looks at her. He's fallen head over heels in love. I know the signs."

"Like what?"

"He preens before she comes over. He keeps the apartment immaculate and doesn't ask her to lift a finger. He sports a goofy grin on his face whenever he looks at her."

"So? It sounds like he's treating her well. What's wrong with that?"

"Just that he'll be bummed out when she finishes that book. She has no intention of staying with him."

"I still don't get how this involves you."

"I let him stay because he worked on my murder case. But the precedent's been set by my allowing a roommate. Dottie will try to rent my pad again and again and again, and you know I'll drive off anyone who moves in."

Morgaine smirked and shook her head. "Now it makes sense."

"Don't you witches have some kind of code about not hurting others?"

"But how do you know she's planning to break up with him?"

"She told me she was going to…what was it? Tell him to go catch tadpoles in another lily pond."

"She said that? When?"

"Yesterday."

Morgaine frowned. "Yeah, that's not good. It doesn't sound like she's really taking the Witches' Rede seriously, if she knows how hurt Joe will be. Maybe she doesn't realize he's in love with her. Has he ever told her?"

"Not when I was around. But I told her. She didn't seem to care."

"Shit. That doesn't sound like the Gwyneth I know. Let me talk to her before you say anything to Joe, okay?"

Chad emitted a loud sigh and floated toward the door. *"Fine. I'll wait. But if I have to listen to a grown man cry—"*

Morgaine folded her arms. "You'll what?"

"Try something I've been saving for a special occasion. You'll see."

Morgaine cringed.

"You've got to be kidding!" Roz stood toe to toe with Konrad and jammed her hands on her hips. "I will not film our sex. Body issues, remember?"

"I thought we put those fears to rest." Konrad grabbed his jeans and stepped into them. Their lovemaking had been fantastic. Was it so bad to want a little souvenir?

"Yeah, they're resting, not dead. Show me my naked body through a medium that adds ten pounds and see how quickly those feelings of shame and disgust wake up."

He reared back. "Shame and disgust? Roz, how can you possibly—" *Careful, guy. You don't want her thinking she's stupid as well as overweight.* "Never mind. I just thought it would be fun. And I thought you were over that silly belief that you're somehow not the most beautiful woman in Boston because of your weight. I find nothing disgusting about you. You're the most exquisite woman I know."

She smiled, but there was a sadness in her beautiful blue eyes. "I...I know you think that, but you make a grand total of one."

"I guess I've got my work cut out for me."

Roz picked up her clothes from the floor. "What do you mean?"

"I won't be satisfied until you believe it too." Konrad swept her into his arms and held her close. He cupped the back of her head and kissed her hair. "Should I tell you again how I see you?"

"No, it'll just embarrass me."

"Man, you're really putting yourself in a no-win situation, Roz. Look at me." He stepped back slightly and lifted her chin until she stared into his eyes. "You have the softest, creamiest skin and the most magnificent blue eyes that stand out even more, because of your dark hair, perfect eyebrows, and thick lashes. The highlights you added couldn't make you more radiant. And I love the new haircut. Very cool. I know most guys don't comment on things like that, but we notice them."

"Seriously?"

"Yeah, seriously. And you're not fat. You're voluptuous. I like grabbing onto you and finding a real woman, not a bag of bones. I'm sure I'm not the only guy on earth like that. You've dated a few guys before, right?"

"Yes. I haven't had any long-term relationships, but I dated a couple of guys in high school. A few guys in college. One in law school. The occasional drunk hits on me, but that doesn't count."

"Why doesn't that count? They have eyes."

"Yeah, and they're probably seeing double. Maybe they think I'm twins."

Konrad shook his head. "Roz, Roz, Roz, what am I going to do with you?"

She smiled again, and most of the sadness was gone. "I don't know. Love me? That might work...eventually."

"I can do that." He dipped his head and captured her lips in a long, sweet kiss.

When he finally released her, he said, "I have things you could find fault with too, you know."

"Like what?"

"Like the fact that I'm poor now. Or poorer, I should say." He spoke softly. "I don't think I can make the rent this month."

"Oh, no! I shouldn't have let you pay for all our dates. And the bail money must have wiped you out." She grabbed his arms and tried to shake him. "Why didn't you tell me?"

"Pride."

"Stupid pride. Let me help you this month, and don't say—"

"No."

I was just going to tell you not to say that."

"I know." He sighed and pulled his T-shirt over his head. "Dottie will have to understand."

"Does she seem understanding to you?"

He smirked. "No. But I've never been late with the rent before. That has to count for something." He grabbed her hand. "Let's go up to my place. I'll make you lunch."

"I should make *you* lunch. Food isn't cheap either, especially all the steak you eat."

A loud bang and what sounded like two females yelling at each other filtered through Roz's closed door.

Konrad wandered toward the sound. "What the—"

As soon as he opened the door, he recognized the

voices. Gwyneth and Morgaine were getting into it. They must have been on the third floor, but outside their apartment, since even without his wolfish hearing he could make out every harsh word.

"Are you calling me a slut?"

"Are you acting like one?"

"No! I'm only making the most of what the Goddess gave me."

"Even if it goes against the Witches' Rede?"

"I ain't hurtin' nobody."

"Oh yeah? Then why did Chad say you used Joe and were about to dump him?"

"How do I know? The fact of the matter is it ain't none of y'all's business!"

A huge ruckus ensued. Worried about what they could do to each other if they used their powers, Konrad rushed up the stairs. What he saw at the top of the third floor landing made him stop. It was like watching a train wreck. The two women were rolling around on the floor, grabbing clothes, pulling hair, and scratching. As Gwyneth was about to bite, he charged in.

"That's enough, ladies." He grubbed Gwyneth by her macramé belt and lifted her off Morgaine. While he held her suspended in midair, Morgaine scrambled to her feet.

"Now, what's this all about?" he asked.

Morgaine adjusted her black blouse and blew a piece of hair out of her mouth. "Chad told me Gwyneth was using Joe to write her book, and now that it's finished, she's planning to dump him."

"Gwyneth, if I put you down, will you retract your claws and talk to your cousin calmly?"

"Sure, if she minds her own beeswax."

Konrad set Gwyneth on her feet.

Morgaine crossed her arms. "So you aren't denying it."

"Denying what?"

"What Chad said, that you were going to tell Joe to go fishing for tadpoles in another lily pond."

"He wants kids. I don't. I think it's called basic incompatibility. It's got nothin' to do with usin' and dumpin'."

Morgaine shook her head. "Uh, I wouldn't use that metaphor if I were you. I should know better than to believe Chad. He's probably watching us right now."

"Yeah, and laughin' his ass off." Gwyneth cocked her head. "I can't hear him, though. Can you?"

"No."

Konrad rested his hands on his hips. "He must know better than to piss off a couple of powerful witches. That's why I came rushing up here. I wondered if you two might start throwing lightning bolts at each other."

Both women laughed.

Gwyneth drawled, "We can't shoot lightnin' out of our fingertips like buckshot, sugar."

"And if we could, we wouldn't," Morgaine added. "To attack with our powers would be black magic, and we know better than to dabble in that."

"So instead you attack each other with your vicious words, long fingernails, and teeth?"

The women looked at each other and shrugged.

Morgaine sighed. "I know how it must look." She eyed her cousin. "We really should know better than to handle things this way."

"Scrappin' ain't agin the Witch's Rede, so far as I know."

Konrad frowned. "What happens now? Are you going to be able to live together again?"

Gwyneth crossed her arms. "Depends. Is my buttinski cousin gonna stop tryin' to run my life?"

The door to 3A clicked and opened. A dejected-looking Joe strolled into the hallway. "Let me save you girls some trouble," he said. "I'm moving out."

Morgaine gasped and narrowed her gaze on Gwyneth.

Gwyneth sidled up next to Joe and stroked his arm. "Y'all don't have to go on account of little ol' me."

"No, I want to be, uh, closer to the beach. Yeah. Summer's coming, and I thought I'd rent a beach house."

"Well, that sounds like fun!" Gwyneth said. "I hope y'all still want to be friends."

Morgaine gave her the hairy eyeball.

Konrad coughed discreetly and mumbled, "Well, I'll let all of you work this out." Just as he was about to descend the stairs, he pivoted. "Don't kill each other." He mumbled under his breath, "It's not worth the guilt."

The trio stared at him wide eyed as he turned to jog back downstairs to Roz's apartment.

Roz was glad Konrad was upstairs when her phone rang. It was Shawn at B.A.S.H. Apparently Morgaine's validity as a medium had checked out.

"I thought you said you debunked ninety percent of haunting reports."

"We do," Shawn said. "Unfortunately, it looks as if the museum is one of the other ten percent. Our sensitive confirmed the presence of a spirit, neither friendly nor unfriendly. It's what we call a benign haunting."

"Well, there's nothing benign about what this spirit is trying to do to my client by framing him."

Shawn cleared his throat. "With all due respect, did it ever occur to you that your client might be guilty?"

Roz's jaw dropped. *Konrad, guilty?* She felt like a fool. No, she hadn't considered it. Not for a moment. And why not? Was her judgment clouded because she was sleeping with him?

"Ma'am? Is there anything else we can do for you?"

"Ah, no. Thank you for investigating it and getting back to me so quickly."

"Our pleasure. It was an interesting place. I might go back there just to enjoy the atmosphere."

"Be careful you don't piss off the resident ghost." Roz hung up.

Konrad returned and let himself in. "Is everything okay?"

Damn, I need to work on my poker face. "Uh, yeah. Didn't you say you had an alibi for the night of the theft?"

"Yeah, but I also told you it can't be proven."

"Why not?"

Konrad stared at the ceiling. "Oh, boy."

"What is it? *Tell* me!"

"Okay, okay. I guess now that you know about me, I can tell you more. I was with my pack."

"Oh, you have a…pack?"

"And the trial lands on the full moon. That means they probably won't testify for fear of being caught in the city when they shift."

"But don't you shift at midnight? And you *live* in the city. Somehow you manage to handle it."

Konrad hung his head. "There's something else I never told you. I was kicked out of the pack in disgrace."

Roz didn't have the heart to be angry with him for withholding more facts from her. His shame showed plainly on his face.

—~~—

Roz sat woodenly on the edge of a chair. *I wonder how many of the people who work here are werewolves?* Konrad had said his pack ran the school, so it could mean several were, even the nice secretary she'd just spoken to.

The current dean of Newton Prep had refused to see her, but his secretary told her not to leave. Apparently she knew others who would be willing to talk with her about Konrad.

At last the secretary returned.

"If you'll follow me to the faculty lounge, I can introduce you to several staff members who'd love to talk with you."

Roz rose. *Love to?* She followed the woman out the door and down a long corridor, heels tapping loudly. "It's unusual for lawyers to be welcomed with open arms. Usually we're met with reactions more like that of your dean."

"Oh, no. I think you'll find there's a great deal of interest among the faculty as far as Konrad is concerned. Can you tell me where he is now? Is he okay?"

Roz raised her eyebrows in surprise. "Doesn't he keep in touch?"

The woman dropped her gaze. "Sadly, no. And I can't say I blame him. We made a terrible mistake and treated him horribly. I think it's safe to say that all's forgiven now, at least on our end."

"He told me he was kicked out. I don't think he's angry, just sad."

The woman stopped in front of the door that said "Faculty Lounge" in bold letters on the window. "I wish I could stay with you, but I'd be missed if the phone rings."

Roz stiffened. "Why? Am I not safe alone in there?"

She chuckled. "No, it's not that. You're perfectly safe. I just have to get back to my ass hat of a boss."

"Oh." Roz smiled at the woman's candor. "Well, thanks. Maybe I'll see you later."

"That would be nice, but the others will fill me in." She opened the door for her. "It's better if the dean doesn't see you talking to any of us."

A normal-looking group sat around a table. They glanced up and stopped eating as soon as she entered the room. The men stood.

One of the gentlemen pulled out a chair for her. "Have a seat, Miss Wells."

"Thank you." Fortunately, her seat was close to the door, in case anyone looked hungry.

Before he even returned to his seat, he said, "We're all very curious about how Konrad is doing. You said you were his lawyer. Is he in trouble?"

"Unfortunately he might be. I need to verify his alibi. He said he was with some of you here on the evening of March 18, 1990."

The group looked at each other. Finally a woman spoke up. "How are we supposed to remember where we were on a particular evening more than twenty years ago?"

Roz cleared her throat. "It was the night of the burglary at the Isabella Stewart Gardener Museum."

A collective gasp filled the room. The woman who

had spoken before said, "You can't possibly think he had anything to do with the stolen art."

Roz still didn't want to commit to a position, but the fact that these people seemed to find it impossible to believe helped.

"It doesn't matter what I think. The state thinks there's enough evidence to bring him to trial."

Several people began speaking at once. Some asked Roz more questions. Some expressed outrage. Others were having one-on-one conversations.

"Hold on!" the gentleman who had seated her said. "This isn't going to get us anywhere. Let's all think, and if anyone remembers anything from that night, share it, one at a time."

"And please give me your names as you do," Roz added.

An older gentleman raised his hand. "Wendell is my name. I have one question first." He glanced around the room. "I think we need to know what she knows… about us."

Roz nodded, and they all stared at her. As casually as she could manage, she said, "Are you referring to the fact that some of you are werewolves?"

She saw several raised eyebrows, but the room remained deathly quiet. She waited. Someone *had* to respond.

"Are you a werewolf?" Wendell asked.

"No."

The gentleman who spoke to her first bristled. "What makes you think werewolves exist?"

"Your name, sir, is?"

"Barrett."

She tried to keep her cool. This was no time to show

fear or back down. She hadn't seen Konrad shift as he claimed he could, but the whole telepathy thing was certainly supernatural.

"Well, Mr. Barrett, I know this because I'm his lawyer, and I needed to know."

The woman who had spoken previously shook her head and said, "No, he wouldn't divulge that to his lawyer, even if his life depended on it."

"Your name, ma'am?"

She hesitated, folded her arms, and bit out, "Lois."

"All right, Lois. To whom would he divulge that information, if not to his lawyer?"

"No one," she said indignantly.

Roz decided to go with Konrad's truth, even if she wasn't totally there yet. "Not even his mate?"

More eyebrows shot up.

Finally, Barrett spoke. "Are you saying *you're* his mate?"

Roz raised her chin proudly. "I am."

More agitated conversation broke out around the table. She heard the word "human" spoken as if it tasted like rotting meat.

Lois raised her hand, and everyone quieted. "Prove it," she said. "Show us your mark."

Roz straightened her back. "I will not," she said as if deeply offended. *I hope whatever that mark is, it appears in some really personal place. I'm guessing if my mate put it there, it could be on my ass, and I wouldn't even know. He probably guessed I'd never look there.*

To answer their question with another question, Roz tipped her head. "How about telepathic communication? Does that do it for ya?"

Amid the stunned silence, she heard a sigh of relief,

or maybe it was some other kind of sigh, like one at the end of a sappy movie.

Lois smiled. "Yes, that helps."

Wendell scrutinized her. "And you don't mind that he's a—"

"Werewolf?" Roz supplied. "I'm not crazy about it, but I *am* crazy about him."

The group nodded and murmured.

"Good, then if you're as concerned about Konrad as you seem to be, maybe you can all help me help him."

"How?" Wendell asked.

"I'm hoping for an alibi. Does anyone remember being with him at that time?"

They all glanced around the room at each other. Eventually a few pack members shook their heads, followed by more. Eventually it seemed as if everyone had weighed in, and the answer was "No."

"Wait a minute," Wendell said. "I think I remember something."

Roz's ears perked up with hope.

Chapter 16

KONRAD JOGGED DOWN THE STAIRCASE, OUT THE DOOR, and down the front steps. Even though it was a cool day, he wore only his black T-shirt and jeans. He stopped at a table set up on the busy street corner. "Morgaine, what's all this?"

Morgaine nodded toward the table covered with plates of cookies, loaves of bread, cakes, and tarts.

Gwyneth stood in the gutter, talking to a couple of women in a car. She held up one finger to the car behind, which had stopped at the same traffic light and rolled down its window to see what was going on.

Morgaine grinned. "We're having a bake sale, to help pay your rent."

Gwyneth backed away from the cars and skipped over to the table.

Konrad was taken aback. "Pay my rent? Why?"

"Because you're flat broke, sugar," Gwyneth answered.

"Huh? How did you know? Oh, yeah. You're psychics."

"Not only that, but Roz confirmed it for us."

He tried to keep his temper under control. "I wonder what gave her the idea that I'm a charity case."

"It's not charity. We're not giving you *our* money," Gwyneth said.

"Minor detail."

Morgaine laid a hand on his arm. "Look, we wanted to help, so we all put our heads together and hatched this idea. Roz knew you wouldn't take charity, but you've done so much for us—"

Roz?

At that moment, Roz opened the door and came trotting down the stairs with another plate.

"*Yes, lover?*"

He waited until she arrived at the table. The smell of warm oatmeal cookies wafted up to his nose. "You organized this?"

"We all did."

"Why?"

"Didn't you see the eviction notice on your door this morning?"

He stuffed his hands in his pockets and kicked at the sidewalk. "I saw it. I was going to wait until Jason and Merry got back before I took it seriously. *He's* the landlord, after all."

"Yes, but we didn't want Dottie on your case."

He nodded. "She can be a nuisance. But you didn't have to do this."

Gwyneth chimed in. "We wanted to. Besides, it's fun. It's one of those things that brings neighbors and kin together."

The front door opened again, and Nathan jogged down the steps with a few dollars in his hand.

When he got to the table, he said, "Sorry, I don't bake, big guy. But I can eat my weight in tollhouse cookies."

He handed a five over to Morgaine, and she handed him a plate of cookies.

"Where's my change?"

She gaped at him. "You want change?"

Nathan stared at the plate. "Five bucks for eight cookies?"

Roz placed a hand on her hip. "We're doing this for our friend and neighbor, Nathan. Don't be a cheapskate."

He stared at the cookies. "Fine. But they'd better be good."

Gwyneth smirked. "Oh, they're *good* all right. Don't be surprised if y'all come back for more."

Nathan sniffed and examined the cookies. "I don't see any *special* ingredients."

Gwyneth returned to the opposite side of the table. "They were baked with love, silly. We wouldn't put any wacky tobaccky in them."

He sniffed them again. "Hmm. Well, they sure smell good. I guess I'll just have to take my chances." He peeled back the cellophane and stuck the plate under Konrad's nose. "Here, try one."

Konrad laughed. "Sure, buddy. Don't mind if I do."

Gwyneth looked over her shoulder at the street. "Oh, another red light! I'll take the oatmeal ones this time. They smell too good to pass up, even without a spell on 'em."

She grabbed the plate and sidled up to the car window, calling out, "Y'all want something delicious?"

The guy in the car grinned like a love-struck teenager and rolled down his window.

"Spell?" Nathan dropped the cookie in his hand back onto the plate.

Morgaine waved him off. "Don't worry. It won't work on you. I worded the spell so that only human beings who could afford them would be susceptible. At first we were giving one free with every purchase."

Nathan smirked. "Good idea."

"Well, it was until the same cars drove around the block and wanted more every five minutes."

Nathan held the plate in front of her. "Can you add a few words to make my boss give me a raise? Then I'll bring them into work."

Morgaine whirled on him. "Oh, just eat the damn things."

Roz patted her on the shoulder. "Relax. I'll get back inside and make another batch of *normal* ones. Gwyneth's sales pitch seems to be working just fine without a spell."

Morgaine pouted. "Yeah, her sex appeal's in overdrive. But we're making boatloads of money, so it wouldn't be right to complain."

"You don't need to complain. You're every bit as pretty as she is," Nathan said.

Everyone stared at him in shock.

He shrugged. "What?"

Morgaine recovered first. "I think I heard you give me a compliment, and it wasn't followed by some kind of smartass remark that negates the whole thing."

"You seemed to need one."

She rolled her eyes. "And there it is."

―⁓―

Roz and Konrad were making out on her sofa when she heard a knock on her door. They reluctantly broke their lip lock. "Before I answer it, would you mind closeting yourself in my bedroom again, just in case it's my dimwit stepfather?"

"Sure, if I have to."

"I think it's best until after the case."

Konrad removed himself as Roz crossed to the door.

She glanced over her shoulder to be sure he was out of sight and then opened it.

Of all the people she hadn't expected. "Merry!"

Her best friend rushed in to hug her. "I couldn't wait to get home. I've missed you so much!"

Roz welcomed the firm embrace and almost cried, she was so glad to see her. "Oh, Merry, I'm so glad you're back. I've missed you too. A lot!"

"Well, tell me what's going on. Are you still seeing Konrad?"

Roz turned toward her bedroom. "Hey, sweetie, it's okay. You can come out."

"He's here?" Merry strode to meet him as he rounded the corner and gave him a big hug too.

"Great to see you, Merry," Konrad said. "Is Jason home? I need to talk to him."

"Yeah, he should be upstairs talking to Dottie."

His face fell. "Oh. I'll wait a while, then."

"Is anything wrong?"

Roz groaned. "You could say that. Konrad's been arrested for a crime he didn't commit and posting bail wiped out his bank account. He was a little late on his rent, and Dottie sent him an eviction notice yesterday."

Merry gasped. "What? You've got to be kidding me!"

"Sorry, Merry," Konrad said. "It's no joke."

"I can't friggin' believe it. I'll be right back, guys. I'm going to have a word with Jason and his aunt."

Roz didn't stop her. She flew out the door and up the stairs.

Konrad yelled, "Wait!"

Merry didn't even slow down.

—*w*—

Konrad charged up the stairs and heard Merry demand, "What the hell do you think you're doing, Dottie? Evicting Konrad for one late payment is ridiculous. Jason, set her straight!"

Konrad appeared at the door she had left wide open.

Dottie reared back and stared at Merry wide eyed. "Excuse me?"

"Honey, that's not necessary." Jason put an arm around his furious wife. "I'm taking care of it."

Konrad quickly interjected, "Merry, Roz didn't get a chance to tell you. I'm getting the money."

Dottie crossed her arms. "Oh? And when are *we* getting it?"

Just as Merry opened her mouth, Jason held up his hand. "We'll get it when he has it, Aunt Dottie. There's no need to rush him."

Whew. I knew I could count on Jason to be reasonable.

"But his aunt better stay out of choking reach," he heard Roz think from downstairs. Apparently their telepathy was growing stronger, traveling over greater distances.

Dottie's jaw dropped. "I thought *I* was the manager."

Jason rested his hands on his hips. "And I thought *I* was the landlord."

Her lips thinned into a tight line.

Merry took a deep breath. "Dottie, if it weren't for Konrad, I might not be alive. He saved me from a would-be rapist with a knife to my throat. Don't you remember that night?"

Konrad stared at Dottie and waited to see what she'd say to that.

She relaxed a bit, but her arms remained folded in front of her. "I remember. But does that mean he gets a free ride? How are the other tenants who pay their rent regularly going to feel?"

Merry folded her arms too. "They don't have to know."

Konrad coughed. "Um, Merry, they already know. They held a bake sale to help me out."

Dottie had a smug look of satisfaction on her face. "You see? They all know. I watched the whole thing from that window." She pointed to the bay window facing Beacon Street. "Roz and Morgaine set up a folding table on the corner, and Gwyneth risked her neck walking into oncoming traffic to sell the goodies. Nathan bought some, so he knew about it. In fact, the only one I didn't see was Joe."

"And he already gets a break on his rent," Merry added.

Konrad's eyebrows shot up. "He does? Why?"

"Because his roommate is an officious ghost," Dottie said. "And for some reason, he won't let anyone stay there except Joe, so it's half the rent or none at all."

Konrad scratched his head. "I heard Joe is moving out. I can give you half the rent right now."

Dottie gasped. "Joe's moving out? Oh, no. We'll never get that place rented again."

Konrad stuck in hands in his pockets. "I don't know. He seems to like me. Maybe he'll let me move in."

"You're kidding. Now I know he hates me," Dottie wailed.

"What makes you say that?"

"Apparently I'm the only one he plays tricks on."

"Tricks?"

"Yes. Last fall, before we held the séance and he was

still trying to frighten potential renters away from what he considers *his* apartment, I was showing it to someone, and he moved boxes from the closet right into my path, causing me to trip. I could have broken my neck!"

"Are you sure that was his doing?"

"Don't you start questioning my sanity too. I get enough of that from my husband and nephew."

"Sorry."

Dottie jammed her hands on her hips. "But why would he like you? It's not like you can protect him from anything. He's already dead. You can't talk to him like Morgaine and Gwyneth can. You can't even see him to know he wants you to turn on the TV, like Nathan does." Dottie threw her hands in the air. "I give up."

Jason patted her shoulder. "I'm sure he doesn't hate you. He probably just knows he can get a reaction from you. If you ignore him, he'll probably leave you alone."

"Oh, no. I tried that." She shook her head, vehemently. "If I ignore him, he keeps upping the ante until I lose my temper and scream at him."

"What does he do?" Konrad asked.

"Irritating things. He sees me waiting for the lottery numbers to be read with my ticket in hand then causes static on the TV. He turns the oven off as soon as I put a roast in. He shakes up my cans of soda in the fridge."

Konrad bit his lip. *Don't laugh, don't laugh, don't laugh.*

Jason sighed. "I don't know what to tell you, Aunt Dottie. There's nothing we can do about a ghost."

Ralph walked in from the hallway. "What's going on? Did I hear Dottie telling you some stupid ghost stories again? By the way, welcome home, Jason."

Dottie put her hands over her face, but Konrad saw the skin around them turning red. Jason and his uncle clasped hands and patted each other's backs in a man hug.

At last, Dottie balled her fists and yelled, "I can't do this anymore."

Jason raised his eyebrows. "Can't do what, Aunt Dottie?"

"This! All of this. Managing an apartment building full of miscreants, trying to rent unrentable units, using what little authority I have to collect the rent and being undermined at every turn. I've had it!" She stormed off toward her bedroom.

Ralph shook his head. "She's been like this ever since she published that travel article. Now she wants to take off in an RV and tour destinations all over the country."

Merry and Jason spoke at the same time. "She published the article?"

"What article?" Konrad asked.

Ralph scratched his chin. "When we were in the Caribbean scouting hotels for Jason and Merry's honeymoon, Dottie found her calling. She had a ball touring the various facilities and grilling the managers. Later she used all her notes to write an article describing each place in detail and submitted it to a few travel magazines."

Dottie strode back into the living room with a magazine in her hand. "And not only did a magazine offer me a good paycheck for it, the editor wanted me to write more."

Jason took the magazine from her. "That's great! Is it in this issue?"

"Page twenty-three," she announced proudly.

Ralph cleared his throat. "Um, Jason, after you get settled, there's something I'd like to discuss with you."

"Sure. Give us a couple of hours to unpack."

"When you're free, can I speak with you too?" Konrad asked.

"If it's about the rent, don't worry about it." Jason clapped him on the back. "My wife's right. If not for you, she might not have survived the attack in the alley. Take that eviction notice and tear it up."

Whew. Dodged one bullet. Now all I have to worry about is a grand jury.

While Roz was at the courthouse, trying to change the date of the big trial to a waxing or waning moon, Konrad decided he should bone up on the law. Unfortunately he didn't have any law books, so he pulled out his copy of John Grisham's *The Jury.*

He remembered enjoying the story the first time he'd read it, but now he was a defendant. *I might as well prepare myself for the inevitable.*

He had barely started reading when he heard a commotion from upstairs. It sounded like women yelling, and not in ecstasy, so he put down the book and hoped the witches weren't killing each other again.

"I should mind my own business," he said out loud.

He retrieved the book and tried to read. After he had scanned the same sentence three times, he realized it was no use. He had to intervene.

Upon opening his door, he was able to identify the voices. Yup. Morgaine and Gwyneth were at it again. Suddenly a new voice was added to the cacophony. *Joe?*

"Look, it's not her fault. I told her I like to listen," he said.

"That doesn't mean she should forward *all* the calls to your apartment. I didn't receive a single phone call for two days. I thought all my customers deserted me. Instead I find out my dear cousin is stealing them!"

"It ain't like that, Morgaine."

"Oh, yeah? Then what *is* it like?"

"Like Joe said, he likes to listen to me handle the sex calls."

Joe cleared his throat. "If you ladies will excuse me…" He retreated to his apartment and closed the door.

"So you just did it because you were being nice to him and didn't think about how that would affect me?"

"Yeah. I'm not mean, just stupid sometimes."

Morgaine covered her mouth as if trying not to laugh.

"I see you smirkin'." Gwyneth advanced on her cousin, but Konrad inserted himself between them.

"Hold on, you two."

Morgaine peered around him and continued to talk to Gwyneth as if there weren't a six-foot-four-inch werewolf standing between them. "Why not just invite Joe to *our* apartment?"

"I can't."

"Why not?"

"On account o' he gets horny from all the dirty talk comin' out of my mouth. Then he just has to start—"

Konrad cleared his throat. "Not to change the subject or anything, but I thought Joe was moving out."

"He is."

"What?" Morgaine seemed shocked. "I thought you changed his mind."

"Well, he changed it back."

Konrad folded his arms. "It might be for the best. You two have been fighting ever since he moved in. You were the best of friends before that. Isn't that true?" He looked from one witch to the other. "I never heard fights in the hallway before."

At last Morgaine answered. "We've had our disagreements, but not like this."

Gwyneth sniffed. "You liked me better when you were my teacher. Now I find I can do things on my own that you can't, like writin' dirty books."

Morgaine lowered her voice. "Yeah, how will you do that, if Joe moves out and can't correct your grammar for you?"

"I'll think of somethin'. Maybe Konrad here can do it. You used to be a teacher, didn't ya, Konrad?"

He held up both hands and took a step back. "I'm not getting involved in anything that might make one of you furious or my girlfriend insecure."

"Aw." Gwyneth tipped her head. "Y'all are a right stand-up guy, Konrad. I wish I had someone as dedicated to me as y'all are to Roz."

"What about Joe?" Morgaine asked.

"That was just sex."

"Ah-ha! You finally admitted you were just using him!"

"Did not."

"Did too."

Dottie appeared at the stair landing and called, "What's going on up there?"

Gwyneth leaned over the railing. "None of your bees—"

Konrad slapped a hand over Gwyneth's mouth. "Just

a little disagreement, Dottie. I'm sure the girls will work it out."

"Well, do it quietly, for God's sake. I can't hear myself think."

As soon as the door slammed, Morgaine snorted. "Dottie thinks?"

Konrad smiled. "I guess now that she's a magazine writer, she needs to use her brain."

Gwyneth's eyes widened. "She's a what?"

"A writer."

Gwyneth practically flew down the stairs, not bad for a witch without a broom.

Morgaine groaned.

Konrad scratched his head. "Maybe I shouldn't have told her that, since she was looking for someone to edit her books."

"What's that, Chad?" Morgaine cupped her ear. "He says Dottie will do it. He heard her offer to help Jason write his memoirs."

Konrad stuffed his hands in his pockets. "I'm sorry. I totally didn't see that coming."

"No worries." Morgaine tipped her head. "Hang on, Chad has something else to say." She chuckled. "He said that once Dottie reads Gwyneth's erotic novels, she'll probably jump Ralph's bones, and maybe that'll help her relax."

"Hey, can you ask Chad something for me, since you're talking with him right now?"

Morgaine paused a moment and laughed. "He said, 'Sure.' Go ahead and ask him yourself. He's invisible, not deaf. I'll just let you know what he says in response."

"Oh, okay. Uh, Chad, would you allow another

roommate to move in when Joe moves out? If it's some-one you know and like, one of us, I mean."

She cocked her head and listened. "He wants to know why you want to move in with a ghost."

"Dottie said half the rent is better than none, and since I only have half the rent and will be spending a lot of time at my girlfriend's place anyway—"

Morgaine nodded. "Makes sense, but maybe Gwyneth could move over there for a while, if not permanently. Since we're not getting along all that well, maybe put-ting a little distance between us would help. What do you think, Chad? Would you be willing to have Konrad or Gwyneth as a roommate?"

She paused and then said, "He's thinking it over."

She tipped her head back and forth as if ticking off the seconds it took to answer a question on *Jeopardy*. At last she had an answer. "He says he's still not sure, but if he did allow it, he's partial to Gwyneth."

"Why?"

She listened another minute, crossed her arms, and sighed. "He said, not only can she talk to him, she's wicked pretty and walks around in the buff."

Konrad sighed. "Oh, well, it was worth a shot."

Morgaine straightened, and her eyes lit up. "I don't think you need to worry. You might be moving in with your girlfriend soon anyway."

He balled his fists. "I won't sponge off my girlfriend."

"I'm not saying that." She smiled, and there was this knowing look on her face.

"Do you know something I don't? Did you get one of your psychic flashes?"

"Maaaaybe."

He leaned back and studied her for a moment. "If anything I'd rather she move in with me. I can't imagine finding room to house my whole library. Her place is smaller than mine."

"It sounds like you've thought about it."

Konrad chuckled. "Maaaaybe."

―――∾∾―――

Roz took her fighting stance. Hands on hips. Eyebrows knit. Torso leaning forward. She wasn't going to let some client tell her how to do her job, even if he was her two-hundred-thirty-pound werewolf boyfriend.

"Don't give me that look," Konrad said.

"What look?"

"The one that says you'd like to wipe the floor with me."

"Sometimes I wish I could. This is one of those times."

He threw his hands in the air and paced across his living room. "There's got to be another way. I don't want you using the pack for my alibi. Besides, it's not as if any of them would remember where I was on any particular evening in the early 1990s."

"I beg to differ. It sounded as if some of them remembered a meeting that took place that night."

His jaw dropped. "You…you spoke to them?"

"Oh course I spoke to them. How would I know if you had an alibi or not?"

"How?"

"I did my research and found the only private school once run by a certain Konrad Wolfensen, and then I went to Newton and asked to meet with the faculty."

"What did you tell them?"

"Well, at first I just said that I was your lawyer and that you were being accused of a crime I believed you were innocent of committing and that we needed an alibi if they could provide one."

"Roz, these are the same people who ran me out of town and threw me out of the pack."

"Well, they wanted to help. It seems like the guy who replaced you as the dean is a real ass hat. His secretary's words, not mine."

He laughed. "Good. What else did you talk about?"

"Well, they wanted to know how you were, and how much I knew about you."

He looked at her askance. "What do you mean?"

"They seemed really concerned for you."

"Not that. The other thing. What did you tell them you knew?"

"That you were a werewolf."

Konrad gasped. "Why the hell…Do you know how much danger you were in?"

Roz shook her head. "No, they seemed really nice." *I sounded really lame, saying that just now.*

Konrad dropped onto his sofa and covered his face with his hands. "That was insane. I thought I told you that the number-one responsibility of werewolves was to keep humans from finding out we exist. I don't know why they didn't kill you."

"Well, they were getting their hackles up until I told them I was your mate."

He looked up at her in wonder. "You said that?"

"Yes."

"How did they take it?"

"They wanted me to prove it, and when I told

them we had telepathic communication, it seemed to change everything."

He patted the seat next to him.

"Does that mean you don't think I'm insane anymore," Roz said.

"Oh, I'm still sure you're certifiable. I just want to make sure I heard you right."

She sat next to him. "Heard what right?"

"It sounded like you've finally accepted me as your mate."

Roz folded her hands in her lap and stared at them. *You may have showed your hand a little too soon, Roz. Now what?*

"Now we celebrate, my love…in the bedroom."

Roz chuckled. "I should have known you'd hear that. And react that way, too."

He scooped her up in his arms, carried her to his bed, and said, "You and I are two of the luckiest creatures on earth. So many people never find their soul mate." He gently placed her in the middle and crawled in beside her. "I love you, Roz."

He wasted no time pulling her into his tight embrace and kissed her senseless.

Roz found nerve endings she never knew existed tingling to life. His shadowy stubble subtly scraped her face.

He pulled back a moment. "Do you know how rare this is?"

"You mean making love with your soul mate?"

She noticed the tiny lines crinkling outward from the outer corners of his eyes as he smiled at her. "Yeah. Making love, not just having sex."

"Rare and beautiful."

He delivered another intoxicating kiss and stroked her back all the way to her buttocks, which he cupped tenderly.

She inhaled deeply, loving his scent, loving *him* so much it almost moved her to tears.

Chapter 17

"KONRAD?"

"Mmm?" He ran the backs of his fingers down the column of her neck, his touch so light and feathery she trembled. "Are you cold, love?"

"No. On the contrary, I'm heating up big time." It was true. Heat raced up her chest to her face.

"Your sexy blush turns me inside out."

She laughed. "I've never heard that one before, but I don't think anyone but you has ever turned my cheeks pink, either."

He began unbuttoning her blouse. As his fingers reached her breasts, he slipped his big hand inside and fondled one. Excitement ripped through her body.

"Oh, God," she said breathlessly as she arched into his hand. Her nipple must have poked through the stretch lace of her bra, because he gave it a gentle squeeze.

"Oh." Her knees went weak. She couldn't wait for a slow seduction. She grasped the hem of her blouse and undid the remaining buttons quickly. "I want you, right now."

He chuckled. "Eager, are we?"

"Uh-huh." She sat up, peeled off her blouse, and tossed it to the floor.

"Well, I intend to seduce you a little longer, so lean back and enjoy it."

She giggled but flopped backward on the bed as he'd asked.

He leaned over, and his hot, moist lips slid softly against hers. She inhaled his faint exotic scent, some kind of musk-scented toiletry, if she had to guess. Or maybe it was just pure him. The movement of his lips over hers intensified, and soon he was demanding entrance.

She parted her lips and met his tongue as their mouths fused. The bliss she experienced when he kissed her like that was beyond description. Warm, undulating waves of pleasure invaded her from head to curling toes.

He tasted good, slightly sweet. He ran his velvet tongue around hers in an erotic dance and then sucked it. The resulting vacuum sealed their lives together as well as their lips.

She inadvertently moaned. He lifted his face, dipped into the hollow of her neck, and feathered kisses from her ear to her collarbone. His hand found her breast again and massaged it. She arched into his hand and begged, "Please, Konrad. Please—"

"What do you need, angel?"

"I need to get rid of these barriers. My bra. Our jeans. Everything."

He smiled at her, stood, and peeled off his clothing while she lay there, doing the same. When he freed his enormous cock, it bounced up full and erect.

"Oh, God. You're so—" Words failed her.

"Turned on?"

"I hope so. Either that or you took an overdose of Viagra."

He laughed. "I don't need any help making love to you, Roz. *You're* my aphrodisiac."

Crawling back onto the bed, he stared at her like he

was starving and she was a juicy steak. The intensity of his gaze alone sent her heartbeat skittering. When he reached her breast he took the puckered nipple into his mouth and sucked. Meanwhile, his hand slid down her torso until he cupped her mons. His fingers teased her labia, collecting and spreading her moisture.

She moaned and arched with the pleasurable on-slaught of sensations. Just as she thought she couldn't take any more, he broke the suction and turned to her other breast. As he suckled her thoroughly, he slipped one finger into her passage and then two. He thrust and withdrew until she was desperate for his cock.

"Please… I need you."

He rose on his hands and locked his elbows. Gazing down at her, he smiled. "How about a little sixty-nine?"

"Ooo—" was all she had to say.

He turned around and straddled her.

No sooner had she taken his beautiful cock in her hand than he lapped her slit from the bottom of her labia to the top of her apex. She jolted.

"So not fair," she cried.

"Why not?"

"I can't get your whole cock in my mouth from this position. I think it's the height difference."

"Yeah, I'm pretty long in the torso. I guess you'll just have to wait." He went back to licking her clit.

"Ohhh…mmm…" She was able to run her tongue around the tip of his cock, so she wet it thoroughly, sucked the head, and pumped the shaft with her hand. His groan let her know he was getting plenty of enjoyment.

He increased his pace, flicking her clit with his tongue almost as fast as a hummingbird flutters its

wings. The glorious friction created that familiar welling up of sensation deep in her core. Moaning, she had
to let his cock pop out of her mouth. Tremors took over
her legs as sensation shot through her. She exploded
in pleasure and cried out. Ripples of bliss spread out
to every nerve ending. Her orgasm lasted longer than
usual and left her weak.

"Can I have your cock now?"

He peered down between his legs and grinned at her.
"I think that can be arranged."

Instead of moving a few inches, he vaulted over her
and turned around so they were facing the same way,
lying on their backs.

"You're going to make me move?" She stuck out her
lower lip in a fake pout.

"Only if you want to. I can skip—"

"Oh, no you don't."

She scrambled up onto her hands and knees and positioned her mouth over his erect cock.

"You don't have to, you know."

"What?"

"Some women find that distasteful."

"Not me. I know it makes you feel good, and it gives
me pleasure knowing I can do something so erotic for
you. I love you, Konrad."

He grinned.

She positioned herself between his knees so she
could look up and see his face. He smiled and folded his
hands behind his head. She sunk her lips down over his
shaft and withdrew, applying suction. His eyes closed
as he moaned.

She flicked the cock head with her tongue a few times

until he moaned again and then took the length of his
erection into her mouth—or as much of it as she could
fit. She teased his balls with her fingers while she sucked
his cock. His face held a look of pleasure and pain, yet
he reached down and ran his fingers through her hair.

Knowing she and Konrad could bring each other such
intense joy filled her with sexual power. He'd taken her
to the brink and over. She wanted to do the same for
him, and she knew she could, if he'd let her.

She let his cock slide from her lips long enough to
whisper, "I want you to come in my mouth."

His eyes widened and he stared at her. "Are you sure?"

She nodded. "I've never wanted to do that before you."

He grinned. "Well, if it's really what you want—"

"It is."

She went down on his cock as if she had "Hoover"
stamped across her forehead.

"Jeez, Roz!"

She glanced up and thought she saw his eyes roll
back in his head. Should she stop abruptly or not? "Are
you okay?"

"Hell, yeah. It just felt…really, really good. There's
not much you can do to hurt me, as long as you keep
your teeth out of the way."

"Oh, my God! Did I bite you?"

He laughed. "No. You were doing it perfectly."

"Oh, okay." She smiled, secretly satisfied that she'd
figured out what gave him the intense sensations he always gifted her with. She returned to what she had been
doing and watched his face. His eyes drifted shut and
his mouth opened. He didn't cry out like before, but his
breathing deepened.

Eventually, just as her mouth was tiring, he trembled and jerked, coming in spurts. He tasted vaguely salty. She swallowed and continued until he stilled. Except for his panting breaths, he didn't move.

"Are you all right, lover?"

A smile spread across his face, but his eyes remained closed. "Oh, yeah. I'm more than all right."

He finally opened his eyes and grabbed Roz by her arms. He hauled her up on top of him and cradled her head with one hand as he stroked her back with the other. "I can't wait to get hard again."

She settled into his big, warm body and smiled.

A commotion in the hall eventually roused them from their satisfied afterglow. Konrad hopped out of bed and dressed quickly.

Roz followed suit. "Don't tell me Morgaine and Gwyneth are fighting again?"

"I don't know. It doesn't sound like women yelling. More like grunting."

He jogged out of his apartment and up the stairs to the third floor with Roz right behind him. Sure enough, Gwyneth was helping Joe move. She grunted under the weight of a heavy box. What surprised him, though, was Morgaine pushing a dresser from her apartment across the hall to Joe's.

Konrad took the box from Gwyneth, lifting it as though it weighed no more than a cube of sugar. "What's going on?"

"Joe's movin' out of 3A, and I'm movin' in. Thanks for helpin'. That musta been a box of rocks."

Morgaine stopped pushing and snickered. She whispered something to Roz behind her hand.

"Hold on, Morgaine. I'll be there in a minute, and I'll help you with the furniture."

"I can help her," Roz said.

"Well, don't hurt yourselves."

She blew him a kiss.

Morgaine elbowed her. "I guess you two have made up."

"Oh, yeah. And then some."

Konrad used his super-acute hearing to listen in as the two women continued to talk.

"What do you mean? Are you in love?"

He didn't detect a response from Roz, but he felt better when he heard what Morgaine said.

"Finally! It's about time. You'll be moving next."

Roz said, "Huh? Why? Do you know something I don't?"

Morgaine chuckled. "Maaaaybe."

Konrad wanted to get upstairs before Morgaine repeated the conversation he'd had with her about it, so he ran the rest of the way to the truck and back up the stairs.

He spotted Gwyneth coming out of Joe's place with another box.

"Why aren't you using the elevator, Gwyneth?" Roz asked.

"Joe's had it all tied up with his furniture. I reckon he's done with it now, though."

"Yeah, he was just loading his headboard into the truck." Konrad noticed she wasn't struggling with this load, so he punched the button for the elevator, and it whirred to life.

"Let me help you ladies with the furniture going across the hall. Can you two lift that end if I lift this one?"

"I imagine so," Morgaine said. "Why? You don't want to scratch the floors?"

"Do you want to give Dottie one more thing to complain about?"

"Good point."

The three of them lifted it fairly easily. With Konrad walking backward and Morgaine and Roz on the opposite side, they managed to walk it into the only bedroom.

When they had set it down, Roz asked, "Is Chad here?"

Morgaine laughed. "He's been chattering away, telling me where to place things. He said if Gwyneth wants to live with him, she has to make the place appealing, but not girly. I can hardly wait to see what he thinks of her flowered bedspread." She paused. "Oh, he says he's seen it."

"Hey!" Morgaine stuck a fist on her hip. "That means you've been in our bedroom. You promised you'd stay out of there."

Roz's eyes widened, and she stared at Konrad.

He cleared his throat. "Uh, Morgaine, can you please ask Chad to stay out of our bedrooms too?"

She listened a moment. "He wants you to say 'pretty please.'"

"Oh, for God's sake."

Roz piped up. "Pretty, pretty please, Chad?"

She glared at Konrad.

"Oh, all right. Pretty please?"

Morgaine paused. "That's enough out of you, Chad. Now, excuse us while we go back to playing musical apartments."

—*m*—

"I guess I'm stuck in a job I hate."

Roz picked at her food as she sat across from Merry. They had decided to go out to a nice restaurant for lunch. Finally they could catch up without any drama from the other residents in their building interrupting them.

"Don't give up. You never know what may happen next. Six months ago I'd never have predicted that Jason and I would be married."

Roz swallowed. "Sure, it's almost exactly the same thing as me getting involved with an unemployed teacher slash 'security expert.'" She made air quotes with her fingers.

Merry's brow knit. "What do you mean?"

Roz sighed. *Should I tell her? She's my best friend, but she's also the landlord's wife.* "Merry, whatever I tell you is in strictest confidence, right?"

"Of course…well, except for Jason. I have to be able to talk to my husband if it comes up. I won't outright lie to him, even for you."

"Oh." *Better not tell her their tenant is, or was, a thief.*

Roz must have paused a little too long, because Merry cocked her head and stared at her.

"Oh, no. It's nothing."

"Look, Roz, you can tell me anything. I won't re-peat it. I just won't lie *if it comes up*. So ask yourself how likely Jason is to ask me what you want to tell me. Especially the day before Fenway's opening day. Unless the building is on fire, he won't be thinking of anything besides baseball."

Roz took a few moments to think it over and decided

she could talk about her job situation. That was a safe topic, for now.

"Well, Konrad and I made a list of all the possible jobs we might like and could train for quickly. Then we tried each one to see if anything clicked with either of us. We made these experiments into some of our dates."

Merry brightened. "What a good idea! What did you try?"

"Oh, boy." Roz shook her head as she recalled some of their more spectacular failures. "Okay, first we tried ballroom dancing. We figured if celebrities could do it in a few weeks, anyone could."

"That sounds like fun. Didn't you enjoy it?"

"Unfortunately I'm a klutz and Konrad's two left feet are really heavy, so when he stepped on my foot, I had to be rushed to the hospital."

Merry gasped. "Oh, my God, are you all right? Why didn't you call me?"

Roz shrugged. "It was only a minor sprain. I used ice, Arnica gel, and stayed off of it for a few days."

"How's the foot now?"

"It was my ankle, and it's all better. See?" Roz stuck out her legs so Merry could see them without the tablecloth in the way. "They're both the same size and everything."

"Well, you were lucky. Some sprains can be worse than breaks. A bad sprain that isn't treated properly can take two or three months to heal. Cute shoes, by the way!"

"Spoken like a fashionista nurse. But like I said, it wasn't that bad."

"What else did you try? To find new jobs, I mean."

"Well, we tried some career counseling online. We even tried to divine the future with a tarot reading."

Merry laughed. "I did that too. With Morgaine and Gwyneth reading my tea leaves."

Roz raised her eyebrows. "Really? How did that go?"

Merry shuddered. "Not good. But I think the danger they predicted is over now. I'm pretty sure it had to do with Lila Crum, the paparazzi that tried to blackmail Jason. But anyway, what did your readings show?"

"Just that we were only good at our old jobs, the ones we wanted to leave."

Merry grimaced.

"Yeah, that's how I felt too. Anyway, we tried a few more dates. Bartending was a disappointment. My klutziness got in the way again. I broke a bottle and a glass, and Konrad almost busted up the place defending me from some angry goon. Then we tried a cooking class and almost burned the place down. We even tried to skydive."

Merry sat up straighter. "You skydived?"

"Yeah, Konrad made a tree landing and almost got killed. But he was completely healed the same night. I mean, no cuts, no bruises, not a mark on him. That's when I knew there was something very…um…different about him."

"You mean that he's a—"

"Shhh!" Roz cautioned. "The first rule of supernatural club is you never talk about supernatural club."

Merry snickered. "I get that. But how are you adjusting? I remember when you called me you were pretty shocked."

Roz nodded. "I still wonder about my sanity sometimes. Am I a complete idiot to think I'm safe with him? Or with the rest of his kind?"

"Have you met others?"

"Oops. I almost forgot the first rule."

Merry waved a hand. "Whatever. If you need to talk about it, I'm here. I might have an inkling of what you're going through."

Roz snorted. "Yeah. Again, there's a teeny bit of a difference between finding out you're in love with a bird versus a wolf."

Merry lowered her voice. "Look, a predator is a predator. But you can trust the human half that loves you. I was afraid Jason might get confused and think my pet rabbit was dinner. But he says he knows the difference, even in his other form."

"I hope you're right, because I don't have a pet, and dinner might be *me*!"

The waitress came over to their table. "Is there anything else I can get you?"

Roz shook her head. "No thanks." *Get out of here, blondie*. "We're fine."

When the waitress left, Roz took another bite and let Merry talk for a while, except it looked as if Merry just wanted to ask more questions.

"What happened after the skydiving accident? You said he healed too fast. Did you confront him?"

Roz nodded and swallowed. "Hell, yeah. We had a big fight. I knew he was keeping a big secret from me, and then he gave me a partial truth, so I thought that was all there was to it. I was really mad that he misled me, and I called him a liar."

"Oh, that must not have gone over well."

"We broke up for a short time. Then he was arrested again and needed my help. I learned that no matter how much I wished I didn't love him, it was no use. I had to try to help him."

"Arrested? Again? Wait a minute. You never told me about this."

"Oh, yeah. It must have slipped my mind. Tiny detail."

"Yeah, right." Merry frowned. "Come on, Roz. Spill it."

Roz took a deep breath. "Okay. The day after I moved in, Konrad was arrested. He said he had no real job and couldn't afford an attorney, so I was appointed his public defender. I got him off, then we went back to his place, and he got me off. Don't judge."

"I wasn't going to."

"Good. Anyway, I believed in my heart of hearts that he was innocent. No excuse."

"No need to explain. Go on," Merry prompted.

"Okay, so everything's swell. Then on the way home he kisses me, and guess what."

"You kissed him back?"

"Besides that. Never mind. I'll just tell you. He nicked my tongue with his fang, and presto…we have telepathic communication."

Merry's eyes rounded. "You what? Did…did you just say—"

"You heard me. We can read each other's minds."

"Christ on a cracker, Roz! That's…well, that's—"

"Crazy? Nuts? Impossible? Yeah, but for some reason it happens when a werewolf finds his mate."

"No, I was going to say wicked inconvenient!"

Roz chuckled. "You're picking up the Boston vernacular."

"Yeah, the nurses at work say it, and it seemed appropriate for the occasion."

Roz added, "It only happens when we're talking loudly, in our heads. Usually when something surprises us or something. We can do it on purpose too."

Merry scratched her head. "I'm speechless. I don't know what to say. Congratulations?"

Roz grinned. "That makes as much sense as anything."

"I'm really glad you found a wonderful man, even if…well, you know."

"There's one silver lining in all this mate business. I think you'll understand and appreciate it, since you have the same blessing."

Merry tipped her head and hesitated. "Blessing? Are you pregnant?"

"Huh?" Roz's jaw dropped. "No. Are you saying that you are?"

Her best friend grinned. "We haven't told anyone yet. I thought maybe you could read my mind too."

Roz whooped and jumped out of her chair. Hurrying around to the other side of the table, she grabbed Merry and hugged her. "Holy crap! Congratulations." She held Merry's arms and leaned away so she could see her face. "Are you happy about it?"

Merry grinned. "Very. We both are. We want you to be the baby's godmother."

"Then I'm over the moon." She glanced around the restaurant and noticed people were staring at them. "Hey, it's not every day you find out you're going to be a god-mother." People smiled and returned to their own conver-sations. "Can you teach the baby to call me Auntie Roz?"

"Well, not right away. Maybe when he or she learns to talk."

Roz laughed and went back to her chair.

"What were you going to tell me? What's the blessing we share?" Merry asked.

"Oh, yeah, in all the excitement I almost forgot what we were talking about. Well, apparently wolves mate for life just as falcons do, so no more losing the latest guy to someone skinnier than me."

Merry looked at the ceiling. "Hallelujah!"

Roz grinned. "Let's raise our water glasses in a toast."

"What shall we toast to?"

"To apartment 1B, *the love shack*! It seems as if anyone who moves in there finds the love of their lives."

Merry laughed. "To apartment 1B." They clinked glasses and took a sip of water. Suddenly Merry's eyes widened.

"What are you thinking?" Roz asked.

"I know who should move in there next."

"Hey, I haven't even moved out yet."

"You will. Konrad will probably ask you to share his larger apartment instead of the other way around, don't you think?"

Roz shrugged. "He hasn't asked me anything yet."

"Then why don't you ask him?"

"Boy, you really want me out of that apartment, don't you?"

Merry chuckled. "Not at all. It just seems inevitable. But I wonder if he's afraid to ask you right now. He needs help with the rent, and if his pride is anything like most men's—"

"Oh, God. You're right. I didn't even think of that. If anything, he's prouder than most. But we're really getting ahead of ourselves. We have a preliminary hearing to deal with first."

"When is that?"

"Next week. It was supposed to be today, but because of the full moon, I postponed it."

"Probably a good idea. What happens to him when the moon is full?"

"Uh… I don't know, and I'm not sure I want to know."

"You should probably ask him. Maybe if you're better prepared than I was, it won't be such a shock."

"Did you see Jason shift?"

Merry laughed. "Oh, yeah. And the timing couldn't have been worse. Believe me, it's better to know what you're in for."

Roz heard herself gulp.

Chapter 18

DOTTIE AND RALPH HAD CALLED EVERYONE TO THEIR apartment. When Konrad arrived, he was nearly the last one.

"Hello, Konrad," Dottie said. "It looks like all the chairs have been taken, so I guess you'll have to stand."

"Nonsense," Ralph said as he sprang out of his chair. "Here, Konrad. Have my seat."

Dottie glared at him.

"No, thanks," Konrad said. "Standing is fine."

Roz patted her armrest and gave him a come-hither look. He balanced on the arm lightly as he pictured upending Dottie's couch, Roz rolling into his lap, and launching a couple of witches into the air.

Gwyneth asked, "Where's Nathan, y'all?"

People murmured, but no one seemed to know. Dottie checked her watch. "Well, I guess we'll have to start without him. You snooze, you lose, as they say."

Nathan walked in at that moment. "I wasn't snoozing. I was watching TV. I hope this is important."

Dottie folded her arms. "I'm glad you could join us. It's very important." She turned to her husband. "Ralph, do you want to tell them?"

"Me? This is all you, dear. I thought you'd want to make this announcement."

She huffed. "Oh, all right. Ralph and I are leaving."

Nathan voiced what most were probably thinking,

"That's great. Happy trails. Can I get back to my apartment now?"

Jason held up one hand. "Whoa. I knew you guys were thinking about a change, but when is this happening? I thought you'd give me some time to find a replacement superintendent."

Ralph clapped Jason on the shoulder. "Don't worry. We wouldn't leave you in the lurch. I found someone interested in taking over the maintenance job. And we won't leave until you find someone else, if he isn't exactly what you want. He sounds perfect though. Loads of experience."

"When can I meet him?"

Dottie glanced at her watch again. "In about five minutes. I asked him to come by."

"Well, this really doesn't concern the rest of us," Nathan said. "Can I get back to my program now?"

"Wait," Roz said. She turned to Dottie and Ralph. "Where are you two going? I hope you have something else lined up."

Dottie brightened. "Oh, yes. We bought an RV. We'll be traveling the country, and I'll be writing magazine articles for the travel industry."

"Well, tarnation," Gwyneth whined. "I was hopin' y'all would be here to help me correct my grammar before I send in my sexy books. Now how am I supposed to make a livin'?"

"In other words," Morgaine said, "congratulations. It sounds like a wonderful opportunity."

Gwyneth shot her a look filled with hostility. "Y'all don't have to correct my manners, Morgaine. I'm not your little prodigy anymore."

Morgaine folded her arms and turned away from her cousin.

Merry jumped up and gave her husband's Aunt Dottie a hug. "Yes, I think congratulations are in order. You're going to make a wonderful travel writer."

Roz added to the distraction. "And what a great way to see this big, beautiful country! Where will you start?"

"We'll be starting in Bar Harbor, Maine, and driving southwest. We'll crisscross the country over the summer ending in San Diego this fall. Then travel across the South during the winter and head to the Pacific Northwest next spring. Then we'll drive the Trans Canada Highway until we arrive back here in New England the following autumn."

"You're going to miss two whole baseball seasons," Jason said.

Ralph piped up, "Not if we're near any of your away games. I'll have to do something to keep myself occupied while Dottie's working."

Jason scratched his head. "I'd love to see a familiar face in the stands, but this is happening so fast."

The doorbell buzzed.

"Oh, that must be *him*," Dottie strode to the intercom beside the door and pressed the button. "Who is it?" she sang out happily.

The unfamiliar male voice said, "Jules Vernon."

Nathan burst out laughing. "Jules Vernon! That's not really his name, is it?"

"As far as we know it is," Ralph said.

Nathan grinned. "I can't wait to meet him."

Dottie shushed him. "Come on up. We're all gathered in 2B." She buzzed the front door open. Pointing at

Nathan, she hissed, "You behave. Or better yet, just go. You don't want to be here anyway."

Ralph opened his mouth to intervene, but Nathan held up his hand. "You don't have to ask me twice." He left the apartment door open and was heard cackling all the way down the stairs.

—⁓—

Roz had to talk to Konrad, so she followed him to his apartment after the tenants meeting. She had decided that Merry was right. She should have some idea of what to expect of her mate every twenty-eight days.

"I have a few questions for you. Some of them might be kind of embarrassing."

"Sure." He patted his lap. "I'll tell you anything you want to know."

She sat on his hard thighs and twined her hands around his neck. "I need to know some things about your…condition at the full moon."

He nodded.

"First of all, what if I have my monthly? Will the scent of blood do something to you if you're in wolf form at the time?"

He laughed. "I might sniff your crotch, but that's all."

Talk about embarrassing questions, and answers!

He chuckled. "Don't be embarrassed. I was teasing. I might nuzzle you a little bit, but I'd do that in human form too."

Jeez, these answers aren't making me any more comfortable. Still, Roz needed to satisfy her curiosity, and embarrassment couldn't get in the way. "It sounds like you expect to be around me as a wolf sometimes."

"Are you worried about your safety? Because, I thought I assured you—"

"No, not that. Merry told me that Jason can tell the difference between her pet rabbit and food when he shifts, so I'm guessing you can too."

"I can guarantee you're safe with me when I'm in wolf form…maybe even more so than at other times. I may be a pussycat as a human, but as a wolf…well, let's just say that I'd chomp someone's ass if I sensed a threat to you."

It was Roz's turn to laugh. "If it ever comes down to that, let me bite the bastard's ass myself before you jump in to defend me, okay?"

"No promises."

They shared a short tender kiss before she continued. "The shift, is it painful?"

"Hell, yeah. Imagine your nose stretching to the size of a wolf's snout, your legs collapsing and jointing the other way, your hands and feet—"

"Okay, I got it. I got it." Her stomach churned.

"It's usually less painful shifting back, Roz. Sometimes I'm so tired from running, I just fall asleep, and it happens without my even knowing it."

"Oh, well, that's good, I guess. Where do you change?"

"Right here in the building. I used to take my clothes off in a park and hide behind the bushes, but almost getting caught a couple of times put the kibosh on that. Now I run down the stairs naked, wedge open the back door, shift, knock the wedge out so the door closes and locks automatically, and I'm on my way."

"That sounds like a lot of trouble, and you could still get caught."

"It's been hard, with Dottie snooping around. I hate to be rude, but I won't miss her."

"I don't think many of the residents will. How do you get in?"

"I paw the basement window. Sly lets me in, as long as I return before the sun comes up. If I'm late getting back, I shift behind the bushes or the Dumpster and knock on Nathan's window until he lets me in."

"Well, that's just nuts. How about if I let you out and back in again?"

Konrad's brows rose. "You'd do that for me?"

"Sure. If I'm your mate, why wouldn't I?"

"You're not afraid to see me in wolf form?"

"I already did, remember?"

"Yeah, but you didn't know it was me."

She shrugged. "Now I will. So, what? Can we try it tonight?"

He punctuated his words with kisses all over her face. "You're *smack* amazing, *smack* Roz. I *smack* love you." He then possessed her lips like never before and kissed her until her toes curled.

Roz moaned and moved against him as he kissed her and rubbed her hips, her sides, and her bare ass on either side of the lacy thong beneath her skirt. Every part of her fit his palms as if made for his touch, and the way she rubbed her hard nipples on his chest nearly took away his control, but he held on.

In seconds, his hand moved between her legs, hiking up her skirt and finding her damp, ready pussy once more. This time, however, he did not stop at her swollen

button. He thrust first one, then two fingers straight inside her.

"More," she begged against his lips.

Konrad laughed. "Patience, angel." As he flicked
his tongue against hers, he fucked her slowly with
his fingers.

She raised one leg and wrapped it around him, then
rode him, moving back and forth, vaginal walls tightening on his digits with each rocking motion.

Konrad slipped his thumb over her clit, and Roz cried
out and shattered.

"Incredible," Konrad murmured. He slid his fingers
out, lifted Roz to his chest, and carried her to bed.

She kissed his broad shoulders while he carried her,
and when he laid her down, she spread her legs wide.

He undid the buttons of her blouse and studied her as
he had when he first saw her revealed. Her full, round
nipples jutted out toward him. Her large breasts seemed
to beg for kneading, for kissing, for sucking. Her shape
pleased him to no end.

She lay still as he removed her clothing. He stared at
the red triangle of her thong, awaiting his hands and his
pulsing cock.

The smell of her womanly musk roused Konrad's desire.

"You are so beautiful. I have never seen, never imagined, a woman as perfect as you."

"I'm not," Roz started to protest, but the words
degenerated to moans as Konrad leaned forward and
snared one hard nipple between his teeth. In seconds his
fingers were back inside her pussy, pumping away as
she writhed and thrust herself against him.

Their connection was so strong he knew every

thought, every muscle was ready for him. He sensed she wanted Konrad as she'd never wanted another man, and that knowledge pleased him.

"Fuck me," Roz begged, her voice heavy with desire. "Your hands, your tongue, your cock. Fuck me anyway you want to."

Mine, he thought-whispered again and again as he sucked her nipples.

Her mind told him what she wanted and he gave it to her with no reservations. Moving down on the bed, he removed her thong and opened her labia. He trailed his tongue around the ridges, occasionally darting inside. Her juices tasted rich and sweet.

She wriggled against his grasp on her hips. "Don't make me wait. *Please.*"

Konrad heard himself growl as he traced the outline of her pussy, stopping to kiss and suck anywhere that struck his fancy.

"Tease!" She beat his shoulder.

He merely laughed. She couldn't punch hard enough to hurt him if she tried.

He inched closer to her swollen center. His tongue moved in slow circles, making promises.

"Damn it, Konrad." Roz's breath came in rough gasps. She thrust her hips higher and rubbed herself against the stubble of his chin.

Giving in to her craving, Konrad slid his lips and tongue over Roz's clit.

She cried out, shivering, as he sucked it gently and stroked it with his tongue. His cock felt close to exploding as she came, and he didn't know how much longer he could ignore his own immense needs.

He guided her through every aftershock, then let up on the pressure, but didn't stop.

She pulled his hair. "Stop," she pleaded, but he didn't. He held her tight, increased his pressure, and built her excitement to another fevered peak. "I can't come again," she cried.

You can and you will.

She let go of her resistance and allowed the intense sensations he offered her. He sensed her insides coiling, tightening.

Angel, there's nothing I won't give you. No pleasure I want you to miss.

Roz came with the power of a volcano. Her legs gripped the sides of his shoulders and shook as she convulsed and screamed into his pillow. When had she grabbed that?

He continued until she whimpered with her release.

Satisfied at last, he pressed kisses to her thighs and mons, letting her recover. Roz's body entered a state of deep relaxation, and Konrad rested his face on her soft pubic hair. *I love you.*

She sighed her accord.

Roz opened her thoughts to him even further. The man was desperate. He hoisted himself from between her legs and lay down beside her. She knew he intended to let her rest, yet his want and need for her burned. She could almost feel his cock ache.

You're an incredible lover. She managed to roll onto her side and stare into his blue eyes.

He ran his hand over her hip, to her thigh, and

stroked her back. "I just follow where your body leads me."

His gaze never wavered. She saw no guile in his expression. Tears burned behind her eyes and came dangerously close to spilling. She could hardly believe how much love they were sharing and enjoying.

Roz sensed deep layers in this man, things she couldn't begin to understand. For the first time in her life, she was in love with someone who loved her just as deeply.

"Lie on your back."

"I had hoped you'd rest awhile. I know I drained you."

She grinned. "Yes, you did. But I want to give you your pleasure now. You need it too."

"What would give me the most pleasure would be if you'd let me take you as a wolf takes his mate. I should warn you, though. I may want to mark you, and you need to be ready for it. I don't want to scare you."

"I've heard about marking. The Newton pack asked to see my mark."

His eyes bulged. "What did you do?"

"I said I had no intention of showing them that, and I acted all huffy."

He chuckled. "And they just dropped it?"

"Well, yeah. There wasn't much they could do. I figured they wouldn't strip search me to find it."

He laughed. "First of all, it wouldn't have been more embarrassing than showing them your bra strap. A male wolf marks his mate with a bite between her neck and shoulder."

It was as if she hadn't heard his words right and had to wait three seconds for a replay. Her heart momentarily lodged in her throat. "B-bite? Did you say you're going to bite me?"

He shrugged. "L'il bit."

She gasped. "Isn't that how you became a were-wolf in the first place? You...you promised I was safe with you!"

"And you are! I can mark you without turning you. But the mark provides more than just official evidence of our bond. You would have been even safer if you'd been able to show them my mark. Then the whole pack would have protected you with their lives. It's our way."

"Oh." What now? She had accepted him for what he was. Didn't that include his customs and traditions? But wait, he'd said he might *want* to. Did that mean he didn't have to?

"Is this marking something you can control? Like, if I don't want you to do it, can you skip it?"

"I'm afraid not. It's instinctual. I've fought it up to now, but I don't know how much longer I can hold off. That's why I had to prepare you."

"I-I see. Once you do it, does it have to be done again, or is it a one-time thing."

"One time. I'll try not to hurt you, but I'll have to break the skin, then the bruise won't go away."

"That's the mark? A bruise? It won't infect me and turn me into a werewolf too?"

"Not if I'm careful, and I will be, unless you *want* to go all the way."

"Not *that* way! Jesus. Become a werewolf? I'm *so* not ready for that." She felt his body stiffen and realized she may have offended him.

He relaxed. "No need to worry about that now. If you change your mind later—"

"I don't think so. I accept all of who you are, but it's not who I am."

He toyed with the hair curling against her cheek. "I just always imagined my mate running beside me under the full moon." He stroked his fingers up and down her neck until she shivered. She remembered that he was waiting for her answer.

"I…uh…I guess it's all right if you can mark me without turning me. But just so you know, I don't need any mark to tell me I'm yours."

He smiled. "I know that, angel. I don't either, but it's not a matter of choice."

At last she relented and reached for him.

He dove into her arms and whispered into her ear. "I promise you won't be sorry. I'll always be good to you, and I know we'll be happy together."

She kissed his neck. "I believe you."

He rose enough to give her a long, deep kiss that stirred her soul. Her chest squeezed with happiness.

He cupped her bottom and pulled her closer. His cock, still hard as steel, throbbed against her thigh.

She pushed on his chest, and as soon as he let go, she rolled onto her hands and knees. "Take me."

He groaned. She sensed his tight coil of desperation dissolve into relief, along with excited anticipation. He positioned himself behind her with his hands on her waist.

Without another word, Konrad drove into her balls deep. When she moaned, he quickly asked, "Did I hurt you?"

"Not even a little bit. It feels good and…right."

"*You feel so* damn *good*," he thought as he started his rhythm.

She answered him with her mind. *Give me everything. Fuck me. Fuck me hard.*

Growling like a wild animal, Konrad hammered into her. She slammed forward with each thrust, but he held her waist in a vice grip and didn't allow her to inch away from him.

"Roz," he roared, pistoning over her, and then in his thoughts, "*My mate, my mate, mine!*"

She threw herself into the moment and sensed, rather than felt, him break into a sweat. Heat poured off him as he escalated into a frenzy. Her breasts jerked and bounced, her sensitive nipples scraping the cotton sheet.

Her heart raced. She gritted her teeth, and then stopped holding back. An enormous orgasm ripped through her. She spasmed hard, buried her face into his pillow, and screamed over and over. When she was hoarse and her body went limp, his grip kept her from collapsing.

And still he fucked her. "*Please let me do this gently,*" he prayed.

Dizziness swept over Roz as she realized what he was about to do. "Mark me!" she cried out, not knowing what else to say.

Minds locked. He bent over her, and his teeth clamped onto the skin between her neck and shoulder. She felt his animal pleasure and embraced it.

"Do it!"

He bore down. *Ouch.* Suddenly her senses came alive in a whole new way. His balls slapped her ass and the smell of sex filled the air. At last he came with a bellow, and she climaxed with him. Her vaginal muscles contracted around his cock and milked every drop of his essence.

They stopped moving and fell forward. Both of them took in deep, gasping breaths.

Konrad's weight on top of her felt good, as if she were covered by his protection, owned and yet not without her desire to be. Possessed, in a splendid, freeing way.

He shifted his weight off of her. Still panting, he murmured, "I love you."

"Mmm…love you too." She touched the ache where her neck met her shoulder. When she looked at her fingers, she saw only a tiny smear of blood.

Then they both drifted into a deep, dreamless sleep.

———~~———

"Are you serious?" The mattress dipped as Konrad propped himself up on his elbow. "You want to *see* me shift?"

Roz nodded.

Why would she want to do that? "Are you sure? It can be frightening for a human to witness. I remember the first time my brother and I watched a whole pack shift. I dropped to my knees, and I'm pretty sure I didn't breathe for a minute or two. I almost passed out."

Roz sat up and hugged her knees. "I want to be part of your life; all of it. This is a big part of who you are."

"No, Roz. It's *what* I am, not who I am."

"Wrong word, same diff'. I should know what to expect. Wouldn't it be better than springing it on me sometime?"

He rubbed her back. "Why would I do that?"

She shook her head. "I don't know. Maybe by accident? Merry said Jason unintentionally shifted in front of her without preparing her for it. She totally freaked."

"That wouldn't happen. I have great control over my shifts. I can arrange to be elsewhere at midnight when it has to happen if I haven't shifted voluntarily before that."

"What if I walked in on you as you're halfway transformed?"

Konrad thought about it as he got out of bed and stepped into his black jeans. *It might not be a bad idea. If she can handle watching, I won't have to send her to another room every time.*

"I know. And if we were away someplace where I didn't have a separate room to go to—"

"Oh, you heard that, huh?"

She smiled. "Yeah."

He pulled his T-shirt over his head. "Well, I'd say, 'I'll think about it,' then put it off until you forget the whole thing, but that's no use."

She chuckled as she got out of bed. "I'm not apt to forget something like this."

"Uh-huh. Besides, you can probably tell what I'm *not* thinking as well as what I *am* thinking."

"Handy, considering how much I hate being lied to."

"And there's that." He hung his head. "Boy, I can tell this is going to be a fun and challenging marriage."

Roz stopped buttoning her blouse, turned, and stared at him. "Did you just say *marriage?*"

"Well, yeah." He lifted his shoulders. "Since we're mates for life, I just assumed—"

Her eyes narrowed. "I don't even get a proposal? You just *assumed* I'd want to marry you?"

He cocked his head. "Don't you? I mean, you're a woman. Don't little girls dream about their wedding day from the time they get their first Barbie doll?"

She folded her arms and didn't look happy.

What the hell did I do wrong?

"*If you don't know, you're an idiot.*"

He sank down onto the edge of the bed. "I-I guess I probably should have had a ring and arranged a fancy candlelit dinner, but I can't afford those things right now, Roz."

She threw her hands in the air. "I don't need those things."

This is damned frustrating. "What *do* you need then? I'm obviously missing something important. Don't make me guess what that is. Just tell me."

She heaved a huge sigh. "You're right about every little girl dreaming of her wedding. And being proposed to is part of it!" "*Stupid.*"

I heard that.

"*I don't care if you did.*" She tried to stomp off, but he caught her wrist before she made it to the bedroom door.

Hanging onto her wrist in an iron grip, he dropped to one knee, rolled his eyes, and asked in a sing-song voice, "Rosalyn Wells, will you?"

She kicked him in the groin.

"Oomph!" He cupped his balls in pain and groaned.

Seconds later, she marched out of his apartment.

Roz ran down the stairs and managed to slam and lock the door to her apartment before he reached her.

"Roz!" The door shook as he pounded on it.

"Go away."

"You don't mean that."

"Don't you *dare* tell me what I mean!"

Konrad slumped, leaned his back against the wall, and slid to the floor.

Chapter 19

"SLY, YOU WERE HAPPILY MARRIED, RIGHT?"

Konrad sat on the basement steps as he discussed the latest Roz quandary with his good friend. He'd always felt sorry for the way Sly lost his wife and child, then became a vampire all in one horrible moment.

"We were extremely happy." Sly gazed at the floor, and his expression grew nostalgic and sad.

"I'm sorry. I wouldn't bring up painful memories, but I need your help."

"No, it's fine. I like remembering those days. They were the happiest of my life." He leaned against a support column. "And will probably continue as such during the rest of my lon-n-n-ng life."

Konrad gave his friend a sad smile. "I hope you won't have to go through the next hundred years or so without a loving partner. That's just cruel."

Sly sighed. "Tell me about it. But it would be unfair to expect any woman to live up to the memory of my wife. Anyway, you had a problem?"

"Yeah. A big one." He raked his fingers over his scalp, pushing the hair out of his eyes. "I asked Roz to marry me."

Sly's expression brightened then turned to one of concern. "I'd offer congratulations, but maybe I should wait until you tell me what the problem is."

"I don't know what I did wrong. Well, I sort of do,

but I thought she'd be happy. Instead she kicked me in the nuts."

Sly laughed. "Ah, you got a feisty one. That's the best kind. You'll never be bored."

Konrad scratched his head. "I suppose so. But I wish I could figure her out a little better."

"She's a woman. There are some things you'll never figure out, but tell me what happened, and maybe I'll see something you missed."

Konrad took a deep breath. "Okay, we were basking in the afterglow of some of the best sex we've ever had in our lives."

"Sounds like a promising start."

"Yeah, I thought so. Hey, I mentioned the thing about how we have telepathy with each other, right?"

"Um, wrong. You two are telepathic?"

"Only with each other."

"I've heard of that happening with vampires, but I didn't know if it was true."

"Really? Vampires experience that too?"

"Only with one person. Their beloved. It's like a soul mate, and supposedly there's one for each of us."

"I guess it's the same for werewolves. When I discovered Roz was my mate, I naturally assumed she'd be my wife someday."

"Uh-oh."

"What? You figured out the problem already?"

"Maybe. If the words 'I just assumed' translate into taking it for granted, yeah, that could lead to a kick in the nuts."

Konrad hung his head. "Fuck."

Sly smirked. "Nailed it, didn't I?"

"I'm afraid so. She said something about dreaming of a proposal since she was a little girl, that she didn't need a ring or candlelight. I tried to do the right thing. I got down on one knee and everything—"

"But it was too late. The damage was done."

"You think so? Is it hopeless? I *can't* lose her."

"You won't, but you'll have to do some world-class groveling."

Konrad groaned. "Shit. I've never groveled in my life."

"If she means that much to you, then you'd damn well better prove it to her. In the five years I was married, I discovered one secret to keeping a woman happy."

"I hope you're not going to say 'a grovel a day keeps the lawyer away' or anything like that."

Sly chuckled. "Hell no, nothing like that. The only thing you have to do is make her feel desired. Make her know you want her."

"But she already knows that."

Sly shook his head. "That's not enough. You can't expect her to retain that feeling constantly. Women are plagued with self-doubt. I don't know why, they just are. You have to show her or tell her, or better yet, both, and reinforce it."

"Every damn day? What if I forget?"

"It's not something you schedule, dumb ass. Good God, you really have no idea, do you?"

Konrad blew out a deep breath. "I guess not."

"Look." Sly sat on the step next to him. "Send her flowers. Slip a mushy card under her door. Do whatever you have to do to make her realize you love her, want her, and that you're sorry."

"Is that what you mean by groveling?"

"Exactly!"

"Oh. That's not too bad. I can do that. I can't afford to send expensive flowers, but I can buy a card."

"Great. You can always *pick* flowers. The more effort you go to, the more it shows you care."

"Where do you pick flowers in the city?"

Sly smirked. "Some bush in an unfenced yard, I guess. If you *borrow* one rose, they'll never miss it. And for some reason, a single rose seems to mean as much to women as a dozen. That's one of those things we'll never figure out."

Konrad stood. "Okay. Thanks, buddy. I think I know where I'll take my midnight run tonight."

"Yeah? Where?"

"There's a public rose garden on the Fenway."

Roz awoke the following morning, pulled the covers over her head, and groaned. Never had a man driven her to drink before. The night before, she thought she had a point. Now she just felt stupid.

But talk about being taken for granted! I wasn't even worth the effort of a genuine, heartfelt proposal. Last night's tears and the lump in her throat resurfaced.

Her logical side took over again. How could he know she wanted a romantic proposal? It wasn't as if he could read her mind. Well, okay, he could, but only if she was thinking loud and clear. As soon as he said the word *marriage*, her mind jumbled.

Now she couldn't quite remember why. Had it really been *only* because he'd taken her answer for granted and forgot to ask the question? She wasn't usually that petty.

The men she'd known before were unromantic and even prone to insensitivity. They made Konrad look like a poet.

She removed the covers from her pounding head and inhaled a deep breath. "Time to face the music, ding-bat." Roz sat on the edge of her bed, straightened her nightshirt, and waited for her head to stop spinning. Finally she braved the ten-foot walk to the bathroom medicine cabinet.

"Oh, gross." Why had she looked in the mirror before grabbing the aspirin? Her cute new bob was plastered to her head. She looked toward the shower and figured the warm steam might make her feel better.

"Okay, shower first, then coffee."

She turned on the water, and while she waited for it to get nice and hot, she plodded to the kitchen to get the coffeemaker started. While transferring the heaping coffee grounds from the can to the pot, her hand shook. Coffee overflowed the little measuring cup and spilled onto the counter.

"Oh, for the love of—" Roz flopped into the folding chair by her little kitchen table and held her still-aching head in her hands.

Why? Why did I do this to myself?

It wasn't as if Roz didn't want to get married. She'd been hoping to find a lover to settle down with, as her best friend had. She could picture Merry and her man cuddling in front of the fireplace in their penthouse. She knew her friend had found a once-in-a-lifetime love, and now it seemed as if it was *her* turn.

"Okay, so it's not marriage itself. What is it? Konrad?" Whenever she thought of him, a smile stole across her face. She didn't even notice she was smiling at first. As soon as she recognized the fact, a warm, squishy feeling invaded her stomach, and it wasn't from drinking too much wine.

The man wasn't the problem. The beast was. Roz returned to the bathroom and removed her nightshirt. Before she stepped into the shower, she examined the bruise on her shoulder. She was marked, all right. Dark imprints in the shape of a jaw full of teeth showed on both her front and back, with some just above her collarbone and others on her upper back near her neck.

She sighed. She loved Konrad, loved him with all her heart. Loved him enough to let him claim her. But he scared her too. What if they had a serious argument sometime? Would she still be perfectly safe with him?

"*Yes, you would,*" his voice answered in her head.

"Oh, crap!" He must be right outside her door. She jumped into the shower and stuck her head under the spray. *Sorry. I'm in the shower. Can we talk later?*

"*I think we should. Meanwhile I have something for you. I'll leave it outside your door. Come upstairs when you're ready.*"

She sighed. Part of her had worried that he'd be angry after she went off on him, but even though he was the animal, she seemed to be the one easily irritated. What was that about?

Maybe that's why the werewolves in the Newton pack seemed less than fond of humans. Maybe she was the unpredictable and dangerous one. She snorted at that, but something about the notion rang true.

Any one of the werewolves could subdue her in a second, but maybe they didn't want to. It would call attention to them. She saw what happened with Konrad when she was being threatened, even slightly. He had to jump in and defend her. She could imagine that situation would get tiring.

After she turned off the water and towel dried her hair, she put on her fluffy robe and took another look in the mirror. Better. Her eyes seemed a little more awake. Glazed, but awake.

She burped. A dinner of popcorn and wine didn't cut it, but she was out of Rocky Road. She hoped her rationale that popcorn was low in calories had saved her from committing diet suicide. Somehow she knew that paired with an entire bottle of Chablis, her dinner might not have been as low calorie as she'd hoped.

Too late now. She walked barefoot to her bedroom and looked in her closet for something to wear. Nothing jumped out. Her brain was too fuzzy for decisions, so she just tossed on a pair of sweatpants and a matching hoodie. At least they were pink and she could tell herself she looked feminine.

Oh yeah. Konrad left something at the door. As soon as she'd donned a pair of socks, she trotted into her living room and opened her door to the hall. A rose with a note lay on her threshold.

She picked up the gorgeous American Beauty rose and smelled it. Its scent was sweet and seductive. Roz opened the note and read, "I'm sorry. Please forgive my insensitivity. I love you and always will."

Nathan opened his door and wheeled his bicycle into the hall. He glanced at the rose and note in her hand and said, "What did he do?"

"What makes you think—"

"Because he left gifts outside your door and because last night when I let him out, he looked dejected as hell."

"Oh."

Nathan scrutinized her from head to toe. "Another truck run you over?"

With one hand on her hip she said, "Yeah. I just washed off the blood, so the paramedics wouldn't have to."

He laughed and started to open the front door.

"Oh, let me get that for you." Roz strode to the heavy front door and held it open.

"Thanks," he said as he wheeled his bike down the steps.

She let go of the door and muttered, "Don't let it hit you in the ass."

He turned and laughed as if he'd heard her. Hmmm. Maybe he had. She kept forgetting that everyone in this building had freakishly acute senses, especially her wolf-man.

<hr />

A knock sounded on Konrad's door. When he opened it, Roz stood there with her hands behind her back, looking contrite.

"Thank you for the rose. It's beautiful."

"Not nearly as beautiful as you."

She turned her head to the side and snorted.

"I mean it. I'm so sorry, Roz. I had no idea how that came across, until…well, until later."

She still stood on his threshold, making no move to come in.

"Look, I get it. I'm the one who constantly tells you that you deserve to be loved. And you *are*. I adore you, Roz."

She looked up into his eyes, expectantly.

"I know I can't always rely on our mind connection. I need to *learn* to understand my mate. But please understand there's a learning curve here, and I'm trying."

She nodded and stepped forward into his waiting arms. He held her reverently.

"I'm sorry I kicked you."

"Apology accepted. Now let's get out of the hallway." He stepped back. She strolled to his couch and made herself comfortable.

Konrad sat next to her and put an arm around her. "The trial's only a few days away. Is there anything I should be doing?"

She looked up at him with questioning eyes.

"What? Is that a dumb question?"

"No. I just thought we'd talk about what happened yesterday first."

"Oh. Right now?" *Crap. I'm barely out of the doghouse. I didn't think she'd want me to propose so soon.*

She tipped her head. "Why not now?"

"I want to do this right, and I still haven't had the chance to—"

She put her finger to his lips and said "Forget that. I told you I don't need a candlelit dinner or fancy engagement ring. None of that is necessary."

"But I want to do something special, because *you're* special."

She leaned back and smiled. Her whole face softened, and her eyes danced whenever she smiled just for him.

He stroked her hair. "I love you more than anything. You know that, right?"

She glanced at her lap. "Yes, I know."

"Okay, good. Keep remembering that. One of these days I'll *show* you how much you mean to me. That's a promise."

"Why not now?"

"Because you'd always wonder if I did it because you wanted me to. No, I thought of something that will take a little planning. If you can be patient. It might be better to wait until after the trial anyway." *You might prefer not to be engaged to a jailbird for who-knows-how-many years.*

She nodded. "Okay. So, what did you want to do? Talk about the trial?"

"We probably should. What kinds of questions should I expect?"

She dragged her feet up onto the couch and hugged her knees, looking more like a little girl than his attorney. "You might never have to testify."

"Seriously? Could they possibly put me in jail without giving me a chance to defend myself?"

"That's not what I meant. Sometimes the evidence can be disputed and the lawyers can create enough reasonable doubt on their own without the defendant ever having to get on the witness stand."

"How can you do that?"

"Well, we found the two guards who had been at the museum that night, and they'll be asked to point out the gunmen who tied them up, *if* either of the thieves are in the courtroom."

"You're expecting them to cooperate? To say they don't see the guys?"

"They'll be under oath."

"But didn't you say before that the public wants someone to hang? Won't they be tempted to point to me just because I'm the defendant?"

"No. I'm sure they'd prefer to convict the guys who really did it. They won't want an innocent man going to jail while letting the real thieves off the hook."

"Okay, but what if they get confused? It's been a long time, and sometimes people see what they want to see."

"According to their police-report descriptions, you're about as far from the men they saw as you can be. Both were under six feet tall and you're what? Six-six?"

He chuckled. "No. Only six-four."

"Ha. *Only* six-four. Okay, well, I doubt anyone would see you as six feet or less."

"Probably not. So you think that's all you have to do to create reasonable doubt? Isn't that putting a lot of power into the hands of two *human* beings?" He didn't want to have to point out how fallible humans were. Most werewolves thought themselves superior, but Konrad didn't think he was one of them. Maybe deep down, he was.

She fluffed her drying hair. "No. I hope to disprove their DNA evidence too."

"How can you do that?"

"I don't want to say just now. It's better if you don't know every detail."

"Are you sure? Maybe I could help come up with other angles."

"No, I've got this. To be honest, I'm feeling pretty confident. I don't want to get cocky, so the team of lawyers will be there if I need them."

His mood lifted considerably. "That sounds great. I'm relieved I won't be going to jail, and all this will be behind us soon."

"I never said that. If the prosecution can make a good case, it may drag on and on. There are no guarantees."

"Shit. I had hoped…well, never mind."

She straightened and put her feet back on the floor. "What?"

"Oh, nothing. It's just the timing. I had hoped we'd have a nice, easy summer."

She squinted as if she didn't quite believe him, but she let it go, thank God.

He'd had a sailboat reserved, but he could cancel it and reschedule after everything was over. It seemed like a romantic idea, and even if it went the way of all of their dates, wolves were great swimmers.

The jury filed in and took seats along one side of the courtroom. Konrad looked them over. A jury of his peers? Wouldn't that have to be twelve werewolves? The only other werewolf in the courtroom that he knew of was his brother, Nick.

Be that as it may, a dozen human beings of mixed ages and races sat there staring back. His hands began to sweat.

"All rise," said the bailiff.

A rumble signified about fifty people getting to their feet.

"This court is in session, the honorable Judge Vader, presiding."

A balding man wearing a long, black robe breezed into the courtroom and up a few steps to his seat on high.

As soon as the judge sat comfortably in his leather chair behind his massive desk, he said, "Be seated."

While everyone was getting resettled, the judge scanned some papers in front of him. Konrad was beginning to think the good judge had fallen asleep, when the man finally looked up and addressed the jury.

"Members of the jury, what you have before you is a great responsibility, to the court, to the Commonwealth, and to yourselves. Our judicial system asks you to listen to all the facts presented during this trial, then take everything into consideration and make a decision regarding the guilt or innocence of the defendant.

"You are not to take this matter lightly. The outcome will affect more than this one man. You are to deliberate until you are absolutely sure of your decision, no matter how long it takes."

As he droned on, Konrad stared at his lap and obsessed about the jury taking forever to deliberate. He wondered what it took to declare a hung jury.

Roz must have heard him. *"Relax, lover. He has to say those things to every jury. It's not unique to this one."*

Konrad tried to slow his breathing. *Correct me if I'm wrong, but isn't a fast decision a good sign?*

"Not necessarily. A long deliberation may just mean they're taking a second or third look at the evidence and trying to get it right. Don't worry."

Konrad noticed his jaw ached from clenching his teeth. *Easy for you to say.*

"No, it's really not. This is the most difficult case I've ever had. And lift up your head. You look guilty as sin."

Thanks for waiting until now to tell me. Konrad snapped his head up, his eyes level.

"In the case of the Commonwealth of Massachusetts versus Konrad Wolfensen, the charges are burglary of the Isabella Stewart Gardener Museum, grand larceny, fraud..."

Konrad shut down his mind to calm himself. As soon as he stopped shaking, he tried to listen again. Just in time, too. The judge had asked him a question. What was it? Oh yeah.

"Yes, I understand the nature of the charges, your honor. May I speak? I'm quite intelligent. I was a dean—"

"Did I ask you about your intelligence or profession?"

"No, your honor."

"Fine. Perhaps you should let your lawyers speak for you from now on."

Roz leaned toward him and whispered, "Don't say another word. We're *supposed* to do the talking for you."

How the hell would I know that? I've never been on trial before.

The attorney next to Roz leaned toward her and whispered angrily, "I thought you spent hours with this guy. What the hell were you doing?"

She sat silent and stoic, eyes forward, as if the man hadn't spoken at all.

"*I'm sorry. I should have prepared you better.*"

The judge nodded to the prosecution and said, "Proceed with your opening argument."

The other long table seated almost as many lawyers as his did. One of them stood, buttoned his jacket, and walked around the table toward the jury.

"Men and women of the jury, this unsolved case has gone on long enough. I intend to prove that Konrad Wolfensen was one of the thieves who broke into the

Isabella Stewart Gardener Museum on March 18, 1990, to steal twelve pieces of art valued at three hundred million dollars."

A murmur from behind him let Konrad know the spectators were blown away by the value of the loot the thieves had taken, whoever they were. And probably many of the jurors were struggling to pay their bills and suspected *he* was living high off the hog.

Who the hell does this guy think he is?

"*He's the district attorney. Don't let him get to you. He's just doing his job, but I'll be doing mine too.*"

His hands began to shake and sweat again.

"Now, what do we know?" the prosecutor continued. "We know that on that cold spring night between the hours of 1:24 a.m. to 2:45 a.m., thieves who had disguised themselves as Boston police officers gained entry to the museum. They did this by advising one of the guards on duty that they were there to investigate a reported disturbance.

"And we know that the defendant has a brother of the same height, weight, and build who happens to be a Boston police officer."

What difference does that make?

"*I suppose they're going to claim you had access to a uniform and could have easily been one of the robbers.*"

But the eye witnesses descriptions—

"*Don't worry. We'll cross-examine them.*"

The prosecuting attorney continued. "Upon entering the facility, they overpowered both guards, handcuffed them, and took them to separate isolated parts of the basement. There they were duct taped to separate structures to immobilize them. They never had the chance to push the panic button hidden behind the guard's desk, so no *actual* police were notified during the robbery. No video surveillance film is available, because they stole that too."

The murmurs behind him sounded like a mixture of amusement and anger, probably depending on how each person valued priceless art. Konrad's mind drifted to the day he heard the news.

He was watching one of the local TV stations, and a special report broke the news. His emotions ran the gamut of disbelief, heartbreak, and outrage. If he'd only known who did it, he'd have gone after them and practiced a little vigilante werewolf justice on their asses.

Anyone who appreciated the creative arts in this courtroom would probably want him hanged on Boston Common. He shuddered. Dragging himself back to reality, he noticed the lawyer seemed pleased with how he'd horrified the listeners.

"Over the years all logical leads were followed up with no positive investigative results. Numerous interviews were conducted. Many were even accompanied by polygraph examinations. And all forensic evidence recovered *at that time* was sent to the FBI for analysis and, eventually, storage. *However*, new evidence recently surfaced."

Are they calling Reginald's cockamamie story evidence? And if it's something else, how do they explain learning about it? An anonymous tip?

"If so, I'll have to prod the appropriate witnesses until someone gives up the ghost, so to speak."

Not Morgaine, I hope.

"*I doubt the jury will be impressed by a psychic. I think the museum curator is our best bet.*"

Konrad almost chuckled, but settled for a quick smile.

The attorney finally seemed satisfied that he'd done sufficient damage to the credibility of the defense, and he sat down.

Roz stood and approached the jury. She took a few moments to gather her thoughts, but began with her own compelling argument. "The judge reminded you of the seriousness of your job as jurors, and I'm certain you'll do your duty to the very best of your ability. But I'd like to quote a statistic that may shock you. More than 230 wrongfully convicted and imprisoned men and women have been exonerated and released from U.S. prisons after conclusively proving their innocence.

"The prosecution mentioned having DNA evidence that would conclusively prove my client guilty. I maintain it's that same evidence that will prove his innocence."

When had the DA said that? Konrad realized it must have been when he was daydreaming, imagining his conviction.

"Furthermore, I intend to prove their anonymous tip was faulty and the evidence was planted long after the incident. DNA can be used to convict a guilty man or used to frame an innocent one.

"The district attorney failed to mention the guards' descriptions of the robbers. These men stood face to face and toe to toe with the perpetrators before they were taken to the basement and bound with duct tape.

"This is what they said on March 18, 1990. 'One suspect was a white male, late twenties to mid-thirties, between five foot seven and five foot ten. Medium build, dark eyes, and short, cropped, black hair.'

"'The other suspect was a white male, early to

mid-thirties, six feet to six one, broad shouldered but lanky from the waist down, with dark eyes and black hair a little longer in back, rounded off just over the collar.'"

Good girl. Those descriptions couldn't possibly be me.

"We're not out of the woods yet," Roz answered him. *"The DA will point out that they were wearing fake mustaches and could have been wearing wigs and dark contacts. He could say you were younger than twenty and must have grown over the years. I'm just hoping he doesn't, and no one on the jury will think of it."*

Fuck. I'm so screwed.

Chapter 20

WHEN ROZ SAT DOWN, THE DISTRICT ATTORNEY CALLED his first witness, a Boston police lieutenant. She had expected that the DA would use someone credible to introduce and verify the prosecutor's bullshit evidence.

"What is your role with the police department, sir?"

"I'm a detective."

"Very good. And are you familiar with this?" The DA held up a plastic bag for the courtroom to see and then handed it to the lieutenant.

"Yes, this is the evidence I collected at the museum."

"Where, exactly?" the DA pressed.

"It was attached to some shelving in the basement of the Isabella Stewart Gardner Museum."

"And what exactly is in the bag?"

"A small shred of duct tape and two strands of hair."

"Thank you." He returned to his seat.

It was Roz's turn, and the judge said, "The defense may cross-examine the witness, if you'd like."

Roz stood and strolled toward the police detective. "Can you describe the hair strands you entered into evidence, lieutenant? I'm not sure anyone in the courtroom could see exactly what they look like. Certainly if I couldn't from my seat up front, I doubt anyone else could." She glanced at the DA, who appeared disinterested as he took notes.

"Uh, yes. They were two long, blond hairs."

"Long and blond, you said, right?"

"Right."

"How long?"

The lieutenant scratched his head. "About two feet."

Roz raised her eyebrows as if the information were a significant surprise. She hoped it would give the jury a clue that it should be. "Two feet? Not two inches. Two whole feet?" She held her hands about two feet apart. "Like that?"

He nodded and said, "Yes."

People whispered behind her. She heard a couple of titters. Those were good signs. She was planting doubt.

"Thank you." As she returned to her seat, she said, "That's all."

The witness was excused.

The DA called his next witness. As soon as the man was sworn in and seated, the DA wasted no time. "Where do you work?"

"I work for the Federal Bureau of Investigation, in the DNA testing lab."

"Very good. And do you recognize this evidence?" He held up the small plastic bag and walked it over to the witness.

"Yes. It appears those are hair strands I tested."

The DA held the bag aloft again. "Let the record show this is the same evidence identified by the Boston police detective that he testified had been gathered at the crime scene." He laid the bag back down and paced with his hands behind his back. "Now tell me. After testing the evidence, did you find a match?"

"Not an exact match, no."

Roz held her breath. She hoped the witness would leave a large enough hole to poke through.

"How close a match did you get?"

The witness leaned back in his seat, as if feeling confident. "Ninety-nine point nine percent."

The DA raised his eyebrows as if impressed. "My, that's very close. Can you explain to whom the close match belonged and why it might be so close but not exact?"

The witness cleared his throat and sat a little straighter. "The closest match was to a Boston police officer named Nicholas Wolfensen."

"I see. And can you surmise why it would be a close match, but not exact?"

The witness matter-of-factly said, "If the hair belonged to an identical twin, it would test that close."

"There's no other way two people could be so close a match?"

"None that I've heard of."

"Thank you. That's all."

The judge offered Roz the opportunity to cross-examine the witness.

Should I? What can he say that will make any difference? Even if the man doesn't know about Konrad's twin, the DA will just prove it later.

She stood. "No questions at this time, your honor."

"*Roz, this is looking bad.*"

She took in a deep breath. *Have patience.*

The witness was excused, and the prosecutor called his next witness. The name snapped Konrad out of his telepathy with Roz.

"Nicholas Wolfensen."

"*Shit. Roz, what can you do to get Nick out of this?*"

Nothing. He can be declared a hostile witness, but I hope he'll just answer the questions honestly.

"*But Roz, the business! What if they ask him about our*

*business? It'll come out that I'm a thief. I was relieved
that they couldn't bring up the prior arrest, but—"*

By that time, Nick was on the witness stand and the bailiff held the Bible for him. He placed his right hand on it.

"Do you swear to tell the truth, the whole truth and
nothing but the truth, so help you God?"

Nick glanced at Konrad quickly and said, "So help
me God."

"That's not what was asked of you," the judge said.
"Bailiff, would you repeat the question?"

"Do you swear to tell the truth—"

"I do," Nick interrupted, and he didn't look happy
about it.

The DA asked him his profession, and Nick stated
that he was a Boston police officer.

"As an officer of the law, I imagine you'd know what
court proceedings are like. Why did you answer the first
question in such a vague manner?"

Nick shrugged. "I just got nervous and forgot."

The DA approached Nick and stared at him for a long
moment. Finally he smiled at the jury. "Hmm, your face
is very familiar. Do you happen to have a twin?"

Nicholas mumbled, "Yes."

"Speak louder, please."

His lips thinned, and he spit out the word, "Yes."

"Is he or she in this courtroom?"

Nick nodded.

"Aloud please."

"Yes." Nick's glare should have given the DA pause.
Hell, it might have unnerved Superman. Konrad knew
his brother wouldn't shift and eat the prosecutor. Talk
about exposure!

"Please point to your twin."

Nick gave a half-hearted nod in Konrad's direction.

"It's hard to interpret a head nod. Did you just indicate that the defendant is your twin?"

Nick almost growled the word "Yes," making Konrad even more nervous.

"And you're identical twins, isn't that true?"

Nick bit his top lip and let out a deep breath. "As far as we know."

"And were you asked for a sample of your DNA at some point?"

"Yes. They took a cheek swab."

"And isn't a cheek swab as much a match for a hair sample as any other human cell?"

"I wouldn't know."

"Of course. You're not an expert. But I'm willing to bet the expert in this case would verify that."

Roz stood and called out, "Objection. Speculation."

The DA almost bowed to her and said, "Quite right, but I'm willing to put the FBI's expert on the stand again if need be." He stared at the jury as he said, "However, since Konrad Wolfensen and Nicholas Wolfensen are identical twins, and Nicholas's cheek swab was a ninety-nine point nine percent DNA match to the hair found at the crime scene, it's fair to assume—"

Roz was on her feet and objecting before the DA finished his sentence.

He withdrew the question and smiled at the jury. "No more questions, your honor." He didn't even look at Roz when he said, "Your witness" and breezed back to his seat with his nose in the air.

Roz had met Nick only briefly. He said he hadn't

known of an alibi or anything else to help the defense then, and he probably wouldn't now. Konrad couldn't imagine what she intended to ask Nick as she stood in front of him. At least she was blocking the view.

"Nicholas, how long have you been a Boston police officer?"

"Eight years."

She tipped her head. "Oh! Only eight years? You weren't a Boston cop twenty years ago?"

He chuckled. "I wasn't a cop anywhere then. I came out of the academy in 2002."

"Why did you want to become a cop?"

"Nine-eleven. I saw heroes running into the World Trade Center, and I knew I could do that. I'm very strong and probably could have carried several adults out of the rubble before getting tired. I wanted to help. Wanted to keep our community safe."

"That's very admirable. Have you had to do anything like that in your eight years on the force?"

"No. I've been thinking about volunteering for the bomb squad, but I haven't done that yet."

"Wow, so you're willing to put yourself in harm's way—"

The DA stood. "Objection. This isn't a coffee klatch, and I don't see what this little chat has to do with the case."

Roz spoke to the judge. "Just establishing what kind of witness we have here. It also speaks to the kind of family my client comes from."

The judge overruled the objection, but warned her to stay on track.

"Okay, so in your years as a police officer, have you

ever run into cases where evidence had been falsified or planted?"

"Yeah, plenty of times."

"Really? It happens a lot?"

"Well, not on a daily basis or anything, but it's not uncommon. Someone who's holding a grudge might plant evidence to put away a rival, or a guilty suspect might try to throw us off his trail and onto someone else's."

"I see. So it's perfectly plausible that someone who had a grudge against my client, or someone who wanted suspicion diverted to someone else, could have gotten hold of and planted some of my client's hair, then called in an anonymous tip?"

The DA leaned toward the other attorneys at his table and whispered furiously.

Ha, that rattled them. Good.

"Yeah, I'd like to see them explain their anonymous tipster was a ghost."

Roz said she had no more questions, and Nick was allowed to leave the witness stand. He didn't leave the courtroom, however. He sat behind Konrad and put a hand on his shoulder. Konrad clapped his own big hand over his brother's and held onto him for a moment of support.

All we need is reasonable doubt, right, Roz?

"I'd like a solidly doubtful jury before they go to deliberate. When I get to call our witnesses, it shouldn't be a problem."

Are they here?

"One of them is. I'd hoped both would be here by now."

Can you stall until they're both here?

"I can try."

The judge asked the DA if he had another witness, and he said, "None at this time."

"Does the defense have any witnesses to call?"

Good. You're up, Roz!

She rose and said, "Yes, your honor. But one of my witnesses hasn't arrived yet. May we recess until all are here?"

The judge fidgeted in his chair and asked, "Does it make any difference if they're all here at the same time?"

"I think so, your honor."

"Fine. Ten-minute recess." The judge banged his gavel, and Konrad let out a deep breath of relief. All the lawyers reached for their cell phones.

Roz looked behind herself for the first time since the trial had begun. Sure enough, jerk-face was there, and he was moving toward her through the crowd as people were filing out for their cigarette breaks.

"Aw, crap," she mumbled.

"What's wrong?" Konrad asked.

"Stan's here."

"Your stepfather?"

"The one and only. Listen, when he gets here, please don't say a word. Not even to defend me."

"You mean I can't punch him out?"

No.

"Are you sure?"

I'm sure.

"C'mon, just one little punch in the face."

Not in the middle of a courtroom. Maybe later. I'll let you know.

Stan finally came within speaking distance. "Roz, how do you think you're doing?"

"Just fine, thank you."

Stan straightened and put his hands in his pants pockets. "Frankly, I think you could use a little advice."

"Nope, I've got all the help I need," she said.

A couple of the other lawyers noticed the interaction and were watching despite being on their phones.

His brows knitted and his lips thinned. She recognized his brewing anger and figured she had two choices. She could placate him, which wasn't going to happen, or she could ignore him and hope he went away. He wouldn't like the second option, but as far as Roz was concerned, he could raise his voice all he wanted, and he'd only embarrass himself.

She shuffled the papers in front of her and leaned forward to speak to Madison, the only lawyer who wasn't talking to someone else. "Can you take a quick look around and see if our witness got lost?" He nodded and was about to leave when the head partner, Jordan, ended his phone call and spoke up.

"He's in the building. I just called downstairs, and they're letting him through security now."

"Thank goodness." Roz said.

"Who's up next?" Stan asked Jordan.

Roz didn't know whether to be insulted or relieved. As the two of them chatted, she picked up her pencil and drew a couple of stick figures with frowns on their faces in the margin of her legal pad. She added a rifle to one's hand, pointing at the other.

She glanced at Konrad, who looked amused at her drawing. He picked up the pencil lying next to her and added hair to the figure with the gun. It was a little longer in the front than the back. He added bullets coming out of the gun, flying toward, and hitting the other figure. When he erased the eyes and replaced them with x's, she chuckled telepathically.

She added a few drops of blood, and their masterpiece was complete. Before anyone could see it, she flipped the paper over. Apparently she hadn't been quick enough, because when she looked up, Stan was glaring at her.

People began drifting back into the courtroom, and thankfully Stan retreated to a bench far behind them.

The bailiff walked down the center aisle and over to Roz. "There's a whole bunch of people who say they're witnesses for the defense," he whispered.

Everyone was still talking and moving around, so Judge Vader banged his gavel. "Let's get this show on the road. Are your witnesses here, Miss Wells?"

She turned to see about a dozen people filing in and standing at the back of the courtroom, including Wendell, Lois, Barrett, and a few other wolves who weren't with them the day she visited the private school. She smiled broadly and glanced over at Konrad. He looked like he was in shock.

She stood. "Yes, you're honor. They're here."

"Well then, get on with it. Call your first witness."

Roz called the first guard. She noticed the other guard had sat beside him, which was good, but she was more curious about what the pack had in mind. An alibi, maybe? At that point, Roz didn't even care if the prettiest one said she was with Konrad all night. She just wanted to win this case. First of all to keep her lover out of jail, and second to tell Stan to shove it up his ass.

The guard was sworn in, and Roz had only one real question, but she might stretch it into two or three, just for fun. "We've heard the descriptions you gave to the police several years ago. Do you stand by those descriptions, or is there anything you'd like to change?"

"No, nothing I'd change," he said.

"Did you get a good look at the men who bound you the night of the theft? I mean a *really* good look?"

"Yes. As you said earlier, I was standing toe to toe with them. As soon as I realized they weren't who we thought they were, I began making mental notes about their size, build, and coloring. I looked for any visible marks or tattoos that might be helpful in identifying them, but didn't see any."

"Very good. So even though it's been twenty years, you'd recognize—"

The DA jumped up and said, "Objection. Leading the witness."

The judge nodded and said to Roz, "Can you rephrase?"

"Absolutely," Roz said. She turned back to the guard. "Would you recognize the thieves if you saw them again?"

"I'm pretty sure I would. I mean, they're older and everything, but if they didn't have plastic surgery, I'd remember their faces."

"Good. Do you see either of them in this courtroom?"

The guard took a good look around. "No, I don't think so."

"Okay, let me be specific." She turned to Konrad. "I'd like the defendant to stand, please."

Konrad rose up to his full six-foot-four height, and held his head high.

"Could the defendant be one of the men you saw?"

The guard chuckled. "No way. He's too tall, light skinned, and light haired, and I can't see his eye color from here, but I don't think they're dark brown."

"Thank you." Roz looked over at the DA. "Your witness."

The DA rose, a serious expression on his face. Before he even arrived in front of the witness stand, he began asking questions. "Did you happen to see the getaway driver?"

The guard shook his head. "I don't know if they had one, but if they did, then no."

"Did you have cameras outside the museum?"

The guard stroked his chin and looked as if he were mentally traveling back in time. He shook his head slowly. "No."

"So this guy could have been outside the museum, and you wouldn't have seen him. Isn't that right?"

The guard nodded. "Yes, I guess so."

"Thank you; that's all."

———

Konrad's nerve endings tingled when Roz leaned toward one of the other lawyers, said something, and excused herself.

Where the hell are you going?

"Relax, I'm just following up on a hunch."

She hurried to the back of the courtroom while the attorney she spoke to rose and called the other guard as the next witness.

Konrad craned his neck, trying to see where Roz had gone. He was hoping she had just run to the bathroom, but deep down he knew the answer.

She was whispering to the pack. One of pack members opened a book and showed her something. Some of them were nodding, and some were looking over at Konrad with sad expressions. *Damn. That could be good or bad.*

He tried to hear what was going on in two places at once, but even werewolves weren't that gifted. Roz's conversation was short, but she looked pleased when she made her way back to her seat.

"What's going on?" he asked, anxiously.

"Just wait."

Wait? I'm dyin' over here!

"*I think your pack just saved the day.*"

Really? He turned around and took another good look at them. He saw no animosity in any of their faces. A few smiles grew and were aimed in his direction. *Well, I'll be damned.*

"*No, you won't. Not today.*"

Konrad couldn't wait for the witness to vacate the stand, to find out what the pack was up to.

Roz sat contentedly with a satisfied smile on her face. Whatever it was, it must be good.

At last the witness was excused and it was Roz's turn again. She approached the bench and whispered to the judge. Because of his superior hearing, Konrad heard everything as if he were standing next to her.

"Your honor, I have a couple of last-minute witnesses."

The judge waved the DA over and waited for him before speaking to Roz.

"We have some new witnesses," he said to the DA. He turned to Roz. "Why aren't they on the list?"

"I didn't know they were coming, but they have pertinent information the jury needs to hear."

The DA looked put out. "Is this some kind of trick? Is there some reason you didn't want me to know about them?"

"No, not at all."

"It's somewhat irregular, but I'll allow it," Judge Vader said.

The DA looked disgruntled, but returned to his seat.

She called her first pack-member witness. "Wendell Wolfe."

Wendell rose and carried a book with him to the stand. Konrad had thought of him as a father figure. Even though he hadn't seen the man in years, he still looked spry, not a day over two hundred.

As soon as he was sworn in and sitting on the witness seat, Roz asked him to state his name and occupation.

"Wendell Wolfe. I teach mathematics at the Newton Preparatory School for Boys."

"And how do you know the defendant?"

"Konrad was our dean at the school."

"The dean?" Roz looked impressed and aimed her expression toward the jury. "Well, then, there must be pictures of him there."

"Oh, yes. I brought an old yearbook."

"May I have it please?"

Wendell handed it to her, and she held it up, walking it down the line of jurors. Right on the cover it said, "Newton Preparatory School for Boys, 1990."

"Now, let's see that picture," she said. Opening the book, she flipped a few pages. Konrad knew she'd find a nice full-page black-and-white photograph of him. He didn't look much different, except his hair was very short, not more than an inch long.

"Ah, here it is." She opened the book wide and walked the picture down the line of jurors again. "As you can see, Mr. Wolfensen's hair is quite short in this picture." She turned back to Wendell. "And when was this taken?"

"In February of 1990. Here, I have the original with the date stamped on it." He fished a four-by-six photograph out of his inner jacket pocket.

Roz walked over to the evidence table and picked up the bag with the two long, blond hairs in it. "Interesting. Here we have evidence of Mr. Wolfensen's DNA, taken from the crime scene, but these hairs are two feet long, as previously stated by a Boston police detective. If he committed this crime on March 18, 1990, his hair would have had to grow an astounding twenty-three inches in one month."

The courtroom laughed, and murmurs broke out everywhere.

"I'm sure I know what my opponent will ask, so I'll just ask it now. How do we know this photograph hasn't been altered?" Roz asked.

"We have a number of ways to prove it. There are the negatives, still catalogued by the photographer, along with the dates. We also had a portrait commissioned the year before, with the date plainly written under the artist's signature."

"I see. You didn't happen to bring that with you, did you?"

"No, but we could go and get it, if you like."

"Or perhaps you could have someone back at the school take a photograph of it and fax it here?"

"Certainly." He looked over at Konrad and smiled.

"The picture still hangs in its place of honor, reminding us all how much we miss him."

Roz smiled at Konrad. *"Did you hear that? I told you they weren't holding any grudges."*

I heard. A lump formed in his throat. He didn't realize how much he'd missed them either, until they had all filed into the courtroom ready to help him out, like in the old days, before Petroski. The next words he heard astounded him so much, he wasn't sure he'd heard right.

"So if I'd called you as a character witness, it sounds as if you'd have given him a good review."

"Absolutely. We'd really like to have him back."

What the—What about Petroski?

"I guess there's no better compliment than that. Is his position open?" Roz asked.

"It is now. The board of directors decided that his replacement wasn't the kind of man the school needed. Mr. Wolfensen is."

Roz let out telepathic sigh. All the courtroom saw, though, was a confident attorney saying, "Your witness." Only Konrad heard her silently add the word *sucker*.

Chapter 21

SOUNDS OF PEOPLE MURMURING AND MILLING ABOUT the restaurant couldn't drown out the pack's conversation, at least not when it came to the Lycans hearing each other. Roz had to lean in to make out some of the softer voices across the large round table.

The pack that surrounded Konrad and Roz seemed festive, almost as happy as he and she were, and Roz didn't think anyone on the planet could be as happy as she and Konrad were at that moment.

The French waiter brought two bottles of champagne, opened one for Wendell to try, and when he nodded, the garçon filled everyone's glasses. The group members waited for the server to leave before raising their glasses.

Wendell's chest swelled with pride. "To Roz!"

The eight weres surrounding the table echoed his sentiments, and glasses clinked all around.

After everyone had taken a sip, Konrad sighed. "I can't thank you enough. I had no idea you'd help if I was in trouble."

Barrett sat next to him and clapped him on the back. "Don't be daft. We always protect our own."

Konrad hung his head. "But last I knew—"

Lois held up one hand. "Last you knew we were taken in by a con man, and all of us made a terrible mistake."

The table grew quiet, and Konrad smiled, sadly. "Everyone makes mistakes. At least it's over now.

Let's not dwell on it. We're here to celebrate." He raised his glass again, and everyone followed his lead. "To renewed friendships."

Everyone clicked their glasses as before and took another sip.

"Those jurors took no time at all deliberating, did they?" Wendell asked Roz. "Did you know it would go as quickly as that?"

Roz laughed. "I knew we were in good shape when they frowned at the DA during his closing argument. Every one of them looked like they were thinking, "What do you take us for, morons?""

Konrad squeezed her hand under the table. "I was worried there for a bit, but I knew you could do it."

Roz blushed and looked at her lap. "I'm afraid I wasn't so confident. Until your pack came to the rescue, it really could have gone either way."

Barrett looked at her askance. "Even with the guards standing by their descriptions?"

She glanced around the table. "That's all we had, before you guys testified. As you heard, the DA tried to say the guards were under so much stress that they could have misestimated his height and build, or that he was involved in another way, like the getaway driver."

"We wouldn't have let them win," Lois said.

Roz raised her eyebrows. "Meaning what?"

Barrette quickly interjected, "Don't worry, we wouldn't have devoured a whole courtroom full of people." The others laughed.

Roz had to smile too. It would take some time before she understood her mate's people. She supposed it was the same for any young woman just getting to know her lover's family. Er, almost.

"Did you have more evidence up your sleeves?" Konrad asked as he glanced around the table.

Lois chuckled. "Just that I'd give you an alibi, if you needed one."

"How?" he asked.

"I'd say we spent the night together."

Konrad's eyes popped. "But that would have been a lie." He glanced at Roz.

She didn't react, just waited for Lois to explain.

"I know. What I'm saying is that I was prepared to commit perjury on your behalf, and the rest of the staff was willing to back me up."

Roz leaned back. "But what if you got caught in that lie, and they came after you?"

Lois grinned, showing her elongated canines. "I'd tell them to bite me."

The whole table laughed.

When the group quieted, Konrad stared at Wendell. "Did you mean what you said about offering me my job back?"

"Absolutely. The board discussed it as soon as we knew we could find you. You did a good job of disappearing."

Konrad nodded. "I didn't know if there would be more retribution, so I went completely off the radar. You knew where Nick was, though."

"And your brother is one hundred percent loyal to you. He refused to give us any information. I mean, not one word. We didn't know if you were dead or alive."

Konrad nodded, slowly. "I swore him to secrecy. We had our own business, so I paid myself in cash and used my brother's name on our business account. We purposely didn't live close to each other." He gave Roz a long, soft stare. "Now I'm glad I moved where I did, or I wouldn't have met Roz, at least under the right circumstances." He winked, and she grinned back at him.

Lois leaned toward her. "I was thinking of going to law school at some point. The school could use some free legal consultation from time to time. Tell us what it's like to be a defense lawyer, Roz."

She groaned. "To tell you the truth, I hate it. I've spent the last several months trying to think of something else I could do for a living."

"Really? That's too bad. What have you come up with?"

She and Konrad exchanged glances and chuckled.

"Oh, let's see. We tried ballroom dancing. It turns out I'm a klutz with no timing, and I sprained my ankle. Then when I got better, we tried bartending. Same thing, only some guy was being a jerk to me, and Konrad got into a fist fight with him. We narrowly escaped being arrested by paying for the damage to the bar."

The group laughed.

"Then there was skydiving," Konrad added.

Roz heard a few gasps around the table. "It turns out you can't jump before your instructor is ready. I kind of landed in the trees."

Now the others were guffawing; some laughed until they had tears in their eyes.

"The icing on the cake, so to speak," Roz said, "was when we took a cooking class, and I set my hair on fire."

"I have to take responsibility for that," Konrad said. "I was kissing and tickling her when I was supposed to be pouring oil into the pan. I wound up pouring it right onto the gas burner."

"But look—" She turned her head and showed them how the stylist cut off the damage in such a clever way. "I got a cute new haircut out of it. I even talked to the stylist about what it would take to become a hairdresser."

Lois looked directly at Wendell. "Are you thinking what I'm thinking?"

"I'm right there with you." Wendell turned toward Roz and said, "I'd have to run it past the board, of course, but how would you like to be our new career counselor? We've talked about adding the position, and since you've experienced quite a few jobs, and you know what it takes to succeed in them—"

Lois piped up, "Plus we could use your legal expertise once in a while."

Roz stared at Konrad open-mouthed. "It sounds perfect," she whispered.

"Yes, it does."

Wendell fidgeted. "There's just one more thing, and we, ahem, need to know for sure."

Konrad nodded as if he understood. "Show them your mark, angel."

"Oh." She hadn't expected this request, but now that they'd asked, it made perfect sense. She'd need to know she was safe.

She removed her suit jacket and hung it over the back of her chair. After unbuttoning the top two buttons of her white blouse, she was able to slide it aside and expose her neck and shoulder. Even her wide bra strap didn't cover it, so she left it where it was.

Everyone around the table smiled.

"Welcome to the pack," Wendell said. "We'll have a formal ceremony at the next full moon."

"Oh, no. Does she have to endure that?" Konrad asked.

Roz's eyes flew open. "Endure what?"

"Oh, nothing will happen to you. You'll just have to put up with a whole bunch of wolves taking their turns sniffing you so they can distinguish your scent in their other form."

Roz smirked. *As long as they stay away from my crotch, everything will be fine.*

Konrad glanced around the table. "*They'd better.*"

Their group sailing lessons had finally ended, and Roz and Konrad were taking an O'Day sailboat for their maiden solo voyage. The autumn wind could be strong, but that day it was perfect, ten knots, winds from the southwest. There was a clear blue sky overhead, and Roz had applied plenty of sunscreen.

The instructor who had spent several weeks with them beamed as he watched them stow the canvases covering the sails. Roz knew she and Konrad worked as a team in perfect synchronicity, yet the instructor would never understand why. *It really helps to communicate directions to each other telepathically.*

"*Yeah, and no need to shout over the wind.*"

As soon as Konrad had tightened the ropes in the widgets, the instructor asked, "Ready to cast off?"

Konrad saluted the instructor. "Aye, aye, captain."

The seasoned sailor laughed. "*You're* the captain now."

"Co-captain." He pointed to Roz with his thumb.

Konrad started the motor. Roz waved to the instructor

as she used the stick to guide them out of the marina. Navigating the harbor required a little mechanical power before raising the sails.

Eventually they cleared the buoys and most of the islands dotting Boston harbor. Konrad cut the power, and Roz stood, ready to raise the jib. He clamped his big hand around her wrist. "Wait a minute. There's something I want to ask you."

"Ask me while I'm at the bow. As you said, there's no need to shout over the wind." She tried to pull away, but he didn't let go.

"Roz, sit down."

He sounded so serious that her warning bells went off. "What's wrong?"

"Nothing," he said. "Everything's perfect." He smiled and patted the seat.

She sat back down, slowly.

He lowered himself to one knee.

Her loud internal gasp may have communicated itself to him, but he didn't comment on it.

He took her right hand in both of his and rubbed the surface gently with one of his thumbs. "Roz, you mean the world to me. I can't imagine a future without you, and I don't want to. I love you, I need you, and I want you to be my wife. Will you marry me?"

Tears welled up in her eyes. A lump started to form in her throat, but she wanted to answer out loud. Before it grew and made it difficult to talk, she said, "Yes, I'd love to."

He rose enough to grasp her in his arms and stood, holding her tight. The boat rocked a tiny bit, but not enough to throw them off balance. Nothing was enough to throw them off balance anymore, not the stress of a trial, not the stress of a job search. No more stressors were on the horizon, except moving to Newton…together.

He lowered his lips to hers and kissed her deeply. "*I love you, Roz.*"

I love you too. Thank you for making me so happy.

It seemed that their dating disasters were over.

Acknowledgments

Major thanks to my funny attorney and friend, Richard Leonard, J.D. He's always there to answer my legal questions, but I had so many situations this time, he met me for dinner, and I filled four pages in my notebook.

Thanks again to Emily Bryan, aka Mia Marlowe, the awesome critique partner who's as different from me as two people can be, but gives me a new take on things I wouldn't have come up with on my own. *Viva la difference!*

Thanks also to Arwen Lynch, who helped me with Konrad's tarot reading. I didn't have a firm grasp on his character until she did her "magic." It worked so well, I may ask her to read other characters for me in the future.

To Natanya Wheeler, my extraordinary agent, for her gracious patience. Thank you for putting up with ice storms knocking out my power, explaining the fine points of fifteen-page contracts, and keeping me from imploding over minor mishaps and making a mess all over my carpet. I just had it installed and used my advance to pay for it. *Oh,* and thanks for negotiating that, too! You're a godsend.

Instead of dedicating this book to my husband (again) I decided to acknowledge his invaluable contribution. He not only pays the bills but also listens to the weird problems of a writer and gives me his emotional support as well. I love you so much, honey. Someday when I'm rich and famous, you can retire and be my boy toy.

About the Author

Ashlyn Chase describes herself as an Almond Joy bar, a little nutty, a little flaky, but basically sweet, wanting only to give her readers a scrumptious, satisfying, reading experience.

She holds a degree in behavioral sciences, worked as a psychiatric RN for several years, and spent a few more years working for the American Red Cross, where she still volunteers as an instructor. She credits her sense of humor to her former careers, since comedy helped preserve whatever was left of her sanity. She is a multi-published, award-winning author of humorous erotic romances.

Represented by the Nancy Yost agency in New York, NY, she lives in beautiful New Hampshire with her true-life hero husband and a spoiled brat cat.

Where there's fire, there's Ash:

www.ashlynchase.com Check out my news, contest, videos, and reviews.

http://www.myspace.com/ashlynchase Find me on MySpace and be my friend.

Chat with me: http://groups.yahoo.com/group/ashlynsnewbestfriends/
Yes, I'm on Facebook, and I tweet as GoddessAsh.

Strange Neighbors

BY ASHLYN CHASE

HE'S LOOKING FOR PEACE, QUIET, AND A MAYBE
LITTLE ROMANCE...

Hunky all-star pitcher and shapeshifter Jason Falco invests
in an old Boston brownstone apartment building full of
supernatural creatures, and there's never a dull moment.
But when Merry McKenzie moves into the ground floor
apartment, the playboy pitcher decides he might just be
done playing the field...

What readers say about Ashlyn Chase

"Entertaining and humorous—a winner!"

*"The humor and romance kept me entertained—
a definite page turner!"*

"Sexy, funny stories!"

978-1-4022-3661-7 • $6.99 U.S./$8.99 CAN/£3.99 UK

DEMONS
ARE A
GIRL'S BEST FRIEND
BY LINDA WISDOM

A BEWITCHING WOMAN ON A MISSION...

Feisty witch Maggie enjoys her work as a paranormal law enforcement officer—that is, until she's assigned to protect a teenager with major attitude and plenty of Mayan enemies. Maggie's never going to survive this assignment without the help of a half-fire demon who makes her smolder...

Praise for Linda Wisdom

"Hot talent Wisdom does a truly wonderful job mixing passion, danger, and outrageous antics into a tasty blend that's sure to satisfy."
—RT Book Reviews

"Entertaining and sexy... Ms. Wisdom's stories have something for everyone." —Night Owl

"Wickedly captivating... wildly entertaining... full of magical zest and unrivaled witty prose."
—Suite 101

978-1-4022-5439-0 • $7.99 U.S./£4.99 UK

CATCH
OF A
LIFETIME

by Judi Fennell

"Judi Fennell has one heck of an imagination!" —
Michelle Rowen, author of *Bitten & Smitten*

WHEN HE DISCOVERS WHAT SHE REALLY IS,
○ ○ ○ ○ THEY'RE BOTH IN MORTAL DANGER... ○ ○ ○ ○

Mermaid Angel Tritone has been researching humans from
afar, and when she jumps into a boat to escape a shark
attack, it's her chance to pursue her mission to save the
planet from disaster—but she must keep her identity a
secret. For Logan Hardington, finding a beautiful woman
on his boat is surely not a problem—until he realizes his
life is on the line...

○ ○ ○ ○ PRAISE FOR *IN OVER HER HEAD*: ○ ○ ○ ○

"A charming modern day fairy tale with a twist. Fennell is
a bright star on the horizon of romance." —Judi McCoy,
author of *Hounding the Pavement*

"Fennell's under-the-sea suspense will enchant you with its
wit, humor, and sexiness." —Caridad Pineiro, *NYT* and *USA
Today* Bestseller, *South Beach Chicas Catch Their Man*

978-1-4022-2428-7 • $6.99 U.S. / $8.99 CAN / £3.99 UK